Vanguard

Zombie Castle 5

Vanguard

Chris Harris

PRESS

Published by Vulpine Press in the United Kingdom in 2025

Cover by Vulpine Press
ISBN: 978-1-83919-616-4

www.vulpine-press.com

CHAPTER ONE

Admiral Walker-Jones, as he introduced himself, took salutes and offered handshakes to the military men of our group who had lined up to greet him with me. As the rest of his entourage deplaned he introduced certain ones of them to us, but to be honest, I forgot most of their names as soon as I had been told them. The ten men and women who had accompanied him were most likely his aides or advisers and were all dressed in uniforms of different types, presumably depending on their branch of the military or rank they had attained.

The Admiral moved away from the group and I saw him looking around the airfield. He gave a nod of satisfaction when he saw the armoured car and looked surprised when he noticed the tractor and trailer driven by Shawn as they both patrolled the perimeter of the airfield.

"Sir," I said as I noticed the direction of his gaze and walked over to him. "I was just about to recall the vehicles so we can get back to the castle. It's only about fifteen minutes away and then we can offer you some refreshments and get started on these plans we've been talking about."

He looked at me, smiled, nodded, and said, "Yes, yes. There is no point delaying, we have a job to do."

"We have kept the rear of the armoured car clear for you and your people to use," I said raising the radio to get them to come and pick us up, but stopped when he held up a hand.

"I'd rather prefer to ride in that wonderful looking contraption, if that's all the same to you?" he said, pointing at it with a smile on his face. "I have heard so much about these vehicles you have created. I must say I can't *wait* to see how effective they are."

He paused and added wearing a frown.

"Of course…if you don't mind, that is?"

Chuckling at the eager look that had come across his face, I replied, "Of course not!"

I waved at the other vehicles we had bought with us. Deciding to go 'all in' on this mission, as protecting the VIPs that were arriving was paramount, we had chosen to bring most of our eclectic collection of vehicles. Forming them into the usual protective square close by on the grass area near the airfields tower to act as a fallback position for us if need be.

My Volvo, the bus, and military lorries all converted to survive in the new world we lived in, looked normal to us as we were used to them now, but to anyone who had not seen them before they must look outrageous and Mad Max like.

"We have bought most of the fleet with us today as you can see. Of course, you can ride in the trailer if you want to. It's just as safe as the armoured car and to be fair it will give you a much better view of the surrounding area as we drive along," I then added with a cheeky grin on my face, "I'll even show you how to use the spears if you like. We always come across at least a few of them, maybe more, on every journey we make. We got a fair amount on the way here and more always seem to replace them."

I lifted the radio in my hand and asked the vehicles to return as we were getting ready to depart, updating everyone on the newly changed travel plans at the same time.

"I would be happy to learn. It would do me good to know truly what it is like to kill one if I get the chance. All I've had to go on is reports from the ones sent out to do the dirty work for me. Some first-hand experience will enable me to understand it better," he replied, unable to hide his eagerness.

Nodding with agreement with him and secretly happy that he seemed the type of leader not afraid to get his hands dirty, I walked over to Shawn's tractor that had pulled up near to us. He waited, watching with interest as the rear door opened and the ramp was deployed.

"Ingenious," he said as he walked up it.

Halfway up he bounced on it, as if testing its strength, before turning to someone who must have been an aide.

"Photographs, if you please. We must document everything or no one back at base will believe us!"

We waited whilst items of baggage and other equipment was removed from the plane's hold and loaded onto one of the lorries that Woody ordered to be driven close to it.

The Admiral introduced himself to Shawn and Louise who had stepped from the cab and stood guard on the tractor's enveloping steel cage. He had been told about all the group on one of the many radio conversations we'd had, and his memory and people skills were evident when he recalled their individual stories and commiserated Louise on the tragic loss of her sister.

I could tell he was being genuine. Shawn placed a comforting arm around her as soon as her sister was mentioned, knowing that her emotional wounds were still fresh and in no way healed yet. Mainly we avoided raising memories of the loved ones we had lost as a way of protecting ourselves from the reality of their deaths, though in quiet times the pain of the losses we had all suffered were never far from the surface. When the sadness hit there was always someone who knew exactly what you were going through to offer a shoulder to cry on and some supporting words.

The admiral was mortified he'd upset Louise and climbed over the back of the trailer and onto the cage to envelop her in a fatherly hug. This further reinforced, not only with me but the others of our group who saw it, that he was a genuine and kind individual and not the stuck-up stuffy type you would expect an admiral to be.

When the aircraft was secured with chocks against its wheels and its doors were shut and locked, the convoy departed. We had previously assured them that no zombies we were aware of had made it inside the airfield so far and certainly no live person had, as far as we could tell, visited the airfield either, so it should remain untouched. If zombies did somehow manage to get in, we could deal with them as we had done many times before.

Once we were all in our chosen vehicle, the convoy departed the airfield and when the gates had been closed and secured, we began our journey home.

Another man had chosen to join us in the trailer. He had been introduced to me earlier, but I had forgotten his name. I admitted as much to him, so he introduced himself again.

"Captain Digby, Royal Marines," he said, shaking my hand.

"Are you one of his aides?" I asked, thinking as I did so that he looked more a man of action than of paperwork.

"Oh, good Lord no," he replied in mock horror at the thought of being labelled as such as he held onto the side of the trailer as it rocked along the road, his eyes looking outwards. "I led the operation to clear the Scillies."

"Good job," I said, turning sombre. "I'm sorry you lost so many. That must have been a hell of a fight."

A shadow crossed his face and he looked sad for a moment as he relived the events.

"It was." He said quietly before forcing himself to look more cheerful again. "It was also a steep learning curve. I don't think we would have done half as well without the tips and tactics you gave us. You saved a hell of a lot of my people, so thank you."

He paused as he looked across the countryside that was passing us before continuing.

"It's...it's why I asked to come along, in fact. I've heard about these *knights* of yours and I wanted to see first-hand how well they perform."

"I'm sure we can arrange that. You probably know, but we're all training to wear armour and use medieval weapons now. I've faced them with just a knife before, and having seen the knights in action...trust me...armour, axes, maces, swords...it's the only way to go for me if I'm on foot. It's a mad world when ancient weapons and tactics are better than modern methods. isn't it? Bullets run out, but all a blade needs is a keen edge."

Captain Digby nodded in agreement.

"Yes, we used a hell of a lot of ammo to clear the islands and that was only against thousands of the bastards. There has to be millions roaming around the UK, it's why I wanted to see the knights. Until we can secure a lot more ammunition, hand to hand, so to speak, is going to be the only way to deal with them, unfortunately. What I understand from the many reports of your exploits I've read, is that you guys are the experts who'll hopefully be able to show us the way."

"We'll be happy to, I'm sure," I replied and indicated to the few knights who, still fully kitted out in their armour were accompanying us in the trailer. "Seeing them in action is both a mixture of awesome and just plain terrifying. It's amazing to see."

Ian, dressed in full armour himself had overheard us talking and butted in saying whilst pointing to Simon who was similarly dressed by his side. "Yeh. I'm awesome and he's just plain terrified."

Louise calling over the radio informing us of a small pack of zombies ahead stopped any reply from his friend. I grabbed a spear from one of the many that were secured in the holder we had constructed for them in the trailer and spoke to both Captain Digby and the admiral, who had both stiffened and looked more alert when they heard the radio call.

"Gentlemen, if you'd care to help yourself to a spear?" I asked using a formal tone that seemed out of place given our surroundings.

Looking ahead I could see about twenty zombies ambling jerkily in our direction. I called Shawn over the radio asking him to slow down once he had hit them with the plough, as now was a good a time as any to show our visitors how we dealt with them.

He acknowledged and the trailer lurched as he sped up and aimed at the centre of the shambling group. The Admiral could not contain himself, leaning over the side of the trailer and letting out a cheer as the plough destroyed half of them. Their dismembered bodies flew through the air as the blade of the plough cleaved through the pack and the elated cheer turned into a noise of mixed awe and disgust.

Shawn immediately slowed the tractor to a crawl. I glanced forwards and could see him looking over his shoulder at me, so I smiled and raised a thumb to indicate his speed was good.

"Ok, get ready. I'll show you what to do and then feel free to have a go yourselves," I said holding my spear ready in both hands.

My hands had now healed sufficiently enough for me to handle a spear once more even though they were still lightly bandaged, and I was wearing gloves to further pad them. They hurt if I over did it, but every day I could see the improvement when the bandages were changed, and as long as I kept swallowing pain killers, I was okay.

When the nearest zombie was within range I jabbed the spear downwards and pierced its skull. It fell to the ground, killed instantly as its brain was destroyed. Looking at our visitors I indicated for them to have a go. With faces rigid with concentration, they both steadied themselves and held their spears ready. The Admirals first thrust glanced off his target's head and stuck in its shoulder. He grunted with annoyance, yanked the spear free and tried again, this time hitting its open mouth. When he withdrew the spear, its lower jaw was ripped off and stuck to the blade at the end of the shaft. Letting out a cry of disgust, frustration, and anger he jabbed again, eventually killing it this time.

Slightly breathless after the exertion he said, "It's bloody harder than it looks. We are complete amateurs compared to you chaps."

"A lot harder than bayonet practice!" Captain Digby said, after also taking three attempts to kill his own target.

"Don't worry, we've had a lot more practice than you. Zombie sticking is a time-served skill after all," I said trying to keep my voice from sounding condescending.

The remains of the pack had now come within range. The other occupants of the trailer stood ready, but let our visitors end their existence, which they did with varying degrees of accuracy and skill, but with maximum gusto which ultimately led to them all joining their former reanimated colleagues in a more restful place.

After showing them how to clean the spears by dipping them into a container that held a strong bleach mix, we safely stowed them away and continued our journey.

"Is it like this every time you go out?" asked the Admiral.

"Yes, mainly," I replied. "We've travelled this road a lot, and even though we're in a fairly rural area, there always seem to be more that get in our way every time we drive along it. The noise we make must attract them and they just…hang around waiting for us to return, I guess. Since clearing Warwick of the masses that were there when we arrived, there are always more of them that appear every time we go out. Hopefully they seem to be decreasing now, which we are taking as a positive sign. We still though, try to get everyone we can."

I smiled as I remembered Shawn's instructions to me on the first day we met and pointed to him in the tractor.

"On the first day this happened, when I met Shawn and he'd got his head around what was happening, his mantra that he kept continually repeating to us was to kill every one you can, because if you don't, that'll be the one to get you in the end. It does make sense, because no matter how many millions are out there, one less is still one less."

Captain Digby who had been listening to the conversation spoke up.

"Both your tactics and reasoning are sound. When you do the maths on the probable numbers of the turned that are most likely still out there, it's daunting and sounds rather impossible. But we must start somewhere so yes, I agree completely. One less is still one less."

For the remainder of the journey only a few individual zombies were encountered, and these were easily dealt with by Shawn's plough. Both were shocked though by the huge swathes of corpses littering both sides of the road into Warwick. The gut-churning smell of decay that emanated from them was increasing every day now, and the flocks of carrion birds and swarms of rats barely even moved as we passed by. Either they were too engrossed in feeding or too full to move. Probably both was the best guess.

I explained to the Admiral that we were trying to come up with the best way to deal with them as we were all concerned about the health implications our proximity to so many rotting, bloating corpses could cause. Our issue was that we had been so busy gathering supplies and helping the new community at the farm that we'd been forced to keep putting off dealing with the problem, but it was clearly now becoming a priority.

CHAPTER TWO

We were used to the reaction our new home got from first time visitors. Driving through the grounds everyone's reaction when the castle came into view had been very similar. Awe was a good way to describe it.

Driving through the Barbican also showed off how impressive the defences were, but it was when you emerged from the darkness of the tunnel that the true splendour of the castle was revealed.

The admiral stood silently in the trailer as the engines ticked and cooled after being turned off. He did a full three-hundred-and-sixty-degree turn, his head moving everywhere as he took in the sheer scale and size of the place and summed it up with one word.

"Wow!"

The heart of the castle, The Great Hall, was as full as it had ever been since we arrived. There were a lot of us in there, but it could easily cope with more than twice the number. Maud, as busy as ever, fussed around the new arrivals and insisted they all remained in the room and not wander off to explore so she could serve the refreshments she had been preparing to welcome them properly.

Standing next to Woody, I watched Becky walk over to us and give me a peck on my cheek.

"Simon," she said. "I wonder if we could relieve the children. They've been as good as gold standing guard all day but they must be getting restless by now, especially with all the excitement."

Woody looked at his watch.

"Of course. My apologies Becky, I'll get onto it straight away. The next shift is due to start in thirty minutes, but I'm sure they won't mind at all."

He quickly organized the next ones due on guard duty to start a little early and told his young new recruits via the radio that they could return as soon as their replacements had arrived.

Maud and some helpers were bringing out trays of tea and platters of sandwiches and biscuits from the kitchen, so we joined the crowd that was milling around the centre of the room. When everyone was either sitting or standing sipping on their drinks and eating, Charles, the vicar, not unexpectedly, walked into the middle of us and raised his hands for silence. He welcomed our new guests officially and offered a small prayer of thanks for their safe arrival and the hope our plans would be successful. Heads bowed automatically as he started the prayer, even amongst the not too religious ones of us, as behaviour ingrained from long ago school assemblies took over. The mumbled Amens at the end also blurted unbidden from most lips.

I felt a tug at my sleeve and looked down to see Daisy, Stanley, Eddie, and Princess.

"Hi kids," I said and put my arm around Daisy and ruffled her dog's ears.

Their childhood had stopped the day the apocalypse started, and not once had they moaned or whinged about the responsibilities they now had. They were our primary daytime lookouts which allowed more 'grown-ups' to be allocated to other jobs, although we did try to allow them time to be children again when we could. Despite some of them before all this started probably thinking they were too old for it, the adventure playground at the castle proved a great way for them to have some fun and run off their pent-up energy. They also hadn't tired of exploring the castle, and legends from the guidebooks told of many secret passages hidden everywhere. We had offered rewards for those who could find them, and they spent most evenings, torches in hand, tapping walls and exploring every nook and cranny on the hunt for them.

"I'm told you did a great job keeping guard for us today," I said and pointed to the tray of biscuits Maud had laid out. "Go and grab some of those before they're all gone. Mommy and Daddy are probably going to be busy for a while, so I'm sorry if we aren't going to be able to spend much time with you today."

They beamed with pleasure at the well-deserved praise and then at the mention of biscuits. I watched with a smile as they suddenly forgot all about me, turned and quickly weaved through the crowd with Princess snaking after them, aiming straight for the biscuit plate.

Captain Digby was standing and talking when his eye was drawn to the children sneaking their way through the crowd. He gave a start and stared more closely at the one in the middle with ginger hair as a flash of recognition sped through his brain.

"No, it couldn't be. It's impossible," he muttered quietly to himself.

A few seconds later he was still looking when Eddie, now eating a biscuit, turned in his direction. He stared at him hard trying to remember the last photo he had seen. It was from not long ago when his sister had posted a holiday picture on social media. His heart stopped as recognition, and the impossibility of it, dawned on him.

It IS him, his brain screamed at him silently. Joy rose in him at the thought that his sister may have survived. He scanned the room looking for her before snapping his head back to the boy.

"Eddie? Is that you?" he exclaimed loudly. The room fell silent at the raised voice. Eddie, on hearing his name, looked at the man in uniform who had spoken. The half-eaten biscuit fell from his hand as he stared in disbelief at his uncle Darren.

Being proud to have a Royal Marine for an uncle he idolised the man and had kept a photo of him taken when he was overseas prominently displayed in his room. It was a classic hero pose with him holding his rifle, looking tough, with a background of a destroyed house taken on one of his tours of Afghanistan. Eddie used to study it for hours, dreaming of when he would be old enough to follow in his footsteps. His visits were infrequent, but he treasured every photo he had of him and showed his friends with pride the coveted presents of caps and badges his hero uncle gave him when he did occasionally stay with them for a few days when he was on leave.

"Uncle Darren?" Eddie said, his voice quavering with raw emotion.

Digby hurriedly put his mug down and rushed over to him, lifted him up and enveloped him in a hug; a huge smile of joy and relief beaming on his face.

"Where's Anne? Where's your Mom?" he asked, his eyes still scanning the room for her.

Eddie couldn't reply. At the mention of his mother the heart-break he had suffered broke all over him, and he sobbed loudly and buried his head into his uncle's chest.

The sudden elation Digby had felt was replaced with crushing sorrow and he too found tears streaming down his face as he hugged his nephew harder in an attempt to comfort him.

Not one of us knew what to say or do. The shock of Eddie's uncle being here had knocked us all for six. The sight of their obvious heartbreak intermingled with joy that they had both impossibly found a member of their family alive caused more than a few tears to fall from watching eyes. Becky, with tears running down her own face, approached the two and gently put her hand on Eddie's back offering him comfort. Understanding that they both needed time alone to recover, she put her other hand around the captain's waist. He didn't resist, when speaking to them softly, she ushered them through the watching crowd and led them into another room. Maud who had spent so many countless hours looking after him as well, followed her and closed the door behind them.

The silence lasted for quite some time until the admiral spoke, his own voice quavering with repressed emotion.

"Well, that was a turn up for the books, eh? What a surprise for young Digby."

He smiled as he recovered and continued.

"That just proves you should never give up hope for your loved ones. Miracles, as we have just seen, can happen. And they will again."

He gathered himself and looked towards Steve.

"Captain Hammond, I hate to get back to business at a time like this, but may I suggest you give us the tour so we can get down to the real work? It's why we are here after all. Bring whoever you feel fit along as well, but I'm eager to see what you've done here."

***

By the time a very impressed admiral and his entourage had received the full tour, Eddie and his uncle were waiting in the Great Hall being fussed over by the ever-present Maud.

"Digby," the admiral said as he offered to shake his hand.

We'd recounted Eddie's story when doing the tour, so he knew of the fate of the rest of his family.

"Congratulations on being reunited with your nephew. His sad story must have come as quite a shock to you in having the tragic news of your family confirmed," he paused as he held his gaze for a few seconds and softened his tone. "I hate to ask, but are you quite ready to get down to business? I do promise though to give you as much time with Eddie as time allows later."

Digby, who had stood as soon as the admiral entered the room replied.

"Thank you, sir, and yes, I'm ready. At least I know now, and can grieve for them, which is a lot more than can be said for most I suppose. Finding little Eddie makes me more determined than ever to get the mission completed. I can then begin to look after him properly out of memory and respect for my sister."

"Well said Captain," the admiral responded, and shook his hand again. "Now if we can convene our war council, I'm told they have set aside the dining room for our use."

CHAPTER THREE

Admiral Walker-Jones first set out the proposed plans his staff had decided needed to be done in order of priority, and they contained no surprises. First of all, they wanted to try and rescue the personnel trapped in the bunker at the base we had flown over and reconnoitred at their request. Of those trapped inside a few were considered important enough in what input they would have going forwards, and that their rescue was deemed top priority. Then they needed to concentrate on supplying the population on the Scillies and preparing for a structured land offensive to begin clearing the mainland United Kingdom of the tens of millions of zombies that wandered everywhere.

It was easy to say, but all around the table understood the enormity of the task ahead of us. The only way to approach this was one job at a time, therefore all attention could be concentrated on one task and not divided between many. This should hopefully ensure that every angle was covered and nothing got missed. There were others trapped on other bases, but they were all in the north of England. They still had supplies to last for a few months so were not being forgotten, but when the situation was clearer in what we could achieve working together, their rescue would, if it was deemed possible, be conducted.

An aide spread a huge, large-scale map on the table that covered the central United Kingdom from coast to coast. He had asked earlier for my phone that I had used to take pictures of the base with, and using a printer he had bought with him he downloaded and reproduced the images. These he placed on the table as well. We quickly identified and marked where Warwick and the base the trapped service personnel were located. I stood to trace my finger between them working out in my head the ideal route to take. Stabbing my finger at the map I said, "Well, the route I think I'd use takes us pretty much past the Brough's farm," as I pointed its location out. It was marked on the map by the same aide.

"Wouldn't it make more sense to stage this mission from there? It's closer for one, and we know the roads between here and there are clear of any obstructions."

I looked around the room and added, "Makes sense to me anyway."

There were silent nods of agreement from most around the table as they looked at the route I had pointed out.

"I wanted to visit this farm if time allowed. It would give us an opportunity to see what one of these proposed outposts we have discussed creating would look like," said Walker-Jones as he looked around the table wearing a questioning expression. "Does anyone have anything to add?"

At the negative signals he received he continued.

"Right then. What resources do we need and what tactics do you propose to clear the base and get to the people in the bunker?"

A few of us began to speak at the same time. He held his hand up to stop us.

"Can I suggest one at a time please?" he said with an amused tone to his voice. "How about we let the military-minded among us give their proposals first, and then you civvies can use your hard-earned experience to rip our well-worked out plans apart?"

There was a general ripple of laughter around the table and 'us civvies' sat back and waited to see who was going to speak first. Captain Digby stood up.

"Expanding on our tactics to clear the Scillies," he said confidently. "I propose we use the vehicles that are here to transport us to the site. Then, using helicopter coverage to provide resupply and overwatch, we work our way into the facility as one group on foot until we've cleared the area. Once that's done, we assist the trapped personnel from the bunker and exfil back to the vehicles."

Woody thought for a few moments before responding, his eyebrows raised questioningly towards the admiral. "Sir, am I a civvie or military for the purposes of this conversation?"

He laughed at the suggestion.

"Sergeant Wood, you are most definitely military, but I would value your input from the experiences you've had."

"Well then," he responded looking at Digby. "No disrespect, but that plan could get a lot of you killed. Now I like the idea of the helicopter, if that's possible, as that would add an extra level of protection, but what I would propose is far simpler."

Woody sat back and looked at the faces staring back at him expectantly. He smiled as a pretend look of shock came over his face.

"I'm sorry. You want my ideas *now*? I was waiting for others to put their proposals forwards."

Digby chuckled as he responded, holding both hands in the air in defeat. "No that's the only idea we've had so far so please carry on."

"Okay then," Woody replied, standing up so he could address the room better and see everyone. "Yes, I agree that we should stage out of the Brough's farm. Being closer it makes sense, but my question is, is the mission just to rescue those in the bunker or are there any other supplies or equipment at the base that we would like to get our hands on whilst we are there, as that would change my proposal?"

He looked at the admiral for guidance and waited for his response.

"Thank you, Sergeant Wood. I must admit that we have only discussed retrieving the base occupants, as that is the main priority. But now you mention it, if you think we have the capability to gather other much needed equipment and supplies, we would be foolish not to take the opportunity if we can safely do so."

He glanced to the ham radio we had sitting on a table in the corner of the room. "If we could use your radio equipment that would save time. We've bought our own, naturally, but yours is already set up so if you wouldn't mind that would be useful."

Turning to one of his aides, Walker-Jones spoke affably.

"Corporal Holland, would you kindly relay Sergeant Wood's question to the base? Good man."

Willie stood up and slapped the man on his back as he passed him.

"Come on Laddie, I'll show you how to get the old girl working. It may not be as fancy as one of your modern sets, but in my experience it'll probably work better."

Corporal Holland looked at the radio and muttered loud enough for all to hear.

"Bugger me, looks like what my granddad used in the war. Have we got to let the crystals warm up first?"

"Lot easier since we discovered running water and electricity," Willie chuckled, as the officers in the room grumbled at the perceived lack of respect the young soldier had shown.

Grinning happily at each other as they both knew the younger man had avoided a dressing down, the two sat down and Willie showed him how to operate his Ham radio as Walker-Jones continued.

"I suppose, as we are waiting, I can tell you about some of the other ideas we have...Are any of you familiar with M.O.D Kineton?"

Most of the military people nodded, but all the civilians shook their heads.

"I don't believe you know how fortunate you are to have picked Warwick Castle as your home," the admiral said. "M.O.D Kineton is Her Majesties Armed Forces main ammunition supply base, in fact, it's one of the largest in Europe. The base, which is not far from here, stores and distributes the majority of the munitions for the British Army, Royal Navy, and Royal Air force. You can imagine that a visit to there is high on our list."

Captain Hammond spoke up.

"Could you mark it on the map please Sir. I have heard of it but, I've never been there, so I have no idea where it is."

The admiral nodded to an aide with a marker pen who circled the base.

"What a stroke of luck," Steve exclaimed. "Do we know how much and what it contains?"

"No, unfortunately we don't," Digby replied. "All records are computerised and hence lost, but from reports gathered from those amongst us who have actually been there or been in meetings discussing the facility, it holds vast quantities of every kind of munition used by all branches of the armed forces. Stocks are maintained so they don't fall below predetermined levels which means it should contain enough to arm us for the foreseeable future and beyond."

"You know what this means?" Steve asked Marc, a grin spreading across his face. "No more trips to gun shops for the odd few thousand rounds or cartridges."

Marc held up his shortened arm that was still swathed in bandages and gave a muted, sarcastic cheer which caused another ripple of laughter to spread around the table, including among the newest arrivals who all knew of the incident at the gun shop that had cost him half an arm, but ultimately saved his life.

"Yes," Walker-Jones agreed. "The mission to clear the Scilly Isles used a large portion of our own reserves, particularly in small arms. If we hope to stand any chance in the wider operations to come, then what that base contains is vital."

He stopped when universally from us 'civilians', but especially from the knights, came a low snort of derision.

Looking genuinely shocked he looked around the table. "I'm sorry, have I said something wrong?"

I spoke first, smiling and holding my hands up to quieten a few who were about to speak.

"No, not at all. Yes, I agree that getting as much ammunition and the weapons that fire them as we can get our hands on is vital, but you must remember that for the most part, for the expense of relatively little ammunition, we've travelled a good way across the country and killed plenty of the undead in the process." I paused as I thought for a second. "I suppose what we're trying to say is that there are many ways to rid ourselves of zombies, and a lot don't involve shooting them. We only use our guns when the situation calls for it, but we have, I guess, killed the majority of them in other ways."

"I understand," the admiral said, a tone of humility now in his voice. "Which is why we consider your input vital to our planning."

He looked at the knights, who despite not wearing their armour still stood out from the rest of us due to the few items of medieval period clothing most still seem to favour wearing. They knew that if they were called on to help in an emergency then the padded gambesons and leather greaves they wore would speed up their readiness.

In all honesty, I think most of them thought they looked better in them, imagining they were actually part of a roving band of Vikings or more likely heroic knights of the order of the magic roundabout or whatever order they believed they belonged to.

"I would very much appreciate a demonstration of your techniques as soon as possible gentlemen, but we also need the bullets for the non-superhero types among us."

I leant forwards and spoke.

"I take it this base should contain a lot of everything we'll need and by nature it's going to weigh a lot. How do we get it to where it's needed, because flying it there in that plane of yours will take some time I guess?"

"Yes, it *is* heavy," said one of his aides in a superior sounding voice. "Flying ammunition in, unless it's the only way, is never efficient. Which is why we propose to use road transport to deliver it where it's needed. Once our logistics experts have worked out the mission parameters and requirements, we'll inform you of your orders."

The mood in the room changed immediately as half of the occupants drew in a sharp intake of breath at that statement.

"Excuse me?" I asked in cold reply, bristling with a rising anger.

It seemed to me that decisions which undoubtedly may affect us had already been made without consultation, and also more than exasperated that he thought he had the right to command us. I stared at the officer as I continued, my indignation making my tone sarcastic.

"Have you driven a vehicle around here recently?" I asked still looking at the aide who began to look very uncomfortable as he knew he had played the situation wrong. "No, I didn't think so. Have you felt the terror when your vehicle gets bogged down by the mangled bodies of the undead as it's trying to push through thousands of them? How about when the nearest ones attempt to push their faces through the glass of your window so they can eat you? No, I didn't think so. So, before your logistics experts think they can plan a leisurely drive through the countryside and then give us *orders*, I think you need to get some real-world experience under your belt otherwise you'll get everyone killed."

I sat back, my anger ready to boil over, preparing to have a go at the next arrogant officer who thought we were there to do their bidding.

Before anyone else spoke Walker-Jones interjected.

"I must apologise for the way my aide spoke. I can see how upset you all are and I apologise unreservedly for the misunderstanding. The truth is that we don't know anything yet. Which is why we are here to plan the best way forwards using our combined ideas, but mainly can I add that we need your input on how we can do it successfully and with the least risk. All we have are ideas, no firm plans, and you, if I can put it plainly, are the experts who have actually been there and done it so to speak. If such a time comes when plans require execution, then you would receive a *request*, and not orders."

He looked at some of the people who had arrived with him, but especially at the unfortunate aide who was sitting red faced and squirming with embarrassment.

"Ladies and Gentlemen, we are guests here," the admiral went on. "We are not here to annexe these survivors or take over their home, and I will not broker anyone who thinks they are superior to these fine people just because you have had some very expensive taxpayer funded training. Without their input we wouldn't have been able to clear the Scillies with as few losses as we suffered."

I glanced at Captain Digby, who at the mention of the losses let a dark shadow of grief pass over his face. The admiral's tone hardened as he continued.

"The next person to presume we rule a military dictatorship will not enjoy the personal interest I will take in their wellbeing and future career plans, is that clear?"

After a long, verging on the uncomfortable, silence the aide looked at me and said with as much confidence as he could muster.

"I apologise for my poorly chosen words. They did not come across as I intended, I assure you."

I nodded at him, accepting the apology which as far as I could tell, was truthful. The temperature in the room dropped a few degrees as our tempers subsided as quickly as they had risen.

The admiral slapped the table, breaking the uncomfortable silence and spoke cheerfully, closing the matter.

"Now shall we get on with it? We're here to first plan the mission to the base and will discuss M.O.D Kineton another time."

CHAPTER FOUR

Willie and Corporal Holland, who after spending time with the old, weather-beaten former sergeant was looking at him with a form of hero worship, had finished and returned to the table clutching papers.

"Report please," the admiral ordered. "And for the sake of those who don't already know, do detail who we are attempting to rescue."

The corporal looked at Willie, who gave him a nod of encouragement as he knew what it was like to address vastly superior officers, studied his notes and cleared his throat nervously before starting.

"Yes sir. There are thirty-two personnel in the bunker. Twenty-eight men and four women. Of the thirty-two, twenty are serving forces members made up mainly of…" He paused and looked at his admiral, concern on his face as if he may be overstepping boundaries. "Sir, this is classed as confidential information…"

"No, the time for cloak and dagger stuff has long passed," the admiral snapped.

He nodded and glanced at his notes before continuing.

"They are mainly made up of A Squadron, Two-Two SAS, with a few support personnel who made it to the bunker. The other twelve are two wives, two female base medical nurses and eight attached communication staff and contractors."

At the quizzical looks at the various descriptions given the admiral held up his hand to stop the aide.

"Didn't you know?" he asked, looking across the table at us. "The base is the Regimental HQ for the SAS. Why do you think we want to get to them first? Those soldiers are the best in the world at what they do, and they can't do it whilst stuck twenty feet underground." He looked at his aide again and waved his hand indicating he had finished. "Please continue."

"They've given me an initial list of equipment they would like to retrieve, if possible."

Holland paused as he looked at the list as if to remind himself of what he had just written down.

"It consists mainly of weapons and ammunition as you would expect. They also want their comms gear which consists of…"

"Wait," Walker-Jones said, interrupting him mid flow. "I think what Sergeant Wood needs to know is, are there any larger, bulkier items which will require specialist handling or vehicles they want us to try and reach. If it's just weapons, ammunition, and radios, then if we know where they are stored those decisions can be made on the ground when we're there. I imagine it'll be obvious if we can get to them or not."

"Yes sir," he replied glancing at the list again. "No, there's nothing I can see here that'll require specialist transport."

"Good," the admiral said, looking at Woody again. "If that information helps, can we have your proposal now please?"

Woody who had sat down, regained his feet and cleared his throat. He looked more nervous than I had ever seen him, but then I suppose he was unused to addressing such an illustrious audience. In the military orders usually flowed downhill, and I expected his involvement was normally at a smaller unit level where it was left to him or his immediate superiors to interpret the orders received and communicate them to the ranks below. He glanced at Steve who had been his superior officer since his arrival at the Castle, and who now gave him a reassuring nod, and a wink of support.

"Yes sir, that information does help. What I would propose is to do what we've found worked well in the past. Using the tractors, the armoured car, and scout vehicles – sorry the Land Rover and Volvo – we can get most places without too much trouble. If we include the bus and the up-armoured lorries, they should have the capacity to transport the extra personnel and any equipment we gather at the base. As to who to take, I suggest we go all-in on the mission and include all the knights and every experienced person we can field."

He paused, looking awkward as he glanced guiltily at Digby before continuing.

"Now please don't take this the wrong way, but the best people I can recommend to lead this mission are..." he waved his hand to the ones sitting on our side of the table. "Us lot."

The other side of the table sat in shocked silence but he continued resolutely, as if he was determined to get his point across before anyone interrupted him.

"We've all fought as a combined unit before and our cohesion and capabilities are, in my opinion, pretty remarkable considering most haven't had any military training whatsoever."

He shrugged as if in a way of explanation. "Maybe that's the trick? They haven't been constrained by years of rigid training and discipline like we have, so have been easy to mould into what they have become."

Digby began to rise spluttering with indignation and outrage at the suggestion that civilians would be ranked ahead of military personnel.

"Please," Woody said, holding both hands up in a conciliatory manner. "Let me finish and then we can discuss the merits, or not, of my idea."

"Carry on please, sergeant," the admiral said in a tone that brokered no tolerance for interruptions, but with a small smile flickering across his face as he was clearly enjoying his staff finding out they were not quite the pinnacle of prowess they considered themselves to be. This quietened the room down as others were beginning to join in voicing the captain's objections.

Woody continued after directing a short nod of thanks to the Admiral.

"As I said, we should go all-in and take everyone we can spare. When we get to the base, we use our proven smash, stab, repeat routine to kill or disable as many as we can from the safety of the vehicles. Once it's deemed safe enough, we'll debus our enlarged platoon of knights."

He paused and looked around the table at a few confused faces.

"I'm sorry I'll expand on that. Many of us have been training with the knights, drilling and perfecting larger unit actions. We can field over thirty armoured knights which will be able to face numbers many times that, and if they're supported by ground troops and those who remain in the vehicles to prevent our position getting outflanked, we can then clear our way into the building containing the bunker and extract our targets. As to gathering any other supplies or equipment you want us to get, I suggest we keep it simple and follow the same routine again until the job is done."

He paused again as if he knew what he was going to say next would cause more upset amongst the newly arrived guests.

"I also believe that command on the ground needs to be with Captain Hammond. He has fought alongside us and knows our capabilities and weaknesses. The situation, as we all know, can change rapidly and the chain of command needs to be short to avoid delays and potential confusion. Also, now that we know who we're rescuing it may be a good idea to find out how combat effective they are. Do they need ammunition or weapons? Because once we hopefully free them from the bunker, then twenty bored, pissed off Regiment blokes would be a major force multiplier in my opinion. But if they need us to bring any kit with us, we'll need to know so we can get that sorted too."

Sitting down, he let out a theatrical huff of relief, as if he was glad to get what he had said off his chest.

To stop the rising volume of chatter in the room, which had started between people as soon as Woody had sat down, Walker-Jones began rapping his knuckles on the ancient oak surface of the table. His gentle banging increased in volume as his frustration of being unheard rose, until with a loud crack he smashed his hand onto the table with a noise similar to a shotgun being discharged, causing the ornate candelabra that stood at the table's centre to wobble alarmingly.

"Thank you," he said curtly once the room had fallen immediately silent, reacting to the shock of his act.

After giving those on his side of the table an annoyed glance, he continued.

"Sergeant Wood, I thank you for you report, and on the surface I can see the complete sense of it, but before I sign off I am a firm believer that actions speak louder than words."

He paused to glance at the uniformed people that surrounded him. "I need to see your knights in action, because if they perform as well as I think they will, then it will stop all arguments from those that believe it is their job to advise me."

It took me a few moments to think over what he had said before I spoke.

"Sir, er, admiral," I blurted out, still not really knowing what I should call him without causing offence. "We can't just go out and find some zombies to fight just to appease your curiosity. People can get killed that way."

Jamie, one of the knights, put his hand up and made small grunting noises, as if he wanted the toilet really badly. Ian, who had noticed what he was doing laughed at him loudly and spoke before he could.

"You're not in school now, dickhead. If you've got something to say, just say it."

Jamie looked haughtily at Ian and stood.

"I have manners, unlike you, shit for brains!" he said, before turning bright red and looking guiltily around the table stammering an apology when he remembered who was listening to their banter. The admiral laughed at his embarrassed look.

"Please carry on, and don't feel like you must hold back from your normal discourse on my account. It makes a refreshing change from the usual staid meetings I generally attend."

Jamie threw a look and a one fingered gesture at Ian before he continued.

"Tom, I understand what you are saying, but all the rest of you have done so far is drills and battles against imaginary zombies. I think some carefully selected live fire exercises, so to speak, would be the best way to finish off your training. As far as I and the rest of us are concerned, you're all more than ready."

He looked at the admiral directly, "And I also agree with Woody, sorry Sergeant Wood, about Steve, sorry Captain Hammond, being in command. He knows what we can do and has done a great job looking after us all many times."

Walker-Jones gauged the mood in the room, watching many of us nodding in agreement at what Jamie had said alongside the frowns of consternation and mild disapproval from his own people, who most likely had misgivings about allowing civilians to do what they considered their duty.

"Right then I agree. If you are prepared to demonstrate your abilities, I suggest, as time is precious, that now is a good a time as any. Does anyone have any objections?"

The knights at the table looked at each other with eager grins on their faces at the thought of going into battle again. Ian stood and summed up their mood, oddly electing to affect an Australian accent for the occasion.

"Let's fuck'n do it then, boys."

CHAPTER FIVE

Steve, now adorned with his full kit and weapons including a hand axe attached to his belt, gained our attention and asked us to gather around him.

Most of us now wore a selection of chainmail or armour and shields taken either from the extra equipment the knights had bought with them, or removed from one of the many displays that had either adorned the walls or mannequins around the castle.

We'd adapted these to suit the enemy we were facing and not the enemy they were originally designed to protect the wearer from. The key to the armour was to protect us from bites and not the thrust of a sword or the swing of an axe, therefore there could be no space between each part of what we wore as the smallest gap between plates could allow a tooth to reach your flesh. We had invented a variety of ways to solve this including adding heavy duty fabric or leather to cover areas that could be exposed, to lacing some chainmail to another piece to stop them moving or lifting when in battle.

The weapons we carried were just as varied. Through trial and error we now had, either resting on shoulders or in scabbards attached to belts, our preferred personal weapons. My own choice was now a mace; less precise than the sword I had first chosen, but not as cumbersome as a large battle axe. After trying a few different weapons I had taken my chosen mace from the walls of a display and was informed by those who knew more about such things as I did that it was a flanged mace, and was a fine example of its type. All I knew that it felt right when I swung it and the sharp, heavy blades encircling its head would be great for splitting my enemy's heads apart, and the spike that adorned the end would penetrate skulls satisfactorily if I thrust it forwards. Most of us were also leaning on our pikes, but some who had struggled to handle the weight of them had opted for a shorter, lighter spear taken from one of the many displays of them the castle had. They lacked the reach of a pike, but when those with them were inter-mingled with the pikebearers they had, in theory at least, the po-tential to add another layer of defence to our formation.

The admiral and those with him watched with fascination as we kitted up. One aide with him took photographs of the process and made notes, explaining that, again, if they didn't have picture evidence then those back on the Scillies may have a hard time believing them.

The many hours we had spent practising had paid dividends to all our fitness levels. With our regular morning exercise classes, which we all still moaned about but I think secretly most of us enjoyed, I knew I was as fit as I had ever been. Becky had more than once caught me admiring my improving shape once or twice in the mirror in our bedroom. Of course she mocked me, but in quieter, more personal moments, she admitted liking my new trimmer more muscled look, as I did hers.

"Okay, Gentlemen – and Ladies – sorry," Steve began, offer-ing a small bow of complement to the females in our group.

They had, as usual, grouped together where they seemed to prefer their own conversation, rather than the simpler ones the men seemed to fall back on. The six women, Becky, Louise, Aggie, Lucy, Victoria, and Faye, who had fully recovered from her ordeal in the camping warehouse, had all joined in with the training with as much gusto as the men, often outlasting the older ones of their male colleagues in terms of stamina and fitness. Myself included.

The sight of my wife and the other women dressed as they were, all heavily armed with their weapons of choice, gave them the look of a troop of Amazonian beauties. It was a sight that had taken me a while to get used to and I could see the newly arrived military personnel watching them with a look of either awe, admiration, or fear on most of their faces.

Which one was hard to decide.

A few of us, in our defence, intended more for chivalrous rather than misogynistic reasons, had earlier tried to dissuade the women from joining the patrol we were about to attempt. Personally, I just didn't want Becky putting herself in harm's way and my protests were more out of a sense of love, and fear that if something were to go wrong, how could I forgive myself?

Our well-meant ministrations seemed to make all of them more determined than ever to join in. It took Maud, as usual, to put a stop to the situation. Hearing our pleading to the women and their firm rejections of them, she had put her hand to her mouth and emitted her customary very loud shrill whistle which had quietened us all immediately, before speaking in the tone she reserved for special telling off occasions.

"Just because they are women is no excuse for this behaviour whatsoever. If they want to go, they can and they will. In my opinion they are braver and stronger than you load of full of bluster and hot air men will ever be!" she said firmly, before eyeballing each man in turn.

We knew that look well enough by now. It was the one normally used when you knew to defy it would bring consequences none of us had dared yet to strive for. It was the look that promised a counterargument could result in testicular trauma. The glare that promised pain and humiliation in return for disobedience.

None of us tested her. The decision was made and nothing we could say or do would change it.

"We've planned this but let me go over the details one more time before we leave," Steve continued, inviting the group to close around him.

His voice hardened and he spoke slowly and clearly as if addressing a group of children.

"We'll use the vehicles to reach the main gate and the foot patrol will start from there. We've already checked and there are only a few hanging around by it. When they're dealt with, we will proceed further into the town in marching order until we come across one of the larger concentrations we know are still loitering around. I'll then choose the area best suited to deal with them and will advance or retreat as one to that location on my command. Willie'll use the bucket of his tractor to clear the chosen area free of any debris or bodies while the other vehicles position themselves both behind us and on our flanks to provide cover."

He waved towards Walker-Jones and his entourage who stood to one side observing the bizarre sight of a captain, in full battle kit, adorned with the best weapons the British Army produced with the incongruous addition of a hand axe attached to his body armour, addressing a group of medieval knights.

He indicated to those of his men not dressed as knights, but still in their issued uniform.

"I'll be in the flanks on foot with these men but will only issue the order to fire if the situation dictates. We have practised this drill many times, so those in the shield wall follow the orders of your section leader."

For larger formations the original knights positioned themselves between the more inexperienced of us and led their smaller 'platoons', but still followed the orders of the knight in overall command. Ian had been chosen to command this mission as his height gave him a natural view over everyone's heads so he could survey the whole battlefield and issue orders. Steve would be in overall command but trusted Ian to work with him.

"Once that horde has been dealt with, I'll decide if it is prudent or necessary to go further into the town and do the same again," Steve paused, casting his eyes over us.

"*Please* be careful. Yes, this is an expansion of your training, and I am in no doubt you can do it, but I don't need to remind you that beyond our walls is enemy territory and everything out there wants to eat you. You only get one chance to get it right, so don't think because we are being observed akin to some bizarre experiment, that now is the time for heroics. Do as we have trained, and you will all come home."

I knew what he was doing. Yes, those of us that had not fought as we were about to had not done it for real yet, but it was hard not to feel confident in our abilities. Confidence is good but complacency can kill, and he just wanted one last chance to remind us of that.

With serious faces we nodded our agreement. Steve smiled and waved his arm in a circular motion above his head, calling out, "Okay. Everyone, mount up!"

***

The children, along with the adults who had been chosen to stay behind to keep an eye on them and to help them guard our walls, all waved from their various vantage points as we drove through the grounds.

I stood beside Becky in the trailer, and we waved enthusiastically when we spotted both Stanley and Daisy. Slipping an arm around her shoulder I spoke smoothly.

"Here we go darling, off on another date. Don't say I don't spoil you."

She leant into me, returning my affections and acknowledging my gentle teasing. I turned serious.

"And I do mean it. I don't care that you and your fellow suffragettes have had your little victory and are coming, but to be clear, you are *not* going to leave my side. We fight side by side, or I'll throw you back on to the trailer myself if you think otherwise."

Becky gave me one of her '*and you want to try that?*' looks before tightening her hold around me and speaking softly.

"It's the only place I want to be, Tom. Who else is going to stop you from doing something stupid?"

Once we were through the inner gate that led from the carpark and it was closed behind us, we disembarked from the vehicles. Under Steve and Ian's direction we formed a line facing the main gate where I could see maybe ten zombies, no doubt attracted by the noise we had made. They now pressed against it and gnashed their teeth greedily at the nearness of fresh flesh and tried to force their arms through to reach us. Horace, who had insisted on joining us, snarled and barked at the ones at the gate, giving the impression that he wanted to take them on by himself.

As soon as he had seen Ian climbing the ramp to get into the trailer he had rushed up after him, sat down, and refused to move. Not even the temptation of food changed his mind and he sat resolutely, resisting all efforts to pull him from the trailer whilst issuing huffs of indignation until Ian relented in exasperation.

"Let the lump come if he wants to so bloody much! They wanted to see *all* of us in action after all, and he knows what he's doing."

As soon as the trailer door closed Horace lifted his backside from the deck and trotted around with a smug look on his face to receive the fuss he knew he deserved from his fellow warriors.

"Pikes and spears behind you and shields up," Ian boomed when he saw we were in formation.

He waited while we laid the pikes and spears on the ground behind us and raised our shields before saying, "Jamie, open the gate please mate – *Horace! No! Back!*"

Jamie stepped forwards and used his pike to kill the ones nearest to the padlock. Horace stopped barking and gave Ian what could only be described as a haughty look before plodding obediently back, and sat at the end of the line with a superior look on his face as if to prove he had now scared them enough to let the humans deal with the problem. Jamie, with an ungloved hand, quickly entered the code and removed the padlock. He gave a final glance to ensure we were ready and swung the gate open before running back to rejoin the line.

With the resistance of the gate gone, the zombies staggered before regaining what balance they had and made their way directly to us. Our linked shields formed a solid wall which they soon reached and ineffectually tried to break through. The eleven zombies lacked the strength or weight of numbers to trouble us, but still the unearthly groans and rasps they made and the rotting hands that reached over the wall of shields was not a pleasant experience. Separated by the thin divide of my shield the putrid smell of expelled breath turned my stomach as they lurched and pushed their decomposing corpses against it.

I stood bracing myself, not concerned as I knew they could not harm us as long as we, working together, held them back, but wondered why Ian had not issue the command to attack yet.

"You see?" Ian shouted. "The shields keep you safe! Are you ready to kill them yet?"

When the answering roar had died down, he sucked in a great breath to prepare his parade ground voice.

"On three, push back!"

We knew what the drill was, so I braced myself, stole a quick glance at Becky whose brow was furrowed with concentration and effort, and listened for the countdown. When the count reached one, we all let out a collective grunt of effort and shoved our shields forwards as one. The shockwave we created drove the clawing, reaching zombies off their feet, leaving them struggling to rise on the black tarmac of the car park.

"Weapons ready!" Ian boomed.

We in drilled perfection, took one pace forwards, moved our shields to one side and raised our weapons.

"Strike!"

The next command roared from his throat. We outnumbered the zombies three to one, so not everyone had a target to aim at, but those that did swung or stabbed their weapons at the snarling, snapping heads of the undead writhing on the ground before them, ending their tortured, miserable existence forever. I watched as Becky twisted the sword that she had thrust through her target's eye socket straight into its brain and withdrew it. She calmly cleaned the gore of destroyed eyeball and brain matter from it by wiping it on the remnants of clothing the former man was wearing before turning to me, her eyes bright with adrenalin. Becky had killed many zombies before, but they had mainly been dispatched using a spear, rifle, or shotgun, not up close and personal as this had been. Of course, she'd seen and witnessed uncountable other horrific acts of violence and terror, all in the name of keeping us safe, but in a way, I knew this was different.

"Are you okay?" I asked.

"Yes, why shouldn't I be? It wanted to kill me, so I killed it, and that's the end of it," she said sharply before recognizing the look on my face and softening her tone. "Tom I'm fine. It's what we have to do so we can eventually live a normal life again. No doubt later on we're all going to have to deal with the emotional damage, but that's in the future, when we don't have to hide behind the walls of a castle just so we can sleep at night. So yes, I'm okay thank you my love."

I used the arm still gripping my shield to give her a quick embrace. She'd called the zombie 'it', which I guessed was a way of depersonalising the act of killing a former human being. I decided to talk to her later about it to find out if she had consciously said 'it' or not. I looked up, as out of the corner of my eye I could see Ian and Steve walking to our front, both stepping carefully over those we had just killed.

"Good work," Steve said, smiling with genuine pleasure. "Now we've shown our guests how we deal with a few of them, shall we go and show them what we're capable of against more of the bastards?"

He looked up at Walker-Jones who was standing on the bed of the crane lorry we had gotten from the builders merchants, alongside all of those who had accompanied him. "Are you happy to continue, Sir?"

"Only if you are, captain," he replied. "That was very effective I must say, and despite my concerns it appeared to pose very little risk to your people…but I don't want to put any of you in danger just to satisfy my curiosity. It would be heinous of me to do so."

Steve turned back to us.

"Are you all happy to continue and follow the plan?"

At our unanimous affirmative roar of reply, he turned to Ian.

"Right then, big boy, stay in the centre of the line and I'll watch your flanks. Go slowly and listen out for my orders."

Ian's voice boomed out.

"Grab your pikes and spears guys and gals, and let's get going!"

Our formation wouldn't have passed a parade inspection. We didn't practise marching or drilling with the weapons we had, just how to use them to kill. The column that walked through the gates flanked on either side by the soldiers had the look of a disorganised rabble out for a leisurely Sunday stroll.

Walking with my pike resting on my shoulder and shield slung over my back I heard the vehicles rumbling behind us as they slowly followed our lead. The main thing I noticed again though, was the stomach-churning smell of rot and decay emanating from the bodies we had piled up in droves from our previous outings that didn't just hit you, but smacked you hard around the face like a punch from a prize fighter. Clouds of flies rose, flocks of birds squawked in indignation at having their feast disturbed, and swarms of rats scurried away as we passed them. We'd talked many times about the need to rid ourselves of the potential health hazard we'd created but other needs had always taken precedence.

Walking along trying not to gag and seeing others around me doing the same I decided that it really had to become a priority, once the furore created by our visitors had passed. I smiled ruefully to myself as I decided that there would always be other, more pressing needs that would try and vie to be top of our to-do list. I'd just have to hope others thought it important too.

A call of, "*Zombies. Halt!*" from the head of our column bought me back to the present. The sweet, cloying smell of decay that filled my nostrils and coated my throat immediately forgotten.

CHAPTER SIX

I was in the third row of our column next to Becky, so I could see what was ahead of us. A few hundred meters away a large gathering of maybe two hundred zombies, who had been raised from the immobile stupor they seemed to fall into when nothing drew their attention, were beginning to shamble in our direction, attracted by the noises we were making.

Steve raised his radio and spoke.

"Willie, come up and clear the area in front of us please. This spot is as good as any."

A cheerful reply of, "*On ma way laddie*," came back and I heard the revving of a tractor's engine as he overtook the vehicles in front of him and raced past us. The plough that had been fixed to the bucket of his tractor had been removed for this very purpose. We needed to move bodies out of the way using the scoop of the bucket and not cleave through them, just pushing them aside, as the plough would have done.

As he passed me, he lowered the bucket to the tarmac with a metallic clang and scraped it noisily along the road pushing an ever-growing pile of corpses ahead of him until he had cleared a swathe of them out of the way. With the approaching horde growing nearer with every step they made, Willie kept repeating this, driving up and down the road ahead of us pushing piles of mangled broken bodies aside with each pass, leaving dark streaks of gore in his wake that I tried not to look at, until Steve called over the radio for him to stop when he deemed the area was clear enough.

That and the fact the zombies were almost close enough to engage. Obediently he turned around and headed back, giving a thumbs up and a big smile as he passed by before pulling to the side to get out and stand on the wheel arches of his tractor with his shotgun held ready to provide covering fire if necessary.

"Ian," called Steve. "Make ready."

Before Ian spoke, we had anticipated the order and were already moving into position, the original knights keeping those close to them in line and uttering words of encouragement as we formed up.

"Knights, onward!" Ian cried, and the line began to pace forwards, closing the distance between us and the zombies quickly.

"Halt!" came the next command when they were twenty metres away. We had over fifty metres of cleared ground behind us with which to step back into if the press of the undead became too great and we needed more space.

I looked around, thinking it was a good tactical position to be in. The buildings on the high street and the newly made piles of corpses stacked up kept the ones approaching channelled towards us. A good tactical position, yes, but could we perform as expected?

I muttered a few words of love to Becky as Ian ordered, "Pikes ready." I raised the heavy weapon in my hands and gripped it tightly. Our training showed, as a line of long pikes interspersed with a few spears raised as one, turning the line of medieval knights into a deadly weapon of war.

Straining against the weight, I waited until the first one was in range before thrusting my pike forwards and impaling the skull of what was once a policeman, whose ragged uniform hung from his torn and bloody body in shreds, through its forehead. Withdrawing the spike I watched it crumple lifelessly to the ground, and quickly steadied myself to impale my next target that was stumbling over the blockage I had created. My world shrunk to the area directly in front of me as I fought against the growing weight of the pike and trying to get as many first time kills as I could. Missing with one thrust, due to the zombie stumbling on the growing mound of dead we were creating, I punched the spike through the shoulder of it as it advanced towards me. Pushing it back I was about to yank out the spike when with horror I saw the grotesquely damaged body of what was once a young boy walk under its outstretched arms and head straight towards me.

Time slowed down as I stared at the small, snarling beast as its dark lifeless eyes bored into my soul. Its gait was awkward as one of its ankles was broken causing its foot, which was only attached to the leg by a few scraps of skin and sinew, to collapse sideways when it put weight on it. Swearing in a mix of panic and fear as both of my hands were still holding the pike, I shifted position so I could try and kick it away. I watched as a spear head thrust forwards ending up embedding itself deep in its skull, ending the tortured existence of the young boy forever. A quick glance back up the bloodied shaft showed Becky, implacable and professional in her work. As it collapsed, I freed my pike from the shoulder it was stuck in and, with a renewed burst of adrenaline and energy, killed it on my second attempt.

I risked another glance at Becky, who after killing the young boy was standing ready again her spear held out in front of her with a resolute stare of concentration covering her face.

"Thanks, love," I gasped between my sharp shock filled breaths.

Without casting a glance in my direction as more zombies were still crawling over the growing pile of bodies we had created, she replied through teeth gritted with determination. "What *would* you do without me, darling?"

Chancing a glance at the boy who had fell at my feet I thought, *probably die*…but had no time to verbalise it as the next wave of zombies were closing in. After a few more thrusts with my pike Ian bellowed another order.

"Get ready to push. On my command drop your pikes and make ready!"

At the shouted command we dropped our pikes and spears behind us and raised our shields and made good our footing ready for the next move. A few from the ones guarding our flanks ran forwards to collect our pikes and spears and dropped them fifteen paces further behind us before returning to their position. We waited, catching our breaths until they reached us, and we leant into our shields resisting their advance. After the brief fight at the castle gates earlier, the rasping growls and clawing limbs of the zombies reaching over our shield wall as they pushed against us did not hold the same terror as before. Not that it was an enjoyable experience by any means, but as long as we stuck to our training we knew we would remain as safe as possible.

"Push on three," Ian yelled, his booming voice echoing off the buildings around us.

As one we once again put all our weight into our shields and shoved forwards two paces, tumbling the zombies back into the pile of corpses.

"Prepare to strike…"

We reached for our weapons and gripped them firmly.

"*Strike!*"

We shifted the position of our shields and began swinging and thrusting our weapons at the ones struggling to regain their feet and were crawling over the wall of bodies we had created.

A few minutes of brutal effort later, Ian called out to Steve.

"Steve, we're pulling back. Get ready."

When Steve had confirmed his people were ready, Ian ordered us to disengage and drop back fifteen paces where, now breathing heavily, we picked up our pikes and spears and made ready again.

This routine we had done or watched many times, but this was the first time we had tried it with so many knights and all of us could see the difference the extra numbers made. Already we had thinned out the advancing horde considerably, by at least half by my estimate, as I looked at the ones now awkwardly scrambling over their former comrades.

Others ran forwards with canteens of water which we gratefully drank from, easing our already parched throats, before Ian shouted again.

"One more time, guys."

At a moan from a few in our group he added a little more sheepishly at his inadvertent error.

"Sorry, and gals."

Again, following his commands, we used the pikes, shields and our hand weapons to build another mound of re-killed corpses until only a few remained beyond the gory barrier. Those, due to missing, broken, or mutilated limbs were unable to get over it, naturally flowed around the flanks of the barricade where bullets ended their attempts to reach us.

Ian ordered us back another fifteen paces where he stood and surveyed the field of carnage we had created. Very few zombies were left 'alive'.

A satisfied grin rose on his sweat-covered face, and he turned to Steve who had pulled his troops back to be in line with us.

"I think that's enough of a demonstration, don't you?" Ian enquired politely.

The admiral answered for Steve.

"It certainly is my friend. I can safely say I have never seen *anything* quite as remarkable as that in my life. I have no doubt that we must defer to your tactics from now on."

He turned to take in the shocked faces of his people who had just watched the same demonstration with amazed awe. "Don't you agree?"

To my shock, a small round of applause from the visitors rang out like we'd just performed a recital for their entertainment, until the boom of Willie's shotgun reminded everyone that there were still dangers out there.

"Can we leave off on the love fest until we're back behind our walls?" Willie called out in his gruff, Scottish accent.

He pointed to the few zombies who had got closer whilst our attention was elsewhere. He raised his shotgun again and removed the top of the head of the closest one with a single blast, pumping the action of his gun with a loud and menacing *shuck-shuck* before continuing.

"You're all acting like a load of Sunday school children out for a damned picnic!" he mocked, turning purposely from his position high on the sides of his tractor to face the few remaining zombies that were making their way towards us and acting as if he was the only one on guard, which to our shame we realised he had been.

Instantly contrite, we looked at each other sheepishly as we had almost been caught out by an absolute rookie error caused by excitement and more than a little overconfidence.

"Thank you, Willie." Hammond said, taking back control. "You are, to my shame, correct."

Hammond looked up at the admiral who was as red faced and guilty looking as the rest of us.

"If you could wait for a few minutes while we deal with the stragglers, we can continue this conversation back at the castle…knights, get into marching formation. The soldiers will terminate the rest," Hammond said with a glance towards Sergeant Eddy. "Sergeant? Carry on."

"You heard the captain," Eddy growled. "Form line and fire at will! And for the avoidance of doubt, because I know many of you were dropped on your heads at birth, they are all called bloody Will!"

That raised the mood, and whilst the last few zombies were dealt with by single shots to their heads, we shuffled into a column ready for the march home. With Willie's tractor in the lead and with us following, the rest of the vehicles trailed our trudge back to the castle guarding our backs and flanks.

CHAPTER SEVEN

When we had cleaned ourselves of the blood and gore that had splashed our armour, we removed it and changed into more comfortable clothes before gathering in the Great Hall. The children had been relieved from guard duty and Captain Digby had volunteered to take them, with a detachment of his people acting as guards, to the playground. He was, as he had said earlier in the day, when his job allowed, trying to take his uncle duties to Eddie seriously. Eddie relished any attention he got from his uncle and clearly worshipped him as a hero as I supposed any boy would with an uncle who was a captain in the Royal Marines. He also seemed to have come out of his shell of grief a little more now he knew he had some family left, and no longer felt like an orphan.

After Maud and a few of her 'volunteer' helpers had made sure everyone had a mug of tea in their hands, as hoped for, the admiral got our attention. In conversations between us as we walked back, we had decided that we would let him appraise our performance first and not search out the approbation we knew we deserved. Not that we wanted to play games with him, just that we knew that the demonstration of our skills had been, apart from the end, exemplary, but didn't want that to put a stain on the review of our performance.

"Ladies and Gentlemen," he began with a grave look on his face. "Firstly, permit me to apologise unreservedly for creating the distraction that ultimately could have led to one of you fine people getting in harm's way. I'm mortified that my unforgivable error in breaching the chain of command I'd approved whilst in a battlefield situation could have caused this."

He smiled and opened his arms in an expansive gesture.

"But now I can, without fear of causing any more strife. I must say again that the demonstration of your zombie fighting skills was the most remarkable thing I have ever seen. Never in my wildest imaginations would I believe I would be seeing medieval weaponry and techniques being used with such skill on a modern battlefield. I have listened to your accounts, but until I saw them first-hand, I don't think I truly believed them. Most of you have no prior military or even fighting experience, which in itself is testament to all of your combined determination to survive in the terrible world we now find ourselves in. You are unrestrained by any ingrained training and tactics that as we now understand, tragically hampered the ability of our fighting forces to adapt to the situation. You are a credit to the nation and, If I may, I would now appreciate the chance to applaud you on what you have all achieved."

He waved for his people to stand, and with him leading, they began clapping and cheering.

It went on for many minutes, and I thought that maybe it was a release for them as well. For a long time they had all been struggling with a fast moving and ever-changing situation, where terrible news followed swiftly on the heels of bad. They had fought mutiny among other ship's crews and watched as they were lost.

Desperately trying to hold whatever grip they had on the command structure, the tattered remnants of the Royal Navy and their support ships had gathered from all around the world in the Solent, a stretch of water forever associated with the proud history of the Royal Navy, safe from the terror that assailed their beloved country, but also within sight of it, helpless to do anything about it.

Humanity made them send out the message for all able private crafts to make their way to them where they would extend their umbrella of protection and hope over them, but initially they didn't really know what they could offer. When we first established contact with them using Willie's ancient Ham radio, their plans for finding a safe area for the growing numbers of survivors responding to their radio transmissions and made their way to the only hope they had left, was in its infancy.

Once the Scilly isles had been decided on as a potential safe place for what was left of the British population, it was our input on tactics to adopt and weapons to use that gave them their first taste of victory as they battled to clear the islands and make them safe once more for the living to repopulate.

Now they had established a secure place to survive they had to look outwards again, and we were going to be a part of that plan. What they had just witnessed us do had given them the confidence that all the many ideas and theories they had come up with, were hopefully more than just that, and could work.

I think we all must have felt a bit self-conscious at the applause at first, but I decided, eventually, to enjoy it. It was a confirmation of what we had achieved since it all began when our group had gradually formed and evolved into what we were today. We knew what we'd achieved could only be described as remarkable, and I thought, *You know what? Why not take the praise?*

And I can't have been the only one feeling that way.

The ones to whom the praise was aimed began to celebrate too. We joined in the applause, we cheered, shook hands and hugged each other. Some started dancing around the room like drunken revellers when the clock strikes midnight on New Year's Eve until a loud whistle from Maud bought us all back into order again.

"Yes. Well done all you lot. Don't you all feel proud of your-selves," she said, trying to keep a stern face and not let the smile we could all see trying to emerge, break out. "That's enough of all your tomfoolery. You must have better things to do with your time than pat each other's backs and..." she got no further as Willie picked her up and began whirling her around the room trying to smother her with kisses which set all of us off again.

It took some time for order to be restored but when it was, it was a much more combined group that began to plan the next operation: To free the people trapped in the bunker.

The plan, once many ideas had been put forward, discussed, and either rejected or approved, followed Simon's initial recom-mendation virtually to the letter. The one main addition would be the Merlin helicopter that would fly up from the Scillies and provide overhead cover, resupply, and fire support. I personally couldn't see, apart from the cool factor, what having a helicopter would really do to help us but guessed it couldn't do any harm so I did not see the point in moaning about it.

Time, as we all knew, was of the essence and as the forecasters were predicting the weather would break in four days, which might hamper the ability of the helicopter to provide effective cover, we agreed to begin the mission in two days. The first day would involve moving all the personnel, vehicles, and equipment to the Brough's farm ready for a dawn start to head to the base.

The helicopter that was flying up the next day after refuelling at the airfield, would wait at the castle until the mission was close to the base which was only about thirty minutes flying time away. It would have about four hour's endurance over the base before it needed to return to the airfield to refuel, so we planned to send a small detachment to meet the helicopter at the airfield to provide protection and aide in the refuelling. The detachment would stay there, safe in the control tower, and guard the airfield in case it needed to refuel during the mission. The plan was for them to return to the castle once the mission was over, and the helicopter was refuelled for the last time.

Unsurprisingly, every available fighter wanted to go on the mission so the hard decision was who to pick to stay behind and guard the castle. I knew the children could guard the castle – utterly impregnable to the undead when the gates were closed – even if that concept was so insane in a recent, previous life, so it was more a case of who wanted to stay behind and watch over them and keep the kettle and the lights on.

To my relief, Becky chose to stay. She was more than capable of standing in the fighting line, but I personally didn't want her to keep proving herself by doing so. Nicky, being pregnant, was obviously the only one automatically chosen. The others who chose to stay were Maud, who was more than content with keeping an eye on her brood of youngsters, and Charles, the vicar, who was definitely more a man of words than action, albeit words of value and wisdom. Marc was also still a long way from being allowed back on to active duty, though he now at least had the strength to walk up the steps to the battlements where he insisted, if he was provided with a stool to sit on, he could help the children keep watch.

Two of the aides who had accompanied the admiral were also ordered to stay. They insisted they wanted to continue planning the logistics operation to supply the Scillies, which they claimed was a priority. Both looked more suited to desk work than other military activities and the admiral readily agreed to them staying behind as if putting a seal of approval on their lack of martial ability. He saved their embarrassment by stating he needed them to also monitor their comms gear. Two more fighting men were selected by Steve to provide the main defence force, and those rescued from the pub were also kept behind. They had only been with us for a matter of days, and even though they were all willing to get involved they had not yet had the chance to do much training apart from basic firearms familiarization. We planned to do more, but the arrival of the delegation from the Scillies had put a lot of what we could have done on hold. They could guard the walls, fire a gun if push came to shove, and generally help around the place.

It meant leaving the castle poorly defended, but we were confident that even with so few people, if zombies did breach the outer fences, then the walls and the firepower they could still bring to bear on them would be more than sufficient. To put our minds at rest, the admiral reminded us that the helicopter could also be diverted from the mission and could be overhead providing extra cover in a matter of minutes if the situation became dire and could even land in the central courtyard if necessary to add its occupants to the castle walls defenders.

We'd been told that the Merlin's had all been fitted with extra machine guns on both doors and the rear ramp, and carried extra crew to man them so they resembled a flying machine gun nest and had the capability to pour down a large amount of fire all around them if need be.

With the mission and personnel agreed on, we all got on with sorting and loading the supplies we would take. All the vehicles were refuelled and checked over, and any repairs or maintenance needed were done by Shawn and Willie. The admiral and his aides were relegated to porters as we had done this task many times before and knew what we were doing. I didn't really expect Walker-Jones to enjoy getting his hands dirty, but he enthusiastically joined in with our efforts. By the time the unmistakable *whop-whop-whop* of the approaching helicopter broke the silence the following morning, we were ready to go.

We knew it was approaching as the team at the airfield had reported its departure, and most of us found an excuse to leave the walls and gather near the landing zone marked out with white paint on the field in front of the castle. The children all waved excitedly as it did a low circuit around us, it's downdraft buffeting us mercilessly before landing gently in front of us.

I changed my mind about needing it when I saw it. It looked impressively large and deadly, and, I had to admit, very cool. Two machine guns were mounted in either side door and two more were at the open rear ramp, all manned by crew who thankfully were not aiming them at us but were waving just as enthusiastically as the children as it settled to the ground and the shrieking whine of its engines powered down.

Once the aircraft was secured and the crew had formally greeted the admiral and his staff, they allowed the children who were still eagerly hovering around the helicopter to jump on board and explore it. They didn't need to be told not to touch the weapons that bristled from it as they knew full well how deadly they were. Becky and I smiled as Stanley, sitting in the pilot's seat and wearing an oversized flight helmet, waved at us with a huge smile on his face through the window.

"Where's your phone when you need it?" I said as I took Becky's hand and gave Stanley a thumbs up. "That would make a great picture for the yearly album."

Becky automatically began to pat her pockets to search for her phone, until the reality dawned on her that the phone, she always used to have no more than a grab away, along with everything it could do, was a thing of the past.

When the children and the much older children, including me, had had their fun inspecting the helicopter everyone went back to the castle to finish preparing for the following day.

CHAPTER EIGHT

Dawn was just breaking as we said our farewells. Hugging Becky and my children I turned and climbed into the trailer as Eddie was hugging his Uncle Darren. We were still his primary carers, but ever since he had been reunited with his uncle we were giving them as much time as possible together. We didn't know how long he'd be with us, as his role would clearly fall in with battling to clear the infestation of zombies from the mainland, therefore every memory they could make together would be precious.

After making sure my armour and weapons were stowed away safely at the front of the trailer alongside where everyone else had stacked their kit, I claimed a spot on the side. We decided not to wear our armour for the trip to the Brough's farm as we knew the route should be clear, apart from the occasional wandering zombie. They could be easily dealt with using the plough or spear and if we did need to don our armour it wouldn't take long anyway.

I glanced forlornly at my Volvo, as the decision had been made not to take it as we had enough vehicles to choose from. Simon's Defender and the armoured car would provide us with enough scouting capabilities, and both possessed far more firepower than mine. We also needed maximum feet on the ground and the two or three extra that would have been needed to man the Volvo would be better utilized as armoured knights when we got there.

The convoy consisted of both tractors with their trailers, the bus, the crane lorry, both army trucks and the two scout cars.

Most of the personnel going were in both trailers with just drivers accompanied by someone riding shotgun in the others. From the trailers we could wreak the most havoc with both spears and guns, and the bus was to be the main transport vehicle for those we picked up and the lorries and trailers would hopefully get filled with any equipment and stores we could find when we were there. With a final wave and shouts of love the convoy drove through the Barbican entrance and made its way through the castle grounds.

The route to the Brough's farm was a well-travelled path, and a lot of us knew it reasonably well and were able to mark our progress by the various landmarks we passed on the way. Both Walker-Jones and Digby were travelling in the trailer with me and we passed the time discussing the mission, stabbing the occasional zombie and looking out at the mainly deserted villages and open countryside.

When we passed it, I pointed out where we had rescued the ones from the pub in the village, just visible across the fields, re-telling the story of how fortunate they were when I spotted the flash of their torch they were using to try and get our attention.

Walker-Jones was excited to visit the outpost we had created at the Brough's farm. Apart from the Brough's, it was manned by the detachment of soldiers who had volunteered to be garrisoned there. Steve's sergeant, Geoff Gallon, was still the officer in charge there until Woody or Eddy replaced him for a tour.

The concept of creating outposts dotted strategically around the country, which would provide safe havens from which to begin the ultimate task of clearing the undead from our land, was one the admiral was keen to explore as, logically and militarily, it made sense. Akin to the coaching inns of old that provided refuges for passengers as they made the long journeys around the countryside hundreds of years ago, the outposts would provide bases to rest, refuel and rearm. The thought was that we would start by creating them between the port, which would be the mainland end of the sea bridge we intended to make between the Scillies, and our home at Warwick Castle. Where that port was located had yet to be decided, but the quality of the route and the time it would take to travel would dictate how many outposts, if any, were needed.

We'd discussed the question of which port to use the previous night, deciding that the problem was most of the obvious large deep-water ports were in, or close to, large population centres and so would most likely be packed with the undead. Smaller fishing ports would hopefully be less crowded, but the dockside facilities or mainly the potential lack of them, may make loading and unloading more problematic and time consuming. Plus, larger ships may have too deep a draught to enter them. It was what the two aides who had remained behind were working on, so we hoped by the time we returned they would have the solution for us.

Driving up the track to the Brough's farm I could see that a lot more work had been completed since I was last there. The towers, built on all four corners, dominated the skyline, and the walls I noted had been raised and strengthened, but the ditch was the biggest improvement. The work on it had begun when I was there, but it was now a deep, wide trench that surrounded the whole compound. A wire fence lined the top of it and as we got closer, I could see the whole ditch was filled with sharpened stakes. Under the steep drop into the ditch these stakes were vertical to impale zombies if they behaved as we expected and just blindly fell into it. The stakes nearer the walls were set at an angle to impale them as they walked onwards if they had somehow managed to avoid the initial massed ranks of sharpened wood. The angled gate we'd constructed to protect the main gate had been strengthened and improved. It was clear they had not been idle in our absence.

The admiral stood next to me as I pointed out the works that had been started by us and improved by the residents. The gates were pushed open as we approached, and our convoy rolled into the yard where Sergeant Gallon greeted us and directed us where to park the vehicles. The yard of the farm was large, but our convoy needed organising properly or it would cause chaos when we needed to turn around and leave if they weren't positioned correctly.

The sergeant was a stickler for the right way to do things, and he had his men lined up as if on parade so when the admiral stepped from the trailer he issued a loud command of, "Detail 'shun", and his men smartly followed the order.

Observing protocol, Walker-Jones returned the salute of the sergeant and inspected the troops, shaking a few of their hands and chatting with a few more before ordering Gallon to dismiss the parade so they could get on with the real business of them being here. After greeting the Broughs, he asked Stuart Brough and Sergeant Gallon to give him a tour to show him how the defences they had built worked.

Meanwhile Helen, Stuart's wife, and their daughter bought out trays of tea which we all gratefully accepted. I knew them reasonably well by now, so we chatted amiably until the admiral returned from the tour.

"This is all very impressive," he said when he had a mug of tea in his hands. "It shows what can be achieved in a short time with the right equipment and materials, but most of all skill and determination. This place has been described to me in many reports, and I must say it doesn't disappoint. It can easily become the blueprint for what we hope to build in the future. You should all be very proud of what you have created."

He waved his hand towards his aides that had accompanied us.

"I doubt any of my highly trained staff could have come up with anything like what you have achieved here in such a short space of time, but congratulating you is not why we're here. We're here to rescue every person we can who, without our help, would face certain death in the not-too-distant future. So shall we get on with preparing for that?"

Most of those stationed at the farm were also joining us on the mission as well. It was the benefit of an outpost like this one, and any more we established, would provide a force of trained personnel to bolster any future missions we carried out. It was just more than fortunate that the Brough's farm was in the right place to be of help to us.

Once the supplies brought for the outpost were unloaded and stored away, the main task was to make ourselves comfortable. One of the items they'd brought from the Scillies was another radio set that would enable the farm to communicate with us far easier than how we had been doing it so far. This was the first thing we set up and made sure was operational.

There were far too many of us to be accommodated in the main farmhouse, so everyone mucked in to clear one of the barns to make a temporary dormitory for us. Once camp beds and other items had been set up to make our stay more comfortable, everyone gathered in the courtyard for a final briefing and planning session. This was mainly for the new additions to the mission, the garrison from the farm, to be bought up to speed on what the plan was and what everyone's role would be. The soldiers' main role would be to provide support and extra firepower, if need be, when the knights were in action.

The plan, as all the best ones were, was not complicated. They had all seen action with the knights in the past so they knew what to expect with very few questions being asked before we were all satisfied everyone knew what the plan was and how we were going to achieve it.

Sensibly, the decision to abstain from any alcohol was made as we wanted to commence the mission at daybreak, so the afternoon and evening was spent chatting and rechecking all our equipment. As darkness settled over the farm and after we had eaten, the rasps of sharpening stones rang around the courtyard as those with bladed weapons ensured the edges were honed. My mace didn't need much attention but I, nevertheless, spent time sharpening the spikes adorning its head before giving it a good oil and polish.

Most of us were too full of nervous energy to try and get an early night, so until tiredness eventually made us slip off one by one to grab some sleep, we sat around a fire in the courtyard passing the hours away talking between ourselves.

CHAPTER NINE

Before daybreak we were fed and ready to go, and the sergeants bustled around ensuring everyone had their kit in order and all our supplies were stowed away securely. As everything had been checked and double checked the night before I felt this a little unnecessary, but when I voiced the opinion they smiled with knowing, smug looks on their faces. From their vast experience of dealing with the average soldier whose mind never strayed far from the opposite sex, food, drink, or entertainment there was always something missed which only usually becomes apparent after you leave, and it was their job to make sure it wasn't.

They were satisfied after finding one or two important items, such as misplaced bergens and one unfortunate soldier's melee weapon that had been left behind. After reprimanding the unfortunate individuals publicly, and in my mind with a good dose of humour, and with a future promise of extra duties which would be decided upon depending how they performed on the mission, they boarded their relevant vehicles and just as the first light of dawn was showing we started the engines and drove through the gates.

The sky was clear, and it promised to be another hot, sunny day. Those in the trailer, including me, assumed the roles of lookouts by lining the sides and watching the countryside passing by.

All the knights, of which I was now classed as one, were wearing full kit as the next time we stepped from the trailer would most likely be to fight at the base. Unless something else caused us to dismount the vehicles on the route, that was, in which case the armour we wore would be needed.

The admiral and Captain Digby chose to remain in Shawn's trailer claiming it was the best place to observe the action from. They had a radio set up and the captain was following our progress on a large-scale map, updating the helicopter crew – primed and ready since our departure – with our progress until the order to go came.

We were travelling through unknown territory along an untried and unreconnoitred route. The chosen route, though, had been planned carefully to avoid as many towns and villages as possible for obvious reasons, but some were unavoidable which did make me slightly nervous. We knew what our vehicles were capable of so hoped that whatever lay ahead would be no match for us. Hammond, in the armoured car, was acting as lead scout vehicle ranging ahead of the slower convoy and inspecting the planned route. He kept Shawn, behind the wheel of the tractor with Louise by his side, updated on any blockages or obstructions that lay ahead.

Shawn and Louise's relationship had grown and blossomed and were now not ashamed to tell everyone they were very much in love. The bond they had developed ever since being brought together on Bodmin Moor immediately after the tragedy of her sister's death was strong. Shawn's mates, who had lived with him and known him for years, could not help themselves as they made fun of him, accusing him of breaking the code they had lived their bachelor lives by for years and letting a relationship get in the way of their friendships. It was all good natured and never meant with malice, but when overheard by Maud, who always issued her justice immediately, distributing extra duties or menial work to whoever she had heard speaking, they were accused of being jealous and told to leave the couple alone. They reluctantly agreed, keeping their promises until the next opportunity when Maud was out of earshot. Which she seldom was.

The armoured car stopped at any blockage they couldn't move themselves and waited for Shawn to either use the tractor's power to push whatever was causing it from our route, or less occasionally provide cover for us when we were forced to dismount from the trailer and attach chains to a more stubborn vehicle to drag it from our path.

It was nothing we hadn't done before, so whatever we came across we dealt with quickly and efficiently, much to the delight of Walker-Jones who continually told his aides and soldiers to pay close attention to everything we were doing, as he was repeatedly impressed by our proficiency. Even when occasional zombies staggered into view when we had dismounted from the vehicles, those of us working didn't panic as we trusted those guarding us to deal with the threat, either by blade or bullet.

After one particularly nasty crash we came across, when it took both the armoured car and the tractor to push and drag the mess of vehicles out of the way, we found ourselves disturbed by about twenty zombies approaching. This delayed us as we all stopped what we were doing to help the knights and soldiers deal with them before finishing the job and climbing back on board the vehicles.

Once I'd drunk some water from a bottle and wiped the sweat from my face, I turned cheerily to the admiral.

"Well, at least the way back'll be quicker. We'll do it in less than half the time when we don't have to keep stopping like this."

"I'm sorry if I keep repeating myself," he started with the usual look of shocked amazement reserved for when he saw us in action, "but bloody hell man. How *do* you stay so calm?"

I looked at him and answered seriously.

"Trust. Plain trust."

I stretched my arms out to indicate I was including everyone around me.

"After a hell of a steep learning curve, we know what we're capable of and trust each other to watch our backs. And to know when it's too much."

Smiling, he replied, "And when is it too much?"

"Oh, we'll let you know when we get there," I told him with a wry smile. "You'll probably hear the girly squeals from the knights first…I know you keep telling us how well we're doing, but you must remember we have been doing *this* a lot longer than you. We've lost friends, and none of us ever want to go through that again. Experience has given us the skills we're using now, and all of it was hard-earned."

I shrugged off the seriousness and smiled again.

"Trust me. Give your chaps a few more weeks of what we've been doing and they'll be just as confident, but if you follow our lead and listen to us, you'll avoid some of the mistakes we've made."

Slowly Digby's finger marking our progress on the map crept closer to our target until a signpost told us the village the base was in was only a mile away. Hammond had seen the sign as he was scouting ahead and had stopped by it to wait for us. As we pulled up beside him, he exited the armoured car and whilst his sergeant organised a cordon of soldiers to form a perimeter, he walked over to the trailer.

"Are we all set?" he asked.

I looked around at the ones who were riding in the trailer with me. The knights were checking their own and each other's equipment, tightening buckles and making sure everything was in good order. On seeing this I began to check my own armour and called back to him.

"Yes, give us a couple of minutes to check everything and let's get on with it."

Steve looked the admiral dead in the eye before he spoke.

"If you're happy, Sir, I'll assume command now."

"Yes I am Captain, and good luck."

Steve saluted the man before returning to the armoured car, after telling me he'd await the radio signal to tell him we were ready.

Less than five minutes later, once everyone had confirmed their readiness, the convoy formed up and we rolled on into the village.

We'd studied the plans of the base and knew where the bunker we were heading to was located. As the headquarters of 22 SAS, it was an important military facility but not as large as many others. The regiment, though both feared by its enemies and admired by the rest of the world for its exploits and deeds, probably in equal amounts since its formation, was not large compared to other mainline regiments in the British Army. The base spread

71

out over many acres but was small enough so it would be easy for us to follow the directions we had and not get lost finding the bunker.

With all of us on full alert, we entered the village and began the mission proper.

CHAPTER TEN

The village was as deserted, even more so than the others we had passed through on our journey, where there had always been individuals or small groups of former occupants shambling along waiting for us to send them to a better place.

"Where is everyone?" I asked, voicing what everyone else was likely thinking.

Captain Digby stared out over the empty village beside me.

"At the base, I imagine," he said flatly. "From the photos you took on the fly-over, the numbers gathered at the bunker look far greater than the complement of the base, even including support staff. Most likely the main gates, apart from the vehicle barriers which are manually operated, would have been open, allowing any on foot to enter. And as you've told us they do have a habit of gathering together…That's where we'll find them is my guess."

I looked at him and grinned.

"You see, you know just as much about this crazy world we live in now as I do. I should've known that but I still asked the question. I'm kinda thick like that I guess."

Replying with a chuckle he said, "Oh, I don't think I'm an expert like you…not yet anyway. Give me some time and I'm sure I'll get there. And as to thick? Yeah! It takes a real idiot to survive for so long and to come up with the Mad Max vehicles you lot created."

I would have replied, continuing the banter which we all knew was a key weapon in controlling our nerves, but I could see the main gate of the base approaching so stiffened my stance and gripped my spear a little tighter, just as all the others beside me in the trailer were doing.

As predicted by Captain Digby the gates were open and only the raisable vehicle barrier was lowered to block our progress. Shawn, now leading the convoy didn't slow down as he turned off the road and drove straight at the barrier to disintegrate it on the way through. He hit it with such force that the post supporting the barrier was ripped from the ground and flew into the guard house that sat in between the in and out section of road, smashing it to pieces. I smiled to myself as I could imagine the childish grin on his face as he caused such destruction.

He drove slowly through the base following the directions from Louise beside him, she was holding a map with one hand and a handle with the other to steady herself. Glancing behind me I saw the rest of the vehicles were keeping in tight formation as we drove virtually bumper to bumper deeper into the facility. Rounding a corner, Louise told us via radio that they were slowing down as the target building was in sight. As per our plan, Willie's tractor and trailer detached itself from the convoy and pulled up alongside us as we stopped.

Two hundred meters ahead the road was blocked with a solid mass of the undead and I thought the numbers looked as if they had increased since we had flown over the base previously. It was to be expected, I supposed, if our theories about how they, on whatever level their brains operated at, sought out others to make them stronger as a whole rather than individually was correct. Or perhaps the noise they made shambling along attracted others until they clumped together in groups unable to break apart without an external stimulus.

"*Ok everyone,*" Steve called over the radio. "*Just like we planned until I order differently. Are we all ready?*"

The replies came back immediately that all were ready for the next stage of the operation before Steve wasted no time in telling Shawn and Willie to begin. The plan, working on the tried and proven method was for the tractors to make as many passes as necessary until he deemed they had been thinned out enough for the knights to dismount. Before us knights put our boots on the ground though, Shawn and Willie would lower their ploughs and scrape the area clear in front of the building as best they could to save us having to step over the zombies smashed by the tractors, just in case some still 'lived'.

Under the cover of the guns of those still in the vehicles and the helicopter, they would then secure the bunker entrance and protect the occupants as they boarded the bus.

"*Helicopter is thirty seconds out,*" Captain Digby announced as the faint *whop whop* of its blades cutting through the air reached us. When we were close to the base they had taken off and were timing their arrival to coincide with ours, having been reminded not to fly over the facility before we arrived as it would, most likely, agitate the zombies and cause them to spread out in search of the noise's origin and so make our job more difficult.

"There it is!" shouted someone from the other trailer. I followed the outstretched arm and spotted the rapidly growing dark spot as it sped towards us, until with a roar of its powerful engines it swept low overhead, it's downwash buffeting us and blowing up clouds of dust and litter.

It stopped and hovered over the bunker entrance where the pilot rotated a slow 360 degree turn as he surveyed the mass of zombies below that were becoming more animated by such a noisy arrival and began reaching up as if to grab the machine out of the sky. This was the signal for Shawn and Willie to begin. We all held onto the side of the trailer as it lurched forwards when Shawn set off, rapidly going through the gears as he built up the speed and momentum needed to cleave straight through the meat crowd. Willie was gunning his engine as well as he tried to keep up with the more modern, faster tractor.

Normally I could see the aftereffects of the havoc the plough wreaked on a solid mass of the undead as bodies, or parts of bod-ies, were thrown aside after meeting the solid force of the plough. This was the first time I had had a close-up experience from the front as Willies tractor, which was following us to one side, smashed through them. The heavily reinforced blade of the plough offered no quarter, and the first few bodies seem to disap-pear into sprays of blood and gore. The ones in the third ranks and beyond, cushioned by the bodies in front of them, fared no better and were crushed and mangled before what remained of them was flung to one side.

On and on we drove through the pack, unable by the speed and lurching of the trailer to do more than just hang on and watch the destruction. As soon as we were clear, Shawn slowed his pace to allow Willie to catch up and they turned round on the wide roadway and sped up to repeat the massacre. Three more passes later Louise's voice came through the radio.

"*Shawn thinks one more pass will do it and then he'll start clearing them out of the way. Do you agree, Steve?*"

Steve, watching from the armoured car, replied immediately.

"*Yes, I agree. Excellent job so far guys. There aren't many still standing now so carry on. Once you've cleared the way we'll pull the scout cars and the bus forwards into position.*"

After the next pass, Shawn and Willie slowed down and lowered their ploughs so they scraped noisily along the tarmac road. Pushing into the destruction they had caused they drove side by side and kept the edges of their ploughs almost touching to create a reverse wedge where the bodies collected and weren't pushed aside by the angled blades.

Louise's excited voice came over the radio.

"*It's working.*"

We all knew that she meant the driving formation, which both Shawn and Willie had been wanting to try after discussing it a few days previously when the talk around the table had been about how to clear a large area of dead bodies when we didn't have a bulldozer. Again, it was another example of the solutions we had come up with many times before to solve whatever problems or issues we were facing.

The first pass cleared a swathe through the morass of corpses, some still twitching, until they synchronised their turn and pushed them to the side. Reversing back on to the road they drove on and turned around repeating their manoeuvre four more times until the area in front of the bunker was, apart from long red smears of gore and the occasional ripped off limb, clear.

"Brilliant stuff guys," Steve's voice barked over the radio. *"Now let's get on with it before any more appear."*

His armoured car moved forwards with the bus, lorries, and Land Rover following as Shawn and Willie got their vehicles into position to form a barrier around the entrance with the other vehicles arriving moments later.

As I and others were pulling at the ropes that lowered the ramp into position, I noticed the helicopter flying away. Captain Digby spotted me glance up at it with an inquisitive frown on my face as I watched it depart and he informed me that Captain Hammond had just ordered it to reconnoitre the base and report any other zombies approaching.

Good idea, I thought but had no time to consider it more as the ramp was now down on ours and Willie's trailer, and us armour-clad knights hefted shields, gripped weapons, and descended the ramps.

Steve joined us as we gathered, our eyes looking everywhere for danger which, as yet, had to appear.

"Form the perimeter and we'll get the door to the bunker open. No time to waste, let's take advantage of the excellent work done so far."

He indicated to his sergeant and four of his men to accompany him as he walked to a door in the building we had gathered around.

Ian organized us all into a perimeter surrounding the door to the building and I felt we were in a good position as the vehicles formed an outer cordon that surrounded us where soldiers stood guard ready with their weapons to keep any that approached at bay. Unless something disastrous happened, which I couldn't see was likely at that moment, I was confident that the mission was going better than planned.

"Doors open, we're going in," Steve called out. "Stay alert everyone!"

Glancing around I watched as Steve and his men entered the building. We'd been told that the bunker was housed deep below the building and there was another, more secure door further inside the facility. Those trapped inside had given the code to unlock the door, and the admiral had categorically ordered them to stay inside until our forces let them out. This would, he had explained, avoid any of them thinking they could offer help and emerge before we had made the area safe. We knew they only had a few weapons and very limited ammunition in the bunker, so what use they could offer was practically nil. Even though they were the best trained soldiers in the world, twenty or so of them joining in without knowledge of our tactics and capabilities potentially had disaster written all over it. Walker-Jones knew this so his orders had been firm and final. We had, as requested, brought weapons and ammunition for them once they had joined us, but they wouldn't have access to them until they were safely on the bus.

The reason so many were in the bunker was the building above it contained the mission planning rooms. 'A' Squadron had been having an early morning planning meeting about their next operation when all hell broke loose outside. They knew immediately that the few initial gunshots fired weren't from the range, but much closer. The obvious first thought was a terrorist attack on the base so, bursting into immediate action, they took the few weapons from the locker inside the bunker and with most armed with nothing more than attitude and the need to protect their base they ran outside into a scene from their worst nightmares.

Witnessing the panic and confusion as shambling figures fell upon others and began ripping flesh from their bodies with their teeth, they had tried to help which caused a few of their number including their major in command to be overwhelmed by the masses that soon surrounded them. Quickly realizing that their only chance was to find shelter until help arrived, which was something they expected to happen in no time at all. The ammunition from the few weapons they had soon ran out and they were forced to resort to kicking and shoving those that wanted to inexplicably eat them out of the way, as the well-trained and disciplined group forced their way through the masses, gathering any survivors that ran from buildings or wherever they had been hiding on the way, until they reached the bunker once more. Locking themselves in they immediately began the protocols which in any normal circumstances would have bought the might of Her Majesty's Armed Forces to their aid.

After many hours frantically trying to make sense of the desperate communications they were receiving whilst trying to send their own messages out, the dreaded realism dawned on them that the help they hoped for was not going to arrive any time soon. Maintaining comms with the few other units that were still operating in some form or other they took stock of their situation and settled down to wait it out.

The bunker was designed to operate as a secure facility if the country ever came under attack, enabling them to maintain contact with their remaining squadrons on the ground and direct them to undertake any tasks needed. It was not large and had been designed to accommodate their headquarters staff only for an extended period of time, therefore, it had sleeping, cooking, and washing facilities with enough stores to sustain them for a few months, however it wasn't designed to house thirty-two people. The admiral had told us that that those inside had described their living conditions as 'cosy' which I took to mean claustrophobic.

CHAPTER ELEVEN

As we waited the guns on the helicopter began firing, keeping any approaching zombies as far away from us as possible. I could hear Digby behind me communicating with them, his voice calm, so it looked as if everything was under control. With the firepower we could bring to bear along with the arm power of us knights, it would have to be a huge horde to give us any real trouble, so my anxiety levels didn't rise at the sound of the long bursts of heavy machine gun fire coming from the helicopter a few hundred yards away.

Movement behind me caused me to glance around and I saw Hammond starting to lead those from the bunker outside. The plan was to get most of them on board the waiting bus as quickly as possible whilst he held a quick review meeting with the newly rescued senior officers to see if they had finalised the list of supplies and equipment they wanted to collect if we had the chance. A line of people was half walking, half jogging towards the waiting bus, each carrying either a bergen or something in their arms, clearly carrying all the useful items that could be salvaged from the bunker before it was abandoned forever.

Those in the facility had already given us a list of equipment they wanted to collect from other areas of the base, but we had told them it would be impossible to decide whether or not it would be viable to get them until we had rescued them and did a real-world evaluation of the situation. The lorries we had brought with us could carry a lot of stuff, we just had to decide if it was worth the risk to get it.

Steve shouting my name from behind me caused me to look round again. He was waving for me to join him. I turned and stepped the few paces over to him and the group around him. Two I didn't know were with him and he quickly introduced them to me as Captain Clarke and Sergeant Newman, who I knew from previous briefings were the two most senior men from the bunker. The captain was tall and thin with ginger-blond hair, looking every bit the typical upper-class officer. He was most likely public school educated and with the restrained mannerisms of privilege and wealth, but if he was a captain in the SAS I knew there must be more to him than that. Much more.

His sergeant, Pete Newman, seemed to be cast out of the same mould as Eddy and Woody, albeit a younger model, but one that still bore the scars and attitude of his profession acting as the conduit and buffer between the ranks. Reliable and dependable when the chips were down, and all seemed lost. On first impression I warmed to him more than the captain who, despite us just rescuing him, seemed to carry an air of aloofness around him, as if he was better than us.

All we had time for was a quick nod and a handshake as time was precious and we had much to do before we could head back to the Brough's farm.

"Okay everyone," Steve said with a look at Clarke. "Can I take it that you have everything you need out of the bunker?"

Clarke simply nodded in reply. Despite his demeanour he couldn't help himself and kept looking around at our eclectic range of bastardised vehicles and the stranger sight of most in his view, including myself, wearing armour and carrying ancient battlefield weapons. Steve noticed how distracted he was and said sharply to him, but with a smile on his face as he understood what was going through his mind.

"Captain Clarke, yes, it's a weird bloody world, but you can be a tourist later. We have a job to do and not much time to do it in."

The captain let a momentary flash of annoyance pass over his face at an equal rank branding him a tourist, but he swallowed whatever he was going to say and fixed Steve with a stern stare to nod a response.

Steve ignored the look he had been given and continued.

"Right, I'm in command of the forces we have on the ground. Captain, if you and the Sergeant can join the admiral in the trailer over there you can show us the quickest way to the armoury and I'm sure we'll need your help in getting our hands on what you've told us you want to take from there."

Clarke nodded and turned away before Steve raised his voice to address everyone in earshot.

"Phase one is complete, people. Let's get back on board and start phase two."

In much practised order we climbed back onto our respective vehicles and got ready to move again.

This time Shawn and Willie drove side by side through the base. We'd been told that the roads would be wide enough and so it had made sense when planning this stage of the mission to have the two vehicles that could cleave through whatever we found leading the way. With the occasional chattering of guns from the circling helicopter accompanying our journey it only took us a few minutes to reach the armoury and begin to form the vehicles in a protective ring around its entrance as planned, though unlike our usual wagon-circling formation the lorries were backed up to receive the goods.

The tractors pulled ahead of the armoury and waited as the three lorries, one at a time, passed it and then reversed at an angle towards the entrance. With their rears pointed towards the door they all angled themselves slightly, so each cab ended up against the sides of the one next to it to fill any gaps. The other vehicles, with a bit of forwards and backwards shunting, completed the cordon.

Steve exited the armoured car and once he had inspected what we had created and deemed it good enough, ordered those already planned to be on the ground to exit their vehicles. Captain Clarke and Sergeant Newman joined us as we gathered outside the door.

"Okay chaps," Steve said as he pointed towards the heavy looking door. "Let's start, shall we? Captain Clarke, can you get us in there so we can plan how we're going to get it all out?"

Clarke, still not saying a word, walked towards the door and punched a series of numbers into the keypad beside it. It clicked open and with a pull he opened the door to beckon the rest of us inside.

I found his silence strange. He knew we were coming, knew who and what we were and what we had done since it all began. As a captain in the SAS it went without saying that his training and ability were probably far in excess of an equal rank in the mainstream army. They were the best of the best after all, which many countries tried to copy but could never truly emulate their sheer professionalism and capabilities. Not to mention the accolades the regiment had racked up since its conception.

I thought that maybe his professional pride had been stung by being rescued by a group mainly consisting of civilians, albeit with a lot of help from the military, or maybe he was just the strong, silent type. I knew time would tell, but for the moment I had other things to worry about as I looked around the huge room I had followed him into.

Racks of weapons and stacks of boxes, which I presumed contained ammunition, filled the space. Emptying the armoury had been a priority after we had rescued the trapped personnel, but with the quantity I was looking at I doubted we had brought enough vehicles with us to accomplish that.

I turned full circle and whistled theatrically.

"Bloody Hell…Err, Captain Clarke?" I asked looking at him. "Do you want to take *everything*?"

He regarded me with a flat expression.

"Well, they all work, so yes," he said simply.

He continued staring at me in silence until a small smile played across his face.

"But many of them are a little on the old side. We have a selection of most weapons currently in use worldwide here just in case it's all there is to hand when you need it. Most are just used for training, so they wouldn't be our weapon of choice when going on an operation."

He pointed to the racks on the right-hand side of the room.

"If we start over there first that's where the good stuff is, and then if we have time and space we may as well take what else we can."

"If you direct us what to take first, Clarke, I'll arrange everyone else to act as porters," Steve said, turning to his sergeant. "Get the wheelbarrows in here and get things moving please."

On our initial trip down the motorway gathering supplies, the first lorry we had broken into had contained wheelbarrows. Dave Eddy had noted its location and what it contained at the time, but we had disregarded them as irrelevant. When planning this mission we decided we needed to come up with a way of moving a large quantity of supplies quickly by hand from inside a building and he had reminded us of the abandoned lorry full of brand-new wheelbarrows. A check of his notebook followed by a quick trip out to the motorway had given us more than enough for the job, once more proving that you could never discount items you had once thought as useless to your survival.

Armfuls of weapons and boxes of magazines and ammunition were soon being wheeled out of the armoury to be loaded on to the lorries. By now though, the helicopter had not been able to keep the masses of zombies away from where we were and those left to guard us were now forced to use their own weapons. I had to trust that those protecting us would tell us if we were needed so until the order came to help, I carried on. The helicopter was proving its worth as they, firing at the ones further away from us, were managing to thin them out enough that the numbers did not yet pose a problem, but the continual firing was a reminder to us to get a move on.

Steve changed the plan as the firing increased and ordered the remaining SAS soldiers who were waiting on the bus, to disembark and arm themselves either with what we had brought with us for them to use or with what we were bringing out from the armoury, and to help maintain the perimeter. The others from the bunker were told to either grab a wheelbarrow or to help load the lorries. The elite soldiers didn't need telling twice about getting some payback on those that had trapped them for so long and most likely killed their families and friends. As soon as they had grabbed a weapon and loaded magazines, they manned the line and increased the firepower that was keeping us all safe.

It seemed an endless job, grabbing weapons off racks or lifting heavy boxes into a wheelbarrow to push it outside and then help load them onto a lorry, but with every trip more of the racks emptied and the lorries slowly filled. Most of the weapons I could recognise for what they were, but a few ranging from bulky, futuristic looking things to one's small enough to easily hold in one hand piqued my interest as I was handed them and wheeled them outside to the waiting lorries.

Eventually, a much sweatier and dishevelled looking Steve approached me as I entered the armoury on what, to my arms and legs felt like, the millionth time.

"Clarke reckons we're down to second world war stuff now, so it could be a good time to call it."

"Thank God for that," I gasped in exhaustion. "I don't think I appreciated how hard it would be doing this in armour when we planned it. Where does he want to go next?"

"He wants to try and get some comms gear and then grab a few bushmasters from the vehicle pool."

"Bushmasters?" I asked.

Steve replied with a laugh at my obvious confusion.

"A bit like our armoured car, but smaller. Nice bits of kit and they'd be a good addition for us, so I've told him we'll give it a go."

"Okay then, let's get these last few barrowloads on board and get on with it," I said as I glanced around the now very empty racking of the armoury. One item caught my attention and I turned to it and pointed.

"But you can bring that!" I said gleefully.

Steve looked at what I was indicating at before smiling and nodding before retrieving it. I grabbed the last full wheelbarrow and, grimacing with exhaustion, jogged out of the armoury into the loud, continual gunfire that echoed all around us and helped lift the last few items onto a lorry.

We abandoned the wheelbarrows, knowing we had plenty more if we needed them again in a pile before we all went to our respective vehicles and waited in line to board. Steve walked over to me carrying something that made me smile as he handed it over.

"Thought you'd like your new toy on board with you," he said as he handed me it along with a wooden box he was holding by its rope carrying handle.

"What's in the box?" I asked as I took it off him.

"The magazines for it. Wouldn't be much good without them, would it?"

Arms reached out and helped steady me as I struggled up the ramp carrying my Bren gun and the large box. As I put my newest acquisition carefully in one of the weapons bins we had built against the side of the trailer, I noticed Walker-Jones and Digby looking at me with amused grins on their faces.

"I know, I know," I said smiling back to tell the story. "Years ago, on some holiday or another, I saw an old, deactivated one. I was about to buy it when Becky caught me and put the kibosh on it. She said there *wasn't a wall in her house that bloody thing was going on...*" I then with a bigger grin stated triumphantly. "But I know exactly where it's going. It's going to be my personal machine gun mounted above the driver's seat on my Volvo. No way she can moan then, not if it's there to keep me safe."

Both men raised their eyebrows and shook their heads in mock disbelief, but from the admiring comments from others in the trailer I knew I had something that would top trump most in the silly conversations us boys had when out of earshot of the much more sensible women folk amongst us.

The brief comedic interlude over, it was time to get back to work.

CHAPTER TWELVE

Captain Clarke joined us in the trailer and held a brief shouted conversation with Shawn, still stood on the platform of his tractor, directing him to where he wanted to go next.

One by one the vehicles pulled forward and followed us deeper into the base as we cleaved through the zombies that were still heading towards us or left lying on the ground, each with their heads mangled by a high-powered bullet.

We could tell the ones hit by the machine guns from the helicopter because the gun's larger calibre bullets destroyed everything they hit with less accuracy but far more destruction, leaving unrecognizable lumps of scorched and smoking flesh where only the rotten rags they wore marked them out as formerly human.

After a few turns Clarke told Shawn over the radio that Steve had given him to stop, bringing us to a halt outside a plain, two-storey building of similar design and construction of most of those in the base. Steve stepped out of his armoured car and stood on its high wheel arch to look around and made a quick tactical summary of the situation.

They had left the zombies behind momentarily, but he knew they would catch up with them soon enough. If they entered the building quickly and grabbed what they needed, the chances are they would be back onboard before any shambling pursuit caught up. He turned to the other captain and called over to him.

"Captain Clarke. You know where the items are, so you lead and I'll send some of the knights to protect you."

Clarke shot him a mildly disdainful look.

"My men will suffice, I don't need yours," he said coldly before adding a reluctant but conciliatory, "But thank you."

Steve bristled at the response and seemed about to reply angrily when the admiral interrupted.

"Captain Clarke! Captain Hammond is in command, and you will follow his orders. This is not the time for petty rivalry or bravado. He has experience of the situation we are in, and, captain, you do not. Do I make myself clear?" he said with a hard edge to his voice not yet required among the group.

Left with no reply but, "Yes Sir," Clarke controlled his facial expression and stared at Steve who, staring back at him with a cold stare of barely suppressed anger, called out the six names of the knights he wanted to accompany him.

***

Captain Andrew Clarke was a proud man. Proud of his accomplishments at having reached his position amongst *the* most elite military unit in the world, proud of leading many successful missions that he knew he could never talk about, and proud of the men he led and was confident in their ability to surmount whatever was thrown at them.

His pride had been stung, sliced to the metaphorical bone in fact, when they failed to overcome what had happened on the first day the zombies had appeared at their base, leaving him with the only course open to him, after seeing many of his subordinates and superiors ripped apart in front of them, to retreat back to the bunker, rescuing as many people as they could find while they fought their way through the massing undead.

That retreat, synonymous with failure, tore at him from the insides like a trapped rat seeking escape. Every day spent underground gnawed more flesh away at that unreal wound until the injury festered into malicious frustration at his inability to take the fight to the enemy.

He considered it his *personal* failure, and now he was being told to rely on a man he knew was inferior to him in both training and experience, and a bunch of ridiculous civilians dressed as medieval knights of all things, to do what he knew he and his men could damned well do for themselves.

But he was a soldier, so he swallowed his pride and did exactly what the admiral made painfully clear to him. He followed his orders.

He had, of course, been told about the group of civilians accompanied by a smattering of soldiers from different units who, with apparent ingenuity and skill, had fought their way across the country and made their home at Warwick Castle. He had put a lot of what he had been told down as over exaggeration by excited people desperate to make themselves sound as accomplished as possible to impress those who found themselves now in command. Their stories seemed too farfetched to be anything else.

Even though his pride did not let him show it, he was impressed by what he had seen so far. Their vehicles protected them as they either fired at the surrounding zombies from the high sides of the trailers or smashed through them with the adapted ploughs. Their tactics had been sound and as he observed them, unable to fault their discipline under what was effectively a battlefield situation. He knew that without them he would still be trapped inside a bunker with only starvation and death to look forward to, but now he and his men had been rescued, surely they, with him in command, would assume their rightful place at the top of the fighting food chain and people would look to him as to what to do next.

Clarke, however, also knew when to pick his battles, so he kept his true feelings to himself and obeyed his orders. For now.

***

A huge man dressed in armour appeared and gestured for him to follow them down the ramp.

"Alright mate?" he said and indicated to the other knights around him who were hefting their weapons and shields and getting ready to walk down the ramp. "Just stick close to us and you'll be alright."

Clarke fixed them with a cold stare as once more his pride stung at being issued orders by civilians, and not just ordinary civilians at that, but ones dressed like extras from a low budget medieval B movie.

Ian summed up the situation at the bottom of the ramp.

"Okay lads, this is Captain Clarke of the SAS. He's one of those strong and silent superhero types apparently, but don't let that worry you. We'll just have to show him what we can do before he thinks we are good enough for him."

Clarke recoiled visibly at his words, as if shocked by electricity when his innermost thoughts had been projected. The realisation concerned him because, with all his training, he should be much harder to read.

"Right then, let's see what you can do." He muttered silently to himself as he tried to keep his expression emotionless.

With a huge effort of will he controlled his voice and pointed to a door in the nearest building.

"What we need should just be in a room off the corridor through there."

"Which one?" Ian asked.

The captain thought for a second as he reminded himself where the door he had used so many times was, before replying.

"The second on the left. It's about ten meters in."

"Reckon anyone's still in there?" Ian asked as he stared at the windows facing them.

"Possible. No, *likely*," Clarke replied after brief but careful consideration. "It houses – *housed* – the main admin and comms so it was permanently staffed...God knows now...with all the panic and confusion I can't say for certain but I find it unlikely the building is empty."

"Right then, lads," Ian snapped after a nod to the SAS man. "Usual entry procedure it is then; form on me. Captain? Stay behind us but be ready to cover our flanks if it all goes wrong."

Surprised by the use of military terminology Clarke nodded, checked his weapon and held it ready.

He watched as the knights formed a small semi-circle around the door with their shields held out before them. Ian, in the middle, reached forwards and with his mail clad hand pushed down on the door handle and pulled the unlocked door open before doing something that left the captain slack-jawed and speechless.

He expected a rapid entry, expected violence of action and maximum levels of speed and aggression. He expected them to emulate his own training.

What he didn't expect was a polite greeting.

"*Cooee.* Anyone home?" Ian called out, sounding as if he was a nosey housewife returning next door's Pyrex dish as an excuse to hear fresh gossip.

A rasping, groaning sound came from within which Clarke, even with his own lack of zombie fighting experience, knew couldn't mean anything good. Standing behind the knights his view was impaired, but he could make out shapes approaching out of the gloom of the corridor beyond the doorway. He was surprised at the calm conversations the knights were having between themselves as they discussed who was going to strike first, like they were standing at a bar deciding who should receive the first pints poured for them.

The one holding a mace moved his shield to the side and, with a casual swing of the evil looking weapon, smashed it down into the head of the first one that appeared in the doorway making its eyeballs pop out as smashed brain squirted through the now vacant orifices as it fell to the ground to release a noxious stench so bad Clarke's eyes watered.

"Bugger me, that's worse than one of Horace's farts," a man wielding a sword complained.

"One step back and let the others fall over it," Ian said calmly. "And if you could be so kind as to try and knock 'em to the side next time so we don't have to step over them? And my dog's farts only smell due to all the snacks you bastards keep feeding him, I'll have you know."

"Fuck me Beaver, you now want us to kill them neatly?" one said from within the circle, which made Clarke chuckle involuntarily.

Another weapon swung from within the circle, and an undead soldier in tattered, gore-covered uniform emerging from the doorway slumped lifelessly to the ground looking like a dropped concertina.

"Neat enough for you, knobhead?" The man asked as he grunted to work the wicked blade of his short axe from the ruined skull.

"Better. Solid seven out of ten," Ian said with all the nonchalance of a man unafraid of his situation.

The banter reminded Clarke of his own men and he found his stance softening towards them a little, thinking that maybe they were okay after all. Casual piss-taking and dad jokes while decapitating the hungry undead was balls of steel territory in his mind.

"*Yoo-hoooo*," Ian sang out again, calling any more decaying former inhabitants forward for voluntary execution. When none stepped out to answer the call he rolled his shoulders and spoke.

"Right lads, inside. The door we need is the second on the left. Geoff and Simon block the corridor beyond that with your shields and we'll follow you down and enter the room. Be careful of other doors as we don't know what's behind them. Have we got all that, children?"

When they had all replied they had, Clarke followed them down the corridor until they stopped at the door they needed to enter. Without thinking, he let his weapon drop on its sling and reached out to depress the handle to push the door open.

He was met with the mutilated face of a zombie lunging towards him, its mouth already opening to take a bite out of his flesh. He staggered backwards and fumbled with his weapon. In the tight confines of the narrow hallway he found it was stuck behind his back now pressed against the far wall of the corridor. The terror rose in him as he was trapped with nowhere to go but death.

All his training, the countless hours of weapon drills in scenarios so realistic that the line between training and deployment almost blurred, was lost in a heartbeat. He didn't abandon his primary weapon and reach for the backup pistol holstered precisely where his muscle memory would find it. He didn't try for a blade – his tertiary weapon option in close confines – but simply stopped trying to grab his weapon and began to raise his arms to fend it off in pure, animalistic panic.

He drew in breath to scream, staring at the rotting visage of a soldier and knowing that it would be the last thing he saw when an axe flew upwards in front of him. The noise was as fleeting as the flash of reflected light off the honed blade, sounding oddly like a movie sound effect.

The face of the zombie seemed to lose animation. Gone was the rage and hunger, replaced by calm and shock as the image before him slid away, sheared off from its chin to its hairline. He saw a brief flash of a neat line of bone and brain before it collapsed at his feet to release a still fouler stink than before. He had barely begun to comprehend what had happened and was about to react in disgust as what remained of the zombie's brains spilled over his boots when another zombie appeared in the doorway.

Before he had chance to move an inch another knight shouted, "Mine!" and a sword was thrust upwards through its open mouth to sprout the long blade, dripping blood and gore, out of the back of its head. The knight staggered forwards, holding the dead weight of the zombie on the blade as he walked it back through the doorway like a human shield. Or former human shield. When he was clear of it, he lowered the blade and the now twice dead zombie slid off to drop to the floor. As he had walked forwards holding the thing up, other knights had stepped forwards to cover him, just in case any more were in there.

Clarke was rendered speechless, his knees weak and barely holding him up as he leant ineffectually against the wall. He tried to speak, but only grunts and groans emitted from his moving mouth until the contents of his stomach fountained upwards without warning to humiliate him.

When he had finished spewing the third time Ian rested a hand on his shoulder, bringing him out of the fog that was threatening to overtake his brain.

"Feel better now, numpty? When I said follow us, I meant it. You can't just open any old door without checking it first…honestly thought you'd know better than that. Anyway, don't worry about it. No doubt you'll catch up pretty quick."

A shout of, "All clear!" came from within the room.

"Come on," Ian said, slapping the hand on his back a little harder and threatening to invoke another salvo. "Show us what you need and we can get out of here…won't be long before the zombies following catch up."

Still not trusting his voice, Clarke entered the room and checked his weapon with his returning wits and raised a pointed finger at another door.

"All our comms gear should be in there. If you check it first, I'll show you what we need."

He watched as a knight approached the door and with his ear to it knocked on it and listened for a few seconds before he nodded to the rest. As the others gathered around it with their weapons held ready, he opened it and moved inside.

"*All clear.*"

Clarke followed to show them what he needed before they grabbed the lot and headed back outside. His mind had been racing at a hundred miles an hour since his life had been saved. His analytical brain had quickly formed the conclusion that no matter the training he had had and the experiences he'd gained throughout his career so far, it really did not add up to much to help him survive in the world he found himself in now. He told himself it was a simple matter of training; new enemy meant new tactics, and he hadn't thought to consider that until the world made it clear he had fallen from the apex of his personal pyramid.

They ran up the ramp of the trailer and stowed the comms gear as a few shots rang out indicating that the trailing zombies had eventually caught up with them. Clarke looked at Steve who was still on the wheel arch of his armoured car, weapon held ready. Forcing his voice to sound firm and steady to remove the shame and panic his brain wanted to project, he called out to the man.

"Let's try the vehicle pool and see if we can get some Bushmasters."

A voice came through the radio from the driver of the tractor pulling their trailer.

"*That's left at the next junction, right?*"

"Right, next left," Clarke said with a smile to the man holding the radio beside him, barely able to believe that he was starting to enjoy himself fighting alongside the civilians.

"How many Bushmasters do you want to take?" Steve asked Clarke as they bumped along, the fat tyres turning the odd corpse into a weak speedbump.

Clarke had thought about this when he knew they were to be rescued. The vehicles could take up to ten people, so they could carry all of his twenty fighting men that had been trapped in the bunker in two, but knowing the capabilities of them he had already decided that they would take as many as they could. They could easily be driven by just one person and every one of his men had experience driving them, so if they were there, they would take them. He knew normally that at least four or five of them were kept at the base for training reasons and hoped they were all operational, and not in parts being serviced.

"All of them," he answered, this time not having to control his voice as his mind was now focused on the next task. "They're bloody good bits of kit,"

He smiled as he looked around at the trailer he was in and the other vehicles of their rag tag convoy.

"Or they were until the world went mad."

"There they are!" Clarke shouted as they approached the vehicle pool. He could see four of them parked near the back of the mass of vehicles on the hardstanding, their size and bulk making them easily recognisable.

Steve, once his vehicle had stopped, stood on the wheel arch once more and looked to where he was pointing before scanning the surrounding area and jumping down to walk over to the trailer. A few zombies were shambling around, not in enough numbers to be of concern but he knew that the one meant two, and two meant ten and so on, so as always, time was of the essence.

"Okay," Steve called over to Clarke. "The knights will escort you and your men. I'd recommend only a driver and someone riding shotgun in each."

He reached up and handed him a small bag.

"Extra radios. Give one to each driver so you can all be in the loop enroute. When we set off, position your vehicles in the middle of the convoy."

Clarke reached for the bag, but Steve didn't let it go as he tried to take it and looked him in the eye.

"No heroics. Let the knights protect you and let's get back to the farm safe."

Once more Clarke's first instinct was to be annoyed at being told what to do by a regular soldier but then he remembered the axe flashing in front of his eyes and watching powerlessly as the suddenly faceless zombie who had been about to bite him fell to the floor. Far from being the tip of the metaphorical spear he had been reduced to a vomiting, helpless victim only minutes before, so he bit back any reply to give a firm nod instead.

While the knights prepared themselves and gathered in a defensive formation by the rear of the trailer, Clarke handed out the radios to his men, including his sergeant, who had exited the bus with their rifles ready to go.

Weapons at the ready, he and his men stood in the middle of the phalanx of knights making their way through the large area of vehicle-filled tarmac. He watched as, without pause, they smashed, hacked, and stabbed any undead threatening to impede their progress. The way they communicated between themselves would, if he didn't know better, lead him to think he was observing his or any of the other squadrons that made up the SAS partaking in some weird exercise dreamed up by the top command of their regiment.

What he saw he could not fault, and as he walked in the middle of them he stopped raising his weapon in preparation to fire every time an attacker approached just in case it broke through the cordon surrounding him as his trust in their abilities grew. If need be, it would take less than a second to raise and snap-fire his weapon, but still, every one of the undead he saw raised his heart level and more adrenaline pumped into his already overloaded system.

In contrast those protecting him seemed to treat it more like a leisurely Sunday stroll through the countryside than a daring rescue against potentially overwhelming enemy numbers.

He couldn't help but compare their desperate struggle weeks ago on the first day of the apocalypse to what he was witnessing now. If only they'd known what to do and how to do it, and had the weapons to hand, they would have had a chance to save the base and most in it. With a wry smile he dismissed the notion as soon as it entered his head, as who would ever have been mad enough to think that medieval knights and matching weaponry would have been the answer?

They had modern equivalents – replica equipment from police and prisons in case they were deployed covertly – and his mind wandered to him wearing the hard plastic armour and carrying a Perspex shield with a long club in his free hand.

They reached the vehicles in no time, and while the knights continued to protect them by slaying any that got within reach, they all climbed into the vehicles to seal themselves safely inside. As soon as the last door was shut, the knights gave them a cheery wave and made their way back to the trailer, hacking and swinging their weapons past the barricade of their loose shield cordon at everything trying mindlessly to stop them.

Sergeant Newman climbed into the vehicle with Clarke and after starting it and checking the gauges to make sure they had enough fuel and everything else looked okay on it, they sat in silence as they waited for those in the three other vehicles to signal they were ready to depart.

Vehicles shuffled into position as the convoy formed up, and Clarke relaxed as if their escape was all but complete.

"What's your take on them, Pete?" he asked.

The sergeant looked thoughtful for a few moments before replying.

"I know we talked and reckoned their stories seemed too farfetched to be true…but…"

Newman's shoulders slumped as his head slowly shook.

"A bunch of civvies with a few regulars? I mean, fair enough they were supported by a helicopter which helped…well boss, they've just given me the best display on how to survive in this fucked-up world. Can't fault any of their tactics or methods. It's like watching the bloody Romans at work."

He chuckled as he summed up exactly how the captain was feeling.

"Any other theatre we're the biggest swinging dicks around. We bloody know it, everyone else bloody knows it, but now we're the weekend wankers compared to them. We've got a lot to learn, and we need to learn it from the civvies."

The captain contemplated his words as they rolled out of the camp in convoy without a backwards glance.

"I think you're right, Pete. I fucked up badly at the admin block. Almost got my face chewed off like a damned cadet until one of them saved me…"

Clarke sighed, leaving out the part where he lost his lunch but doubted the smell hadn't already given him away.

"I think we all need to learn, but especially me," he said. "I also need to eat a bit of humble pie for a while until we can emulate what they're doing."

CHAPTER THIRTEEN

I relaxed as the gates to the farm opened as we approached. Passing through the gates meant we were back, that we were safe, and that we'd completed a complex mission with far too many moving parts without a hitch. I couldn't help myself and began cheering, whooping and hugging my friends who were in the trailer with me as much for myself as to announce the return of the victors until they all joined in with me in celebration.

The admiral, standing beside me, did try hard for a while to maintain his decorum but our obvious delight was infectious, and even though he was not as exuberant as everyone else, he eventually let out a typical, "Huzzaah!".

Those at the farm had already been told via the radio that the mission had been a success and when to expect our arrival, so we were greeted by more cheering and applause as we drove in. On the way we had discussed it and it had been decided that we now had too many vehicles to fit into the courtyard of the farm so the lorries and Bushmasters were instructed to park up outside under the protection of the walls. We weren't planning to stay for long anyway as there was still enough daylight, if we didn't hang around too long that was, to make it back to the castle before dark. The plan was to drop off the soldiers of the garrison who'd joined us for the mission, sink a quick cup of celebratory tea while the vehicles were checked over, and then set out again for home.

When everyone had got down from whatever vehicle they were in, our large group gathered in the courtyard. Once again, as I had noticed when we joined the ones at the church all those weeks ago, everyone seemed to huddle in their original groups like penguins sticking to their own cliques in cold weather. It was understandable, and time would bond us all into a larger single group after all, but I took a few seconds to watch human nature play me a familiar tune.

Trays and trays of tea were produced by the Broughs, who must have had every single saucepan or kettle that could boil water on the go to produce so many in such a short time. The mood was light and even the newest arrivals, disorientated by their almost feudal surroundings and the duress of the last few hours, joined in with the laughter and the many conversations that were taking place.

The admiral, Captain Digby, and Steve gravitated over to where I was chatting with Shawn, Willie, and Sergeant Gallon about what we needed to do before we left. The admiral glanced at his watch poignantly and we fell silent.

"Brilliant job gents, and I could stay here chatting for hours about how it all went..." he indicated to Digby by his side, "but Digby here has reminded me of the need to get back to the—"

"Yes, we know," I said, interrupting him and seeing a flash of annoyance cross his face. It was gone as fast as it appeared so I carried on. "We were just discussing it in fact. Shawn's already given the vehicles a quick once over and there's nothing that can't wait until we are back to be sorted. Apart from that it is just a matter of making sure those staying behind to garrison this place don't leave anything behind."

Sergeant Gallon's cheerful Geordie accent spoke up.

"Aye. I'll go and make sure my lads are squared away."

He went to walk away, hesitated, then turned back to point at the closed gates and the lorries and bushmasters parked beyond.

"I did notice a few GPMG's and some 40mm grenade machine guns being bought out of the armoury. A few of those wouldn't go amiss here, admiral. It'd certainly help me sleep better at night."

He smiled, waiting for the admiral to concede the destructive weaponry before looking at me with a cheeky grin on his face. "I also observed a lovely looking Bren gun being squirreled away—"

"Bugger off, that's mine!" I interrupted. "I saw it first, so no chance matey. Go find yourself another toy."

"Ah well, cannae blame a man for tryin'," Gallon said defeatedly.

The admiral laughed at the exchange and nodded to him.

"Of course, Sergeant, take what you need. The safety of this outpost is a top priority."

Gallon nodded in thanks and shouted for a few of his men to join him as he headed towards the gates. In no time they were struggling back under the heavy burdens they had unloaded from the lorries, smiling like children about to unbox a new PlayStation.

Sitting on a log bench and sipping a mug of tea so strong it might have been confused for gravy, Captain Clarke saw what they were doing. His immediate thought was to object, as he considered all the weapons they had just retrieved from the armoury part of his regiment's property, so he began walking swiftly over to the admiral to voice his opinion.

As he was preparing the speech of indignation in his mind, he changed it. He knew that he hadn't endeared himself to the admiral, or indeed anyone, with his surly attitude and behaviour since being rescued, which was a stance he now regretted. He knew he'd been wrong about them after the brutal demonstration of how to survive in the new world, and tried to chalk up his attitude to the stress of confinement.

Although his mind was changed his feet had yet to receive the message, and still carried him with purpose towards the group where the admiral looked up and smiled.

"Ah, Clarke, your chaps alright I trust?"

"Yes sir, thank you," he said with a smile before finding Steve's eyes. "Is there anything you need me and my lads for?"

"There'll be plenty of work for you, but for now we just need to get back to the castle once we have things sorted here. Take a bit of time to get used to breathing fresh air."

Clarke nodded and turned away but the admiral stopped him.

"Why don't you travel with us in the trailer, Captain? We can all discuss matters along the way, eh?"

Clarke agreed immediately, sensing the benefit of staying within the circle of command that seemed to exist between the military and the civilians. He hadn't quite figured out how it worked yet, but he knew time would tell.

"Of course, Sir. I'll get someone else to ride along with my Sergeant." He glanced at Steve again.

"It'd be good to stay out in the fresh air for a bit longer. We've been cooped up underground for too long with nothing but our di…with nothing useful to do. Probably made us all a little anti-social."

Steve nodded at him, understanding and accepting his apology and all the other sentiments he conveyed with that one small, subtle admission.

Once Sergeant Gallon, fussing about his soldiers like a cross between a schoolteacher and a jailer, was satisfied that none of those remaining to garrison the Brough's farm had left anything behind we mounted up again. Everyone waved as we drove through the gates shouting final farewells and messages to all that were remaining. Now they had a radio it added another level of protection for them, and comfort about their security for us. If anything happened, we could saddle up and be with them in a matter of hours if need be, and the knowledge that help was coming always made it easier to hold out a defence.

Our convoy of vehicles stretched out behind us as the drive seemed almost pleasant. The weather was warm, and we were following a well-travelled route which we knew should contain no surprises beyond the occasional lost zombie looking to ask for directions and grab a bite to eat. It didn't stop us being on the alert, as we all knew that complacency could kill, but an air of calm washed over us as we drove.

Captain Clarke, our moody special forces hero, after a long period of silence spent leaning against the side of the trailer and staring into the distance, spoke up.

"I think I owe most of you in this trailer, and others, an apology," he began carefully, evidently expanding on his earlier thoughts. "I wasn't sure what I was expecting when I knew we were going to be rescued in all honesty, but I think the sight of most of you," he waved a vague hand at the ones of us wearing armour, "sent my brain into a tailspin."

"Quite understandable, Clarke," the admiral said warmly, hiding his evident discomfort at the man trying to unburden himself.

"It's arrogant of me, I know," Clarke went on, "but I think I expected to be looked upon as an expert I suppose. The reality is that I am far from it – a bloody amateur compared to everyone else – and that hurt my pride, which led me to acting the way I did For that, all I can do is apologise. I know we're bringing a lot of expertise and firepower, but we need to learn your way of doing things."

Digby smiled and slapped a hand against Clarke's upper arm to convey his feelings better than words could. He was grateful, because he had thought he might need to take his fellow officer into a dark corner and read his horoscope if the man's attitude didn't change for the better on the hurry-up, but he was glad to see that realisation had dawned all by itself.

Mutters of supportive embarrassment at his honesty rippled around until the matter was jointly decided to have been settled. The admiral ended the silence by saying.

"I must say, I admit to holding similar reservations about how civilians with no training could possibly know more about how to go about it than our chaps. I also have to admit to being wholly wrong, because it was they who advised us on the best tactics for clearing the Scilly Isles and, having seen them in action personally a few times now, I can't say I can fault them."

The admiral gestured to the knights, including me.

"I'm sure they would be more than happy to train you in their new methods of warfare."

"Old methods," I corrected, unable to keep the thought in my head.

Ian shuffled closer to put his arm around Clarke in a conspiratorial manner. Clarke winced at the pressure of chainmail and steel plate crushing him.

"Of course we're going to show these new boys how to do it," he said, releasing the pressure. "If they can take orders from a civvy?"

Clarke was astute enough to know that Ian was just trying to pull his leg and attempting to get a rise out of him. He had shared barracks with soldiers for long enough to know how the game was played.

"Oh, I'm sure we'll manage, big boy," Clarke said, finding a gap in his plates and poking a finger in hard enough to prompt a flinch. "Just try not to use any big words to confuse us."

As he withdrew his finger the two men smiled at each other in mutual understanding and newfound respect.

"Well, that's the testosterone levels lowered another notch or two," the admiral said, bringing their informal gathering back to task and acknowledging that he understood what had just transpired.

"When we get back, I was planning to give you new arrivals a few days of rest before we start our next mission. Get to explore the castle and find out what's what and all that," he said with a loaded glance at Clarke.

"But sir?"

"Well I rather suspect you and your chaps might like to get out and about instead, and I believe our next priority is something you might like to be involved in. I won't go over the details again, but for obvious reasons we need to replenish our small arms munitions, and luckily M.O.D Kineton isn't too far away. Are you familiar with the place, Captain?"

"Yes Sir, we run regular training missions there to prepare for an attack on it. I know it very well…but when are you planning to go? Only I know my men, the ones with families which is most, want to try and see if their people made it as soon as possible. I don't think it would be right given the circumstances to get them to do anything before they know one way or the other."

Left unsaid was the fear that those who felt unrestrained by the army's grip on them might simply melt away. Better to support their ventures than order them to remain, he felt, and he had heard many of them quietly discussing the routes they would take with their fellow troopers as they roamed the country rescuing their own.

"Of course," the admiral said. "I apologise for not thinking of that sooner…And you, Captain? Is there anyone you need to check on?"

Clarke's face remained like a stone but the moment of hesitation and the crack in his voice spoke volumes.

"I have a wife and child out there somewhere…"

A look of anguish flared on the admiral's face as he looked at Captain Clarke and then the rest of us in the trailer who had heard what he had said. The admiral recovered and, still a little flustered said, "My deepest sympathy, Captain. In all the discussions I have led I have not considered the personal angle. Of course, I completely understand. The search for your families must come first and to keep those under my command in check I have promised them the same, that when possible, we will do our best to search for them." He waved his arm indicating ours and the other vehicles in the convoy. "Now I know what we can achieve using these amazing contraptions, my previously empty promises now have a chance of being met." Putting his hand on the captain's shoulder as if to confirm his next statement he finished with. "Finding out if yours and your men's families have survived will be the next mission, I promise you."

Clarke looked relieved and thanked the admiral for understanding. It'd been on his mind since they knew they were to be rescued, but his first duty was to those under his command, and he had promised them they would all be able to see if their families had made it. His act of selflessness didn't register as an act of selfishness until he allowed himself to consider his wife in that moment, and tears threatened to sting his eyes when he did.

The admiral opened his mouth to speak but the cry of, "Zombies," made us all turn our attention outwards. I looked ahead and saw a small crowd of twenty or so of them shambling along towards us. Clarke raised his weapon, but the admiral stopped him with a hand on his shoulder, saying quietly so only he could hear.

"Save your ammunition, Captain. Just watch and see how they deal with them."

All of us lining the sides of the trailer had now picked up one of the many spears stored in the racks and waited as Shawn swerved slightly to aim the tractor at the centre of the mass. Without pause he drove straight into them and immediately slowed down as we began thrusting out with our spears at any that remained standing. Once we were satisfied that all had been dispatched, Shawn responded to the shouts we gave him and he increased speed once more.

The admiral and Clarke watched as we dipped the spears into the buckets of cleaning solution fixed to the bulkhead of the trailer and stacked the spears back into the racks.

"You see? Barely a scrap of military training between them and that's how they get the job done. Whatever you might think, these people have a hell of a lot to teach us." Walker-Jones said quietly, his low tone reinforcing the power of his comment.

"If this is the new way we do things, then sign me up right now, sir. Me and my boys have some major catching up to do," Clarke said, fully converted to their cause after the demonstration.

***

When I'd safely dipped my bloodied spear into the bleach bucket and stowed it, I went to stand next to Captain Clarke.

"I heard the conversation between you and the admiral about yours and your men's families, and I fully understand. Steve, sorry Captain Hammond, did the same. I know from the little information I've gleaned about it that it was quite a traumatic experience for them. I'd suggest having a chat to him sometime it might give you some insight as to what to expect and, how the men might react to…"

I trailed off with a shrug, not wanting to use the only words my brain would serve up in case I upset the man who, I could clearly tell, was still trying to keep his emotions in check.

"Thank you, I will," he said earnestly. "I now understand that I'm going to have to learn a lot from you people before we come out here again, and if we are to have any hope of coming back alive."

I clapped him on his shoulder and smiled.

"Oh, don't worry. We'll help you get everything ready," I said, and waved my hand at the Bushmasters following behind us. "I'm sure I'm not the only one who has already started thinking how we can improve those babies. Give us a day and you won't recognise them."

CHAPTER FOURTEEN

As the sun was nearing the horizon the topmost levels of the castle came into view. The sight always stirred something in me, but I had yet to boil it down to one single feeling. The helicopter had flown ahead and had already landed after refuelling at the airfield, releasing the ones left there to guard it to return to the castle and help prepare for our arrival. Maud and her helpers had by no means been idle in our absence. As the children, with adult supervision as ever, had stood sentry on the walls, extra rooms were prepared for the new arrivals. Airbeds had been inflated and camp beds set up in some of the still vacant rooms. Even though they wouldn't feel as homely as we had made the rooms we had all used for some time now they would be infinitely better than the alternative; a cold flag stoned floor. We weren't sure how they would want the sleeping arrangements to be, but it was a start and at least everyone would have somewhere to sleep until more permanent arrangements could be finalised.

We were used to the reaction our new home got from new arrivals, and Captain Clarke, who was standing by my side in the trailer, did not disappoint. He let out a low whistle of admiration as we emerged from the darkness of the Barbican and entered the huge, open central courtyard of the castle which was mostly laid to grass. In all honesty the vista still impressed me, so it was easy to imagine what any newcomers thought.

"What do you think?" I asked him as Shawn, switched from tractor driver to parking warden, directed each vehicle to form a neat line. We'd started parking our eclectic fleet a little more neatly after Maud had pointed out that we were carving up the grass of the courtyard, and that when winter brought the wetter weather along we could be faced with a sticky, wet morass of mud and puddles if we weren't careful. As usual she had a point, so we began to be more cautious and one of the jobs on the ever-growing long job list we always had was to find some hardcore and make a proper hardstanding for our fleet.

"Wow just, wow," Clarke said as he slowly spun around to take in the huge structures towering above him on all sides.

"Come along, let's get inside for a brew," I said as the ramp lowered, then noticed Becky standing by the main door.

"Better go and see the wife first though," I said, pointing out Becky to Clarke. "Follow the others and I'll see you in a minute."

I ran down the ramp and gave my wife the hug I had been longing to give her since not long after we'd left on the mission. Becky hugged me back long enough to be polite until, with her nose wrinkled she pushed me away and theatrically sniffed the air.

"Mister," she said. "I don't know who you are, but my man smells better than that. If you want me to show you how much I missed you later you better go and find him. I think he's hanging around the showers."

This was Becky's way of showing she had missed me.

"Kids been okay?" I asked trying to change the subject away from my personal hygiene.

She held my hand as we walked towards the entrance.

"Yes, they've been great. I knew they were missing you though when they slept in with me last night."

"I hope they don't expect to tonight," I whispered in her ear as we entered the Great Hall.

The huge room was as busy as it had ever been. So many people crowded into the huge room that it seemed to be at capacity. Until you studied it carefully and realized that even with the amount of people that now filled it, it could easily take twice as many with room to spare. The new arrivals milled around in the centre, absorbing the sheer splendour of the space. After the initial hubbub of greetings had died down the room was permeated by the low murmurings of conversations until Charles, our resident Vicar, stepped into the middle of everyone with his hands held aloft and called for quiet.

He proceeded to perform his well-practised welcome speech which seemed well received by the newcomers, as nervous and apprehensive expressions changed to ones filled with hope and joy. Reality dawned on most that they were safe for the moment, and the nightmare of being trapped underground for weeks was truly over. Tears flowed from more than a few eyes as he finished and made way for the admiral, who had stepped onto a sturdy table to ensure all could see him.

"Thank you, Vicar, for that heart-warming welcome," he began. "I've been told these good folk here have prepared quarters for you all, so if you could be a little patient whilst we get round everyone to allocate where you will be staying I would be grateful. Also, I can imagine everyone wishes to explore this fantastic building, but as night will soon be upon us can I request that everyone contains their inquisitiveness until tomorrow when I am sure you will all get the full tour."

He scanned the room and sought out Captain Clarke in the crowd, waving for him to come forward.

"Captain Clarke, for you there is no rest for the wicked I am afraid. If I could request for you and your men to join us in the dining room over there, we can continue our discussion we started earlier." Clarke nodded his understanding and the admiral went on.

"Food is being prepared, so if everyone else could make themselves comfortable and get to know each other we will re-join you presently."

He jumped down from the table and made his way to the dining room as the pop of a champagne cork marked the end of his speech before Willie's voice boomed across the room.

"Enough of the formalities for now, folks. Everyone come and get a wee glass of something to wet your throat while we get everything else organised."

When we were all seated around the dining table the admiral started the meeting by asking a representative of all the groups present to introduce themselves, and to give a brief recap of their story so far for the benefit of Clarke and his SAS troopers.

I stood to introduce the initial castle residents, picking out Maud first as our boss. As I told our story I pointed out the others seated around the table we had gathered along the way handing over to Steve who did the same before the admiral introduced the key members of his own team.

"Now we all know each other formally, I shall begin," he said officially as he shuffled the papers that lay before him on the desk as if to give himself the time to formulate his next sentence. "Our primary mission is, and should always be, to save as many people as we can. Captain Clarke painfully reminded me of this on the journey here, therefore I need a plan to be formulated to assist himself and his men to go and see if their families, by some miracle, have made it. Not until that is done can we look at what the planners both here and, in the Scillies, have for us next."

Clarke shifted in his chair uncomfortably as the admiral's realism soured his thoughts. I saw it and felt a stab of guilt in my chest for having my own family safely with me from the beginning. I caught his eye and made my voice as sincere as I could.

"Where are we going first?"

***

One hour later the bones of a plan had been worked out, and we left the dining room to eat buffet style the remains of the food that had already been served to everyone else. After a few drinks and some more socialising, everyone, conscious of the work that needed to be done over the next few days, went to bed.

CHAPTER FIFTEEN

Captain Clarke addressed his troopers gathered in the courtyard in the dawn's early light with a positivity and confidence they all believed.

"Listen in, boys. You've seen how we need to fight in this new world. We're going to have to put aside a lot of our training we have all had and learn some new, sorry old, *very* old, fighting techniques."

Murmurs rippled around the men as a group of knights, already kitted out in full armour, clanked their way into the courtyard.

"We're getting a crash course from these chaps right now, and remember that we're not the experts now, these people are, and they are the key for us attempting to reach our families. If they can get the vehicles we need today and modify them in time, the plan is to leave tomorrow."

He then turned to where the knights were waiting for the training to begin.

Ian had been selected as chief instructor. He seemed to think it was because his size would give him a natural authority, but everyone else knew that it was his uncontrollable mouth and the inappropriate things that spewed from it without warning, would probably be the best way to train the new recruits in the shortest time possible. The children had therefore been sent to watch duty at the furthest points away from the training ground.

"Morning, ladies," Ian began by signalling to a rack of weapons of all types on one side of the courtyard. "Come and pick a weapon then I'll tell you why it's a stupid idea and will get you killed."

***

I was with another group whose task for the morning was to go out and find another tractor and trailer from one of the many farms that surrounded Warwick. The plan was to modify it for the SAS to use for their mission. At the meeting yesterday evening it had been agreed that two of the Bushmasters and a new tractor with a trailer hitched to it would be sufficient for their needs.

I walked around Shawn's tractor with him, performing the regular visual inspections we did every time we left the safety of the walls to make sure everything was in order. Others were loading the trailer and the armoured car that was going to accompany us with the supplies and equipment we would need for what was hopefully going to be a short mission. The crane lorry was also coming so we could load any items we found that could be useful quickly and easily. With everything in order, a few of the knights broke off from their training duties to follow us to the outer gates in Willies trailer just in case they were needed to help us clear the way. The few zombies hanging around didn't pose any problems and we were soon through and heading out into the countryside.

Our aim was to visit the closest farms first, then to widen our search if necessary. Using a map we had planned our route the night before, once more exploring new routes as we hadn't found much need to venture far into the countryside around us yet. Everyone onboard the three vehicles were staying alert and scanning our surroundings keenly but still we didn't encounter many zombies in the town, and most we thrust our spears at seemed to be damaged in some way and unable to move as the others did.

Some had clearly been either hit by our plough or crushed by the weight of others as they were thrust aside by the force of the blade hitting them. Their damaged limbs made it harder for them to move 'normally' and we found them either stumbling along on broken and bent legs or unable to move and just either standing still or lying on the ground, their uncoordinated struggles unable to help them to their feet again. This seemed strange to us as each time we had left previously, there had always been a lot more for us to dispatch by various means. It was a change we did not dislike, and anything that potentially made our job easier we weren't going to complain about so we, still keeping our spears close, continued our journey.

The first few farms we visited disappointingly contained older tractors which we discounted as we knew a modern, more powerful one would be far better for the work it was required for. We searched the outbuildings on the lookout for materials we knew would be useful to convert whatever we found for its new use. If the farm was still home to their original inhabitants they were quickly dispatched before we hurriedly made a pile, and the crane lifted it onto the bed of the lorry before we moved on.

"That's more like it," I said happily as the fourth farm yielded a large, newish tractor in the yard with the bonus of an equally new looking silage trailer already hooked up to it. The farmhouse looked very old but obviously lovingly maintained. Most farm-yards always seemed to have the dilapidated air of conscious neglect around them, with old broken-down machinery squirreled away in some corner just in case it was needed in the future, but this place was very neat and tidy with large, modern open sided barns surrounding it indicating that the owners were either very successful farmers, or very wealthy. Or both.

As we pulled up six zombies, the most we had seen together all day, emerged from the open front door of the farmhouse. Six well aimed shots from the .22's soon ended what couldn't have even been called a threat but it served as a timely reminder to us all for the need for continued vigilance.

As soon as the last one fell, Dave Eddy jumped from the armoured car and went to inspect the tractor.

"Bollocks. No keys," he called back with a tone of frustration in his voice. "They'll probably be in there," he said with a finger pointed at the farmhouse.

Looking at who was in the trailer he called out the names of the four people he wanted to accompany him into the building before theatrically looking at his watch as he waited for the ramp to be deployed and for the chosen ones to join him.

I watched from the trailer, holding my rifle ready as they cautiously approached the house and shouted inside. None of us were in our armour as we hadn't planned to fight any on foot and to just avoid any unnecessary contact with zombies. Large scale zombie destruction was the name of the game for this mission so it was left behind. The tractor and trailer in the yard were too good an opportunity to pass by, so I reasoned that as six had already left the building and they usually grouped together, the risk Dave was taking was worth it.

Watching, I knew the routine they would be following. After listening for a while to see if their shouting had encouraged any more waiting ghouls to emerge they got ready to enter, forming a tight group with their hand weapons and pistols ready. All went quiet for a few minutes as they entered the house until one of them ran out and shouted excitedly.

"There's a bloody survivor in the cellar! She's just clearing the barricade she's built and she'll be up!"

"What the hell?" I shouted back in surprise.

Everyone in the trailer automatically moved towards the ramp, needing to be involved with such exciting news. Those left in the armoured car had also heard the shout and they too began to exit their vehicle. As one, we all ran towards the open door of the farmhouse, until I remembered the basic rules of zombie survival: Alertness.

I turned back to see Shawn and Louise hadn't forgotten. They had exited the cab of the tractor and were standing guard, weapons held ready on its high wheel arches. Acknowledging my mistake Shawn smiled and gave me a cheeky wink, then held his thumb up to indicate all was in order and that no harm had been done by our mistake, so I turned and joined the others inside the farmhouse.

Entering the house I had to physically push myself through the stench of rot and decay it was so thick. The remains of bodies and scraps of clothing littered the wide hallway. Upended furniture and smashed ornaments were scattered everywhere, and holes I knew were caused by blasts from a shotgun had ripped through

126

the walls. I'd entered houses inhabited by the turned before and knew that the mess wasn't caused by their aimless wandering; a desperate fight had taken place here and we were about to rescue a survivor of it.

As I stepped over the bodies that stretched along the hallway it wasn't difficult to work out what had happened. Bodies of zombies killed by a blast from a shotgun lay intermingled with the gore-covered skeletal remains of the defenders. The last body before I reached the kitchen still had a shotgun clutched in what remains of its hand and I nodded to myself sadly as I surveyed the scene, imagining the terror of desperately fighting a losing battle against things your worst nightmares couldn't conjure up, but by the looks of it one had survived so at least they hadn't given their lives in vain.

The entrance door to the cellar was in the kitchen which was at the end of the hallway. It was large and, to my property developers' eye, a very expensively appointed room. The kitchen was at one end with an aga as its centrepiece, with a large living and dining area overlooking what I could tell were once manicured gardens through floor to ceiling picture windows and patio doors. With a whistle of appreciation, I joined the others who were gathering around the door. Loud bangs and the sounds of heavy objects being dragged out of the way were accompanied by the desperate shouts of a female voice as she fought to free herself from her subterranean prison of months.

Someone had already tried to open the door and help, but it was locked and heavy enough to resist our efforts with the small hand weapons we had with us, so all we could do was wait. Eventually the door shook slightly as the last of whatever was leaning against the other side of it was moved. The voice, now sounding much closer, shouted desperately.

"I'm opening the door! Please don't leave me!"

The door swung inwards and, blinking from the darkness of the cellar steps, came one of the most dishevelled people I had ever seen. Her pale, filthy face, matted hair and torn clothing brought instant sympathy from all of us. The smell of her also brought a tear to my eye but I tried to hide that response.

She stood by the door, shielding her eyes from the bright sunlight streaming through the large windows, sobbing from emotion and the exertion of moving the barricade she had built to voluntarily imprison herself. She was a young woman, probably in her early twenties with a slim figure and blonde hair, but she looked as if she had been dragged through the proverbial hedge backwards at least twice.

We watched silently as, blinking and wiping away the tears that had washed rivulets of dirt from her face, her eyesight slowly adjusted to the brightness of the room. I stepped towards her, trying not to breathe through my nose, and spoke gently.

"It's okay now, you're safe. We killed the ones that were trapping you."

She just stood there staring dumfounded at all of us as we watched her. She looked so lost, so confused and bereft, that my heart went out to her. I repeated my first sentence, but more slowly and with an even gentler voice.

"It really is okay. You're safe now."

She still just stared at me silently, so I continued.

"You can come back with us," I told her, suddenly aware how awkward it might be for her.

Asking a young woman if she wanted to come home with you, when all she could see was a group of armed men standing around her, probably needed a little more explaining.

"We're a group based at Warwick Castle. Some of us have our families with us and the Army has just arrived to help. It really is about as safe as it can be in the mad world we're in now."

She looked at me and then at the others again. Most were just nodding and smiling at her as if to try and silently convey the truth in what I was saying.

Dave stepped closer and confirmed what I was trying to tell her. Maybe his older, weather-beaten and craggy face carried more grandfatherly qualities than mine, but as he repeated that she was safe I could see the dawning of understanding rising on her expression. As the words eventually sunk in she burst out crying and flung herself at Dave to bury her face against his chest. With her arms wrapped around him she began sobbing fiercely. Dave was taken aback momentarily before he wrapped his arms around her protectively and kept repeating that she was safe now.

After a few minutes I remembered that Shawn and Louise were still outside keeping watch for us. Louise was also the only lady in our group and possibly what would help the young woman was a friendly female face to add more reassurance that we were who we were trying to tell her we were. Turning to the man next to me I asked him to go and tell Shawn and Louise what was going on and asked if he could replace Louise so she could come inside and help.

Louise took over from Dave without hesitation, and as Louise comforted her she gave the shocked young woman a very brief recap of what had been going on in the world.

Her name was Hannah, and she had been part of the desperate fight in the hallway when they had been surprised by what they first thought were a group of burglars. It was only when they had started to rip people apart with their teeth that one of them had grabbed the shotgun he had been cleaning on the kitchen table. He had just been getting ready to go out to do some rough shooting and already had some cartridges in his pockets, but it was too little, too late and he'd only managed to get a handful of shots off before he was overcome. The pause in the attack that the few shots had made had given her the time to realise escape was the only option, but being trapped inside the house she could only make it to the shelter of the cellar.

She had all those weeks to wonder what had happened. The only conclusion she could actually come to when her attackers didn't move on or communicate in any way with her, with their shambling footsteps overhead her only company for all this time, was that they were zombies, and she was trapped until help arrived.

We still had a job to complete and I said that we needed to get moving, asking if there was anything in the house she wanted to collect.

"What do you mean?" she asked.

"You may want to get some clothes and maybe some family pictures and such the like. Chances are we won't come back here," I said simply, seeing her face drop.

"I didn't really live here. It's my boyfriends' farm, well, his parents really, so I stay over a fair bit when we are both back from university."

At the mention of her boyfriend she stared at the death and destruction in the hallway and started to cry again. It didn't need explaining that he was most likely one of the ragged bodies there.

I turned and pulled at the handle of the patio door which opened easily.

"Come on, let's go out this way," I said in my best cheerful voice.

I didn't need to explain that it was to avoid her stepping over the bones of her boyfriend and his family as she left as that much was obvious. We moved as a group and walked around the house to where our vehicles were parked.

Back at our vehicles Dave slapped his hand to his forehead when he looked at the tractor and trailer we wanted to take.

"We still haven't got the bloody keys for it," he said with a cringing look on his face as he turned and looked at our latest addition to our numbers.

"I'm sorry to ask, Hannah, but would you have any ideas where the keys for it are?"

"As far as I know all keys are kept on some hooks in the kitchen," Hannah said with her brow creased in thought. "If they aren't in the ignition, that's where they'll be."

Dave nodded his thanks and headed back towards the front door.

A thought came to me, so I asked Hannah, "How did you not starve to death or die from thirst when you were trapped down there?"

She smiled sadly as she told me.

"Neil, my boyfriend's dad, was a bit of a survival nut. We all used to make fun of him for it, but he always said it would come in useful one day. He'd read some books a few years back and they'd convinced him to fill the cellar with supplies and equipment, just in case. He actually befriended one or two local authors whose books he'd read."

Her sad smile changed to a grin of fond memories as she continued.

"I met them when he invited them over for a day's shooting and a BBQ. They were nice guys, Devon and Chris I think their names were, but all their talk of ammunition, food storage and all that prep rubbish gave us all enough material to keep taking the piss out of him for his bromance for months afterwards. Never meet your heroes they say…anyway, the cellar is stocked full of supplies, so I had plenty to eat and even though there was a lot of bottled water, the house is fed by its own spring and there is a toilet and wash hand basin down there, so there was no shortage of water."

"So there's a cellar full of useful stuff in the house as well as the perfect vehicle for us outside?" I asked incredulously, not really beginning to believe the luck we were having today, and she just nodded.

I checked my watch. We had plenty of daylight left and we had already fulfilled the mission we set out to achieve today. We had a tractor and trailer, which when adapted with the materials we already had in stock back at the castle and with what we had scavenged today would be perfect for us to use. If we could combine it with gathering more supplies, it seemed a more than sensible option to do so. Time was a factor though, as the SAS chaps were hoping to leave tomorrow to search for their families.

Dave returned clutching a few sets of keys in his hand, having obviously grabbed what was on the hooks to save time sorting them out where the smell was awful. As he approached I told him about the other surprises the cellar contained and he readily agreed that as we were already here, it would be a good idea to quickly empty it. He went to the tractor and, after trying a few different keys, found the right one to start it up before going to the armoured car and returning with a bag of torches and lanterns which he handed around before quickly organising who would be doing what on the work party and chivvied the chosen ones to the house again.

The cellar revealed a treasure trove of long-life food and other supplies. The bloke who had stocked it hadn't held back on his enthusiasm for prepping and, as his house and farm already showed, he had plenty of money to spend on it. On seeing the sheer volume of what we could take Dave asked me to back the new tractor and trailer up to the front door to hopefully speed up the loading.

Systematically sorting through what was in there, passing items from hand to hand in a chain, we steadily worked our way through the unexpected bounty. Another nice surprise we found was the gun safe with its door open. Hannah's story and the walls hit with blasts from a shotgun in the hallway above us had already informed us of the sad tale of someone eventually realising that guns were the only way to try and survive. It was a shame that more of what it contained could have been used, as it would have given them a real chance.

The gun safe was one of the biggest I'd seen, with separate areas for his rifle and shotgun collection and contained a large quantity of different types of both. Another large, locked cabinet next to it caught my attention. Taking the keys from the open gun safe door I tried a few in its lock before finding the right one and swung the door open.

"Bloody hell," I exclaimed in delight. "He's got more friggin' ammo in here than most gun shops!"

An hour later I walked out of the house with Hannah as she clutched a few photos, mementos of her boyfriend and his family, and some clothes she wanted to take with her. We drove slowly out of the farmyard and headed back to the castle. Just before it went from sight, I sent silent thanks back in the direction we came from for everything the farm had provided.

CHAPTER SIXTEEN

After an uneventful journey back to the castle spent talking to Hannah, telling her more about our adventures so far and how our group had grown from just me and my family desperately escaping St Agnes in Cornwall to the dozens it contained now, I gave a brief description of a few of the key people at the castle. I tried to give as humorous an introduction to them as I could, which to be honest, wasn't hard.

She knew Warwick Castle and had visited it numerous times on family outings, so she was prepared for the splendour of the place as we drove into the courtyard through the Barbican entrance. The military vehicles and others in our fleet, all lined up neatly against one of the outer walls, drew her attention first. Secondly, and as we hadn't quite got round to explaining about the knights yet, she gasped audibly when she spotted them. Most of them were still training the SAS soldiers and were formed in a shield wall with pikes extended, practising fighting against stuffed dummies hanging from a frame.

"What the fuck?" she uttered, her voice barely above an astounded whisper.

"Ah. Sorry," I said with a chuckle. "I didn't tell you about our secret weapon yet. Yes, they look a little frightening, but trust me, they are all as daft as anything and unless you are a zombie you have nothing to fear. They're just training the SAS soldiers we rescued."

I stopped as I realised we hadn't yet told her about our recent mission to rescue them yet. I was about to carry on, but I saw Maud and Becky approaching the trailer. We'd radioed ahead to tell them we had rescued someone and they'd gathered, along with every other person who found the arrival of someone new far more interesting that what they were currently doing to greet Hannah.

As soon as Maud saw the dishevelled state Hannah was in as she walked down the ramp she immediately took over, issuing a string of commands to those that were foolish enough to be nearby and appearing unemployed. Placing a protective arm around her and talking to her softly, Maud led Hannah into the castle.

All other activity had stopped as well. The SAS guys were admiring the new tractor and trailer and Shawn was explaining what he planned to do to modify it. Ian lumbered up to me, his usual half grin on his face.

"How's the training going?" I asked as I shook his hand.

"Pretty good," he replied, a rare serious look now on his face. "They've got the gist of it and I reckon they can learn the rest when they're out there. It's mainly a time-served skill to learn anyhow, and now they know the basics it'll be up to them not to do anything stupid and get themselves killed."

He pointed out Captain Clarke.

"Andy seems a changed man from yesterday and couldn't be a more willing student. I think it'll be a good idea though if Steve has a word with him about getting overenthusiastic because, whatever they may think, they won't be as good as any of us until they get a bit more experience under their belts."

"Good idea," I replied thoughtfully. "Must be hard for them though?"

"How's that?"

"Elite soldiers?" I answered with a shrug. "They're probably not used to being at the bottom of the skills tree."

Ian gave a thoughtful grunt in reply.

"We'll make a start on their vehicles now," I told him. "If you do another hour or so of training, then some of them should come and help us to see what we are doing. If they know how it's all put together, then they'll have a better chance of fixing it if needs must."

With a cheery, "Will do," Ian turned away and began bawling at the ones who had stopped to check out their new vehicle to pick up their weapons and to keep at it.

With many hands making the work light, our much-practised vehicle adaption skills made rapid progress on all the vehicles. The Bushmasters, being armoured, powerful and very robust just needed a wedge to be attached to the front to improve them. Once we'd mastered how to do it on the first one, the work progressed quickly. The tractor and trailer again followed a much practised and improved plan and soon they were both taking shape.

The pace really picked up when the soldiers were released from their training to help with the work, and I was surprised to learn how many of the special forces soldiers were capable mechanics. Shawn's workshop area, set up under a large gazebo erected near to the vehicle parking area, really helped speed up the process. He had taken benches and power tools from the maintenance yard and installed power sockets that ran to the generator. Having the right size piece of metal or timber able to be quickly cut to size or drilled on site made a great difference to the speed of work. With the many willing hands we had, hands desperate to go and find their families, the work was completed just as the last light left the evening sky.

That evening, after dinner had been served and tidied away, a few of us sat down with Captain Clarke and his men to help work out the route they would take. The married ones, including the captain, didn't live far from the base. I realised how agonising it must have been for them yesterday when we rescued them and drove back here, taking them further away from their loved ones and answers to the questions they had so long to ponder. We knew the route was clear to the base, and with a map spread out on the table they worked out the best route to take around the list of addresses they had.

Others were sorting through our medieval supplies, adapting items to fit the individual soldiers for size and comfort. From experience, the original knights knew a loose or ill-fitting item of clothing or equipment could hamper your swing or trip you up right when you didn't need it. The plan we'd devised together was very similar to how we operated. Those who had proved most competent during training would be dressed in the armour and chainmail we provided them with. They would be the ground force who would exit the trailer and search their target property, covered by those remaining onboard and the gunners on both armoured cars. The bushmasters had extra hatches on top of them and we'd mounted some of the GPMG's retrieved from the barracks on them.

The trailer sides had been lined with mounted machine guns and grenade machine guns making it a kind of land-based agricultural battleship proving that there was no subtlety to what we'd created. The soldiers had a mission to complete, and maximum firepower would hopefully ensure their safe and speedy return. The amount of combined fire all the vehicles could lay down should be able to destroy anything they may come up against, even the kind of horde we would normally avoid.

Hannah, meanwhile, had been looked after carefully by Maud and others. After showering and dressing in new clothes she'd spent time just chatting and getting to know those caring for her. I could see from how she jumped and twitched, how her eyes darted everywhere, that it would take her some time to accept that she was truly safe.

Her sorrow, guilt, and grief were newer and fresher for her than the rest of us, but she seemed to be accepting of what had happened and as we all knew and had experienced, time and keeping busy was the best cure.

***

As the early light of dawn began to show we loaded the last few supplies, mainly ammunition, fuel, and food, on to the trailer and into the back of the armoured cars. They didn't need much else as they weren't planning to explore, just to complete their mission as quickly as possible.

With shouts of good luck and waves seeing them off, a few of us escorted them to the main gates to close them once they had left.

Our main task was now to prepare for their return when we would go to M.O.D. Kineton and resupply with ammunition both for us and the Scilly Isles contingent. We already had many lorries filled with foodstuffs set aside for them. The planners had worked out the daily calorific needs for the entire population of the Scillies and they had estimated what we had and roughly calculated we had enough to feed everyone for at least two months. More would clearly be required, but for now what we had was reckoned to be enough.

Every house, shop, and business on the islands had also been emptied of any food or other useful equipment they contained. These supplies had been catalogued and were already supplementing what had been brought with them or unloaded from one of the many container ships that were part of the fleet of ships and other craft occupying every safe anchorage around the islands. Plans were progressing to investigate what was growing on the farms the islands had and to care for and nurture any surviving livestock. The hope was, if the Scillies were to be maintained as a permanent base until the mainland situation changed, it would try to become as self-sufficient as possible.

The one part of the mission the planners had not yet finalised was how to get the supplies to the islands. There were no roll-off facilities on the islands, so it wasn't as simple as driving the lorries on to a car ferry and sailing away. We needed secure dockside facilities where goods could be unloaded and craned onto a waiting ship, then craned off again at the Scillies. The place that the planners were considering as the most favourite was the port of Bristol. It was a major port and therefore should already have good security in place being surrounded by fences and with few points of entry. If it could be secured, it had the potential to be ideal. The benefit of it being close to a route we'd travelled before and its relatively short distance from us when comparing it to other options also weighed in its favour.

When the helicopter had flown to us from the Scillies it had done a few low and slow passes of the area and, from the photographs we had seen that they had taken, it seemed to be, apart from one group surrounding a crane, reasonably zombie free. The planners wanted this confirmed by undertaking a ground mission and once more we were the only ones who could do it, so the planning began.

We knew the road was clear to the port, at least to the exit off the M5 motorway anyway, as most of us had used that route to reach the castle. Anyone who drove along the motorway couldn't fail to see the huge expanse of storage areas that surround the docks when going over the Avonmouth bridge. The problem was, seeing it from the bridge and from the photos taken from the helicopter was about as far as our collective knowledge of the docks went.

An expedition was needed, but we decided that it would be best to prepare for the mission to collect ammunition first. Something we could do ourselves whilst we waited for the SAS soldiers to return. They had first-hand knowledge of the base and so would be critical to the success of that mission. The base, we now knew, was the largest ammunition store in Europe and should hold far more than we could take in just one trip, but if we were going, we wanted to take as much as we practicably could and that meant more lorries.

Most of us had gained some lorry driving experience during the food scavenging expeditions undertaken on the nearby motorway. Yes, we crunched gears and weren't the best at going around corners in them, but most of us were competent enough to at least get them back to the castle, mostly in one piece. Dave Eddy consulted his notebook in which he had noted down what each lorry contained and created a list of curtain-sided lorries already searched but found to be empty, and so had been ignored and left where they had been abandoned.

We decided to use curtain-sided lorries because they'd be the easiest to load with forklift trucks, and as the lorries were covered it would keep whatever we gathered protected from the elements until they could be unloaded. A few lorries we had found and bought back to be unloaded had their own forklift truck attached to their rear. Once Chris, who had experience of them, had shown us how to unhitch them from the lorry and operate them, it had aided greatly in their unloading. Now sitting empty in the castle grounds, it was an easy decision to plan to take them with us just in case the forklifts we expected to find at the base wouldn't start from neglect. Dave's list also highlighted more of this type of vehicle sitting abandoned on the motorway. We'd prioritise taking them over others, even if they were loaded, as it wouldn't take us long to discard their unwanted freight.

The mission should be an easy one as Dave's list showed that just a couple of miles of motorway should give us all the vehicles we'd require. A lot of debate was given to how many vehicles we would need. Ammunition was heavy by nature and bulky to handle in large quantities. For the answer we had to turn to the planners, who not unexpectedly barraged us with statistics and figures which we had to interpret.

After chewing on our pencils for a bit with calculators and notebooks by our side, we roughly calculated, bearing in mind that we would not be restricted by the laws governing kerb weight of vehicles and how much they could carry, that an average artic lorry could carry twenty-five pallets of ammunition which came to over one million bullets.

"A...*million*?" I said, gobsmacked at the mind-boggling numbers.

My mind spun faster when I was told that was just for the standard .556 rounds the SA80 rifles used. We reckoned we could double stack the pallets on the lorries in places, increasing the quantity we could take considerably. The lorries would be overloaded, but as long as we were careful it should pose no problems. It wasn't like the Highways Agency were going to pull us over to check the weight.

The list of ammunition requirements also covered other calibres and types of ammunition needed for all the other weapons we had. From sniper rifles to belt-fed machine guns, mortars, and our latest addition of the grenade machine guns, the list just seemed to go on and on. It was all doing no good sitting in a bunker in Warwickshire and to have it here at the castle or on the Scilly Isles seemed the more sensible option. The planners, understandably, as all records of what the base contained were lost when the computer system stopped working, couldn't provide us with a true tally of the quantities the base held. Until we got there, opened up each bunker and inventoried its contents, we couldn't begin to work out how long it would take us to empty so we worked on the simple formula that it contained the magic figure of, "lots".

Someone made the valid point that it would all also be infinitely better under our, or the armed forces control, than falling into the hands of others who may not follow the ethos of help and cooperation we worked under.

For speed and logical convenience, the plan was to go to the furthest lorry on Eddy's list first and, once we'd got it started and crewed, they would then join our convoy to the next lorry where we would repeat the process until we had all we needed before driving our road train back to the castle. To stop the grounds of the castle looking like a lorry graveyard, we'd moved most of the empty lorries to the main carpark which was between the two gates that protected us from the outside world. It was a large, tarmacked area that could easily accommodate the hundreds of visitors' cars and coaches that brought tourists daily to such a popular attraction. The plan was to park them there and work on zombie-proofing them.

***

We admired the twelve lorries scavenged and parked in a vague semblance of neat lines in the main carpark. The mission had gone without a hitch and now Shawn, myself, and a few others were inspecting them and drawing up a list of supplies and equipment required to uprate them. We didn't plan anything special, just the usual plough on the front, mesh to protect the drivers and skirts around the tractor cab to keep the drive wheels clear of piled bodies. All routine stuff by now.

The one extra thing we all agreed on was the need to clear the piles of bodies we'd created in Warwick, but especially around the gate, was now top priority as the stench from all the rotting corpses was becoming more than unbearable. When the wind blew from a certain direction it was starting to become unpleasant for everyone in the castle. We decided that tomorrow, whilst some were working on the vehicles, others would deal with it. Concluding we would plan how to do it over the evening meal our grumbling bellies and tired bodies hoped would come sooner rather than later.

By the time the washing up was done and the dining area tidied away everyone knew what tasks they would be doing the following day. The admiral and his aides who now, by their own admission, were kicking their heels a bit as most of the planning required had been done and agreed on, were added to the work rotas and allocated jobs that best suited their abilities. Their true work would start again when we secured dock facilities and finished the resupply of much needed ammunition, but until that point they would be at our disposal.

As had become a much welcome custom, the end of most evenings was spent sitting around the fire and sipping on whatever your favourite tipple was before tiredness and the need to be up early in the morning forced us to our beds. The idle chatter and banter strengthened our bonds of friendship and trust, but naturally the conversation turned to wondering how Captain Clarke and his men were getting along.

CHAPTER SEVENTEEN

Clarke

The captain felt nervous as the small convoy sped along their planned route. He knew they had the vehicles, weapons, and newly acquired skills to complete their mission but what they might find weighed heavily on his consciousness. Thoughts of his own family had never left his mind during the time spent trapped in the bunker. The helplessness he felt had been heart-breaking, not knowing if they were alive or dead, all the time hoping beyond hope that they had made it but also wishing that if they had succumbed then it had been as quick and painless as possible.

His logical, military trained mind knew that the chances of them or any of his other comrades' families surviving were virtually nil, but deep down in his heart he held a small glimmer of hope that, despite everything, they would be safe. Every time he thought about it, the vision of his wife and daughter running from their front door into his arms played across his mind. During his incarceration in the bunker, the images of his family on his phone had become his only link with them and he had found himself staring at them, flicking through the hundreds of photos for hours on end, lost in a world of emotion filled memories hoping and praying that he would see his wife Tan, and his beautiful, blonde-haired, eight-year-old daughter Emily again. He yearned for it so much that when he dreamt about it, he woke up elated looking for them, until his mind cleared and the reality of his depressive situation sank in once more.

Captain Hammond had spoken privately to him the night before and recounted what had happened when they had eventually made it to their own barracks near Exeter. The grief he had displayed and the tears that had unashamedly ran down his face when he described the guilt he had felt when he briefly lost control of his men and saw them thrown down; killed either by zombies or their own hand.

It was clear it had left a deep impression on Hammond's soul. Clarke fought back the arrogant assumption that such a loss of control would be through poor training and leadership. When he'd considered though how he himself might act when presented with the same situation, finding that he couldn't truly answer that he would be able to control his own emotions, let alone those of his men.

With this in mind he had tried to prepare them for it as best he could. Imploring them, no matter what they saw, to try and hold it together, for not just their sake but for the future of everyone and everything. They were a hugely important asset that would likely be key to the success of any future missions or plans to take the fight to the undead filling their beloved country. He only hoped that his words would break through any veil of desperation and despair that he feared his men would soon be experiencing.

Driving the planned route through winding country lanes, the drivers and passengers became more practised at the best angle to smash through any zombies they found and at thrusting spears into heads as they passed by. They were surprised at how many they came across on a route that had been driven along and cleared only a few days before. It made them realise the size of the task that faced them in the rest of the country.

They didn't stop at the outpost of the Brough's farm. Depending on how their mission went they planned to either stop the night or, for just a brief rest, when they were on their way back. Messages were exchanged over the radio as they passed, mainly to reassure them that the engine noises they could probably hear were theirs and not an unexpected threat. They had known they would be passing, and Sergeant Gallon's cheery Newcastle accent wishing them well, along with some very sergeantly advice about not doing anything idiotic and get themselves killed, or worse, join the RAF, made a few of them smile for the next mile or so.

The closer they got, the quieter and more serious they became. Soon they would be finding out. Some even expressed doubt if it was a good idea to continue, as the reality of knowing may be worse than the ignorance of not. In their hearts they knew they needed to, and so onwards they went.

***

Heartbreakingly, they didn't even stop at the first house. It was the in-laws house of their youngest member, a twenty-five-year-old trooper who had met his wife shortly after passing selection. After a whirlwind romance and between operations they had married and had been excitedly getting ready for the birth of their first child. He and his wife had moved into her parent's home which was only a few miles from the base so she could get family support when the happy day arrived, as it was always uncertain where he would be at any moment and so may not be there when she went into labour. The front door of their cottage was wide open and the small green that was the centre of the hamlet was awash with the undead. When the desperate trooper saw his father-in-law amongst the crowd heading towards them, he knew his dreams were shattered. In anger and grief, he leant his shoulder into one of the GPMG's that lined the side of the trailer and opened up. One box of their plentiful supply of ammunition later, all that remained of the population of the once peaceful little hamlet was the mangled and smoking corpses of its former population, presided over by a sobbing soldier being comforted by his mates. Grim-faced and with hope fading in all of them, they continued.

Time and time again anguish was the only result of their searching. One house gave hope when they pulled up outside as it looked secure and the curtains were closed as if to not draw attention to themselves. For the first time they prepared to disembark from the trailer and go in on foot to investigate, however when they smashed through the locked front door, all they found was the turned family of the trooper. The husband and father, a veteran soldier of multiple skirmishes with the enemy of half a dozen continents, was overtaken with grief and collapsed to the floor when he saw his wife and children heading down the hallway towards him, their arms reaching out and their mouths open as they snapped their jaws in preparation for biting chunks out of his flesh.

Knowing he was out of the fight his comrades covered him with their shields and dragged him out of the house accompanied by his harrowing howls of raw emotion. Once outside he recovered enough to order that no one else touched his family, cuffing angry tears of pain from his cheeks and growling the order with an intensity none would get in the way of. Pulling his pistol from its holster and shaking with grief he turned and strode with grim determination towards his front door. Four shots sounded from within before he appeared, and without a single word or acknowledgment of the comfort his mates tried to give him, he returned to the trailer wearing a concentrated look of cold fury and grief on his face.

After more disappointment at the next few stops it was a silent convoy that arrived at the last village they needed to visit. By chance it was home to Clarke's family, and that of two other members of his team including his sergeant. The coincidence of a few families living close together worked well, as the shared experience of their husbands' non-regular work hours and sudden disappearances after a phone call at any time of the day or night combined with their long absences drew them together. They had formed a close bond of help and mutual support which made their partners often secretive existence more bearable. Such as the bonds of the special forces broke down the barriers between ranks, it carried over to their families as well.

Clarkes house was planned to be the last visited. His wife, through the unfortunate early death of her parents, had come into a sizeable inheritance which enabled them to buy a large house on the outskirts of the village. It was a home they intended to be their forever house. With an electric security gate and a walled garden surrounding it, Clarke had kept his thoughts from his men, but he knew that his house would be probably the best of everyone's to survive in after what had happened. He hoped, but he could not hope too much.

They needed to pass the other two men's houses to reach it and expectations soon faded as they reached the village. Zombies thronged from all directions towards them, drawn to the sound of their vehicles, and rather than wantonly open up with the sledgehammer-type results of the machine guns, they raised their personal weapons. After identifying whoever they were aiming at wasn't a member of any of their families, a single shot to the head ended their eternal suffering. Driving slowly to not ruin their aim they ended more undead lives until they reached the first target house. Its front door was open and as they stopped outside maybe a dozen zombies shambled out of it to investigate what the new noise was. Not one was the man's family, so they soon joined the kill count for the day. Another man's sobs and curses were added to the growing list of the day's sorrow, the broken sounds accompanying them as they continued.

The next house looked locked up and empty, so with heavy hearts they climbed from the vehicles to search it anyway. They had come so far and witnessed so much torment, but they knew they had to search it just to make sure.

The door gave way easily to a kick and the armour-clad men trooped inside to emerge a minute later with shaking heads, silently signalling to their comrades there was nothing inside making Clarke grip the grab handle on the dashboard of the armoured car tightly; his knuckles turning white as his hand trembled.

He didn't trust himself to speak as he signalled for his sergeant, whose house it had been, to get back on board and continue driving as soon as the last man was on the trailer. Pete, with silent tears of grief unashamedly running down his face, took a few moments to compose himself before setting off with an angry clash of gears and avoiding any eye contact with his captain and friend sitting next to him. The captain, unable to verbalise anything as his own emotions were spinning faster than a washing machine at the climax of the cycle, was only able to offer a pathetic pat of condolence on his friend's knee in an attempt to offer sympathy.

Slowly they continued through the small village, and once they had established the approaching undead weren't any of their families, they ran over, shot, or stabbed any they saw until they entered the lane that led to Clarke's own house. A sliver of hope stabbed at his heart when he saw a large crowd of the undead gathered around the entrance gate to his home, because from what he had been told and from his own experience in the bunker at HQ, the undead never left a place where they knew the living were, until they either got to them or something else attracted their attention.

He shouted over the radio for all his men to get on their feet and get ready for whatever they may find. Energised with hope, he had to forcefully restrain himself from his first reaction which was to jump from the vehicle and run ahead to investigate. Sheer force of will made him remain outwardly calm as the small convoy entered the lane. A body lying at the side of the road caught his attention. It had clearly turned, but that was not what interested him, it was the damaged head of the former zombie that did. It had been partially decapitated with a close-range blast from a shotgun. He'd seen a lot of similar kills on the many missions he could never talk about to not need a second look for confirmation.

He and his wife both held shotgun licences, her being a born and raised country girl, and kept a few in their gun safe. He rarely got the opportunity to attend a game shoot these days because things were so busy, but they did accept invites a few times a year to local friends who held shoot days on their farms, more for the social side than the actual hunting.

When he saw another rotting corpse on the ground with shotgun wounds, his level of hope raised even more. Someone had conducted a fighting retreat down his lane, and there weren't many houses down it. Only his and an elderly couple who lived further on and he knew they didn't own any shotguns.

"You seeing what I'm seeing boss?" Pete asked, his voice hoarse from the effort of his earlier tears.

"Something went down here," Clarke said, unable to keep the excited anticipation out of his voice.

"Still going down, I reckon boss," Pete answered, his emotions now under control again.

The zombies around the gate turned as the noise of their vehicles proved a more tempting prospect than his family home. As they approached his men needed no instructions, and they started to methodically take them down for good. The captain looked at the gate and finally let his feelings show. The gate had his wife's car pressed up against it and lengths of timber had been wedged against it to reinforce it further.

"They must be in there!" he called out excitedly "Why else would they barricade the gate? They've barricaded the gate, Pete!"

Taking a look around him, the last few zombies fell as well aimed single shots removed the tops of their heads, he shouted to his sergeant, the desperation in his voice clearly evident.

"Just drive through the bloody gate and push everything out of the way!"

With a reply of "Yessir." He put the armoured car into gear and slowly approached the gate. The power of the vehicle was more than a match for the gate and with a screech of breaking metal and popping of the timbers that supported it snapping, it did not falter as it pushed the car before it down the drive that led to his house. Turning the wheel slightly the car was pushed to the side, and his sergeant sped up until fifty yards later he skidded to a stop on the gravelled parking area in front of the house.

The captain opened the door to jump out and stare at his house. It looked secure. The wooden shutters on the downstairs windows – more for decorative than security reasons – were all closed. They had never been closed once in all the years they had lived there. In fact, he thought bizarrely as the maelstrom of thoughts ran through his head, he hadn't even known they could be closed. Movement at an upper window caught his eye and a face appeared. He couldn't control himself and his vision blurred as tears began to pour down his features on seeing the face of his wife.

Her scream of shock and joy was clearly audible, followed seconds later by noises as whatever was blocking the front door was dragged clear. He moved towards the door as it was flung open, and she ran out and into his arms sobbing uncontrollably with joy and happiness as she rained kisses on his face and cheeks. His bliss, and dreams from when he was in the bunker, were completed a few seconds later when his daughter screaming 'Daddy' over and over almost knocked him off his feet as she ran into his embrace.

He looked up as more ecstatic shouts sounded out as the two men who also lived in the village had spotted their families running from the house. One didn't even wait for the trailer's ramp to descend and vaulted over the side. His sergeant also flung himself from the front of the armoured car and ran to his family. The three knots of families, reunited against the odds, forgot all about their mission and just revelled in the emotions of knowing each other had survived.

A shot from one of his men standing guard bought everyone back to reality. The zombies left mobile in the village had followed them and were now at the destroyed gate and beginning to make their way down the drive. Clarke, dragged from his emotions at the first shot, stared as more appeared and were quickly felled by accurate shooting. The two other men who had been hugging their families joined him and he released himself from his wife's and child's embrace.

He summed it up, back in leadership mode. "No point hanging around here now, get everyone onboard and let's get moving."

His wife, Tan, had overheard him and interrupted.

"Can we just get the bags we have ready to go from the house first? And do you want me to bring the shotguns?"

Andy Clarke smiled at his wife fondly, filthy clothes and greasy hair included, expecting nothing less from her. Coming from a military family herself and with the current life she lived with him, being prepared was a way of life for her.

"Of course. And Absobloodylutely get the guns."

He waved to two of his men.

"Come on, let's grab their things and get out of here."

Before he went into the house he shouted to Pete, still unashamedly wiping away the tears of joy falling down his face, to reorganise who went where in the vehicles, as he wanted the recently reunited families, including himself, to travel together in the Bushmaster.

A guilty thought came to him as he jogged out of the house carrying two bags. In his own elation he had forgotten the despair that others under his command must be going through. The fact that it was probably made worse because some of the families had survived, ramming home their own upset and heartbreak, was not lost on him also.

After he had ushered his and the other families into the bushmaster, he solemnly went to the trailer and other Bushmaster and got everyone's attention.

"I am sorry, chaps, that you weren't as lucky as Pete, Roy, and myself. I know there's nothing I can say at the moment to ease whatever is going through your mind, but what I can do is thank you for today. We knew it was most likely going to be a terrible day for most, but we got through it. I just hope that it is a small solace to you that some have survived and that will help you through the healing process I know you must all go through now."

He tried to sound cheerful when he spoke next, but even as he said it, he knew it would sound most likely hollow to those he was addressing.

"Let's get going. We should be back at the outpost at the Brough's farm in a few hours for a rest."

CHAPTER EIGHTEEN

With a flaming torch in one hand, I checked around that everyone was clear. The day had been spent fighting down the urge to gag and vomit as we pushed the mounds of stinking, rotting corpses the town was littered with using the tractors and a bulldozer, we had found at a housing site on the edge of town, into a virtual mountain of the undead. Layering timber between them and giving them a good soaking of diesel and petrol, we were ready to set the pyre alight.

The wind was in the right direction, so it would blow the expectedly awful smell away from the castle. Once everyone shouted that they were clear I stepped back a few paces, took a run up, and flung the torch as far as I could into the mass of corpses. The torch flew ponderously, turning end over end before landing where the petrol caught immediately, and tendrils of flame spread throughout the whole disgusting morass.

None of us wanted to spend a minute longer than necessary near the pyre, no matter how enticing the draw of a bonfire was. We were all desperate to get back to the castle to change clothes and wash away the smell of corruption that seemed to coat every pore of our bodies, so as soon as we were sure the fire would take hold, we mounted the vehicles to head home.

The pace was positively glacial as we decided to bring the powerful bulldozer back with us. We crawled along at its top speed, which seemed to be less than walking pace as it clanked and screeched beside us. The heavy, metal tracks did their best to ruin the road as straggling zombies were drawn out to see what the commotion was. They weren't appearing in the numbers we'd previously experienced, but enough of them paid us attention to keep a few of us continually on watch ready to shoot when they came into range.

Lining the trailer sides, we killed a few more on the way back. Each thrust of a spear or blast of a shotgun reminding us that, in the not-too-distant future, we would probably have to repeat the work we'd just done.

Once back at the castle we were pleased that, even though the thick, black column of rising smoke was clearly visible, looming over the town like a beacon of death, our reasoning was bang on and the wind carried the smoke and the stench away.

***

The news that Clarke had completed his mission and rescued three families, his own among them, greeted us on our return. He'd decided to spend the night at the Brough's farm to give his men the chance to rest and either grieve the knowledge that their families were gone forever, or rejoice that they were safe. He reckoned it best for the facts to properly take hold, in the quieter and less crowded environment the farm would provide. They would return in the morning, and he promised they would all soon be ready for the next mission to begin.

Maud began preparing more rooms for the newly arriving families to use as well as improve the rooms the others were using as their barracks. When the SAS soldiers and the others with them arrived initially, they'd been accommodated on air beds and camp beds hurriedly set up in various previously empty rooms around the castle. Maud, with the help of her army of volunteers, was determined to give their sleeping quarters a more permanent and comfortable feel to them even if we didn't know how long they'd be staying with us. Our guess was that it would be for quite a time as the SAS soldiers' talents would be wasted on the Scilly Isles, and as our group controlled the only two known operational mainland bases, the castle would be the logical one of the two to house troops given its central location. It was not, therefore, deemed a wasted effort by any of us to make their rooms as comfortable as possible.

After scrubbing myself clean and changing clothes I made my way downstairs to the Great Hall. It seemed that everyone had finished their jobs for the day and were gathering in anticipation of the meal we could all smell being prepared. After the stink of burning, rotted meat that still felt embedded up my nose the change was welcome. With a glass in hand, I walked over to Shawn who had spent the day with a few others working on the scavenged lorries.

He looked at my face that was still red from scrubbing and sniffed the air as I approached. I knew I still had the odour of disinfectant wafting around me, so I gave him a smile.

"Trust me, pal, I think you'd prefer *eau de Dettol* to how I smelt earlier. *Eau de five-week-old corpse* was *not* a best smeller!"

He grimaced at the pun but I wasn't deterred.

"Anyway, we'll find out in the morning if we got the job done right. How'd you get on today?"

"Good mate," he replied, sipping at the can he held. "We've got most of the main stuff done on the lorries. It'll just need a bit of tinkering in the morning, and they'll be good to go.

"Great," I replied. "Unless I get told to do something else, I'll give you a hand in the morning."

I indicated to where Walker-Jones was chatting to Becky and a few others.

"How'd *he* get on today? He really seemed to want to get his hands dirty last night when he asked if he could help."

"He really seemed to enjoy it to be fair," Shawn answered with a chuckle. "The engineering background he's got was a great help, in fact. He came up with some good ideas which we implemented and made the job easier. Annoyingly, the bugger can actually weld a joint far better than me."

Our eyes had naturally turned to him as we talked which he noticed. Disentangling himself from the group he was speaking to with smiles and apologies, he made his way over to us with raised eyebrows.

"Is that my ears I can feel burning or are you talking about me?"

"Shawn says you were a great help today," I replied after taking a sip of my drink.

He raised his glass in acknowledgment.

"Yes, I really enjoyed it. Reminded me of my early days in the Navy when I was a wet-behind-the-ears second lieutenant. Budget cuts meant we had to get creative with repairs sometimes just to keep the damn things afloat. It taught me a lot about out-of-the-box thinking and making do with what was available instead of what we needed. Now I've worked on the vehicles and know what's involved, it'll be a great help going forwards."

He looked into his drink wistfully for a second before continuing.

"It may be me, but as I was working on the vehicles today I could imagine great, long convoys of our modified lorries running up and down the roads resupplying a network of outposts based all over the country."

"Steady on," I laughed in reply. "Can we get a place sorted for the ships to dock first?"

Nodding, he replied, "Oh, I have no doubt that even though it'll be a lot of work with many more learning experiences along the way, the mission will be a success. The planners have done a fine job despite all the unknowns…I must say I have *never* seen a longer contingency list of alternative plans if something doesn't happen the way it should, and I'm sure you'll be happy to know that once the bridgehead is secured on the dock, we plan to have a lot of personnel ready to disembark and help."

When he saw we were about to ask more questions he stopped us by holding up a hand.

"Oh, let's not get bogged down in all that now. We're expecting Captain Clarke and his boys to return in the morning so I'm sure there will be a lot more meetings ahead of us."

We agreed, and before we all drifted off to bed, the evening passed in pleasant conversation and friendly banter.

CHAPTER NINETEEN

When the radio call came in next morning, Shawn drove the knights to the main gate to get them ready to open while the rest of us gathered in the courtyard to welcome the returning SAS soldiers and their surviving families. We weren't sure if it was going to be a celebration of the successful addition to the UK population of more survivors or a moment to mark lost loved ones, so it was a quiet group who gathered to wait apprehensively in the morning drizzle.

Earlier we'd ventured out to see how successful the funeral pyre had been, finding it still burning despite the light rain that had started falling sometime in the night. Most of the bodies had been reduced to blackened, charred, vaguely human- shaped remnants of what they had once been. Bodies twisted by the heat formed macabre shapes as arms extended from the mound with fingers spread as if in a final farewell. Legs moved as muscles desiccated by the fire contracted, giving the impression that some were still alive. The contorting, deformed, burning spectacle sickened all of us who stood there watching the display of the frailty of life. The wind was still blowing the smoke away from the castle and as we sniffed the air, we knew it had been successful as the cloying, putrid smell of yesterday was greatly reduced. Gratefully we turned our backs to the pyre and returned home.

The admiral, as the senior officer present, addressed the SAS men after they gathered around once they had all disembarked the vehicles. He thanked them for their efforts and offered genuine heartfelt condolences for their losses.

It went without saying that there were far more people, both in our group and on the Scillies, who could only guess the fate of their families and friends. At least they knew for certain and could deal with it in whatever way they could to continue their lives. After he'd shaken all of their hands and said a few words individually to each of them, Sergeant Newman dismissed the men officially and the gathering broke up and merged into those grouped around them.

Once the introductions of the newest additions had been made and they'd all been shown their new quarters, everyone, apart from those on guard duty, gathered back in the Great Hall where Maud was making the new families welcome. She and her people fussed over the young ones, introducing them to the other children, who for this very reason had been excused their sentry duties. She'd learned the ages of the children who were arriving and given those who were closest in age the roles of being their guides and a friendly face before they were whisked off to play or explore the castle with their new friends. The smiles, shouting, and laughter that faded into the distance as they left to get up to whatever mischief had been planned made the adults smile regretfully as they remembered their own families they would never see again, or smile in gratitude and relief with the knowledge that they might now have the chance to live as normal as life as the new crazy world they were now living in allowed. Eventually, one of the admiral's aides asked a select few to attend a quick meeting in the dining room.

***

He'd kept the numbers small; just a few of us civvies, sergeants, and higher ranks from the military contingents.

"This won't take long," the admiral explained as he waved us to sit down. "I'm not in command of this Castle as you all know Maud is, but I thought I'd hold a quick meeting to explain what I hope to achieve in the next few days."

He picked out Clarke with his eyes.

"As you've just got back, I suggest we give you today and tomorrow to get some rest and get settled in. We will then, at first light in three days' time, head off to M.O.D Kineton…That's it for now. We'll hold a detailed planning meeting the day after tomorrow."

***

The convoy snaking out of the main gate of the castle was by far the largest and most complicated venture we had ever attempted. Led by Shawn driving his tractor and trailer, our crane lorry and bus, accompanied by fifteen arctic lorries and protected by Steve's armoured car and two Bushmasters driving interspersed between them started the journey. Our trailer had more machine guns lining its sides, courtesy of the armoury at the SAS base, and most of the lorries now had a gunner standing on the passenger seat, their upper bodies sticking out of a hole cut in its roof with a machine gun mounted on a homemade bracket ready for use.

We knew the route to the base was passable as, whilst the new arrivals were settling in, Shawn drove the tractor minus its trailer and Steve Hammond behind the wheel of the armoured car had conducted a quick reconnaissance mission as far as the gates of the base. It was less than fifteen miles from the castle, and we'd travelled past the exit on the motorway when scavenging for lorries for the mission. They reported back that they'd cleared the few blockages caused by crashed vehicles on the side roads to the base, and also that the main gates to the base remained closed where only a few of its former inhabitants could be seen shambling around inside the perimeter. Due to the size of the garrison they'd expected to see more, but they could only report what they'd witnessed, and fewer of the undead to deal with was only a positive. Killing the few in sight with the silenced .22 rifles so as not to attract attention to themselves, they took photos to help add visual details for the briefing and returned home.

With the firepower available and the known strength and capabilities of our vehicles our confidence was high as I took my position in the trailer. The journey should only take about thirty minutes and from what we had been told, apart from the undead which could do us no harm protected by the vehicles as we were, it was the logistics of loading so many vehicles and keeping such a large unwieldy convoy in order that was going to give us a headache.

Captain Clarke had visited the base many times for training missions to simulate protecting the facility from an attack by terrorists or rogue forces. He'd given us a detailed description of what the place was like in the group briefing and planning session held the day before.

It was a huge base covering over two thousand acres, which I found mind-boggling in itself. The munitions were stored in a vast series of armoured warehouses set in the middle of a forested area at the heart of the base, and were even served by their own railway line connected to the national network. Along with wide roads naturally designed for heavy vehicle use, he could foresee no problems accessing all areas of the base.

The base was supposed to have a sizeable garrison and work-force accommodated in the substantial housing and admin area, which was a concern as our reconnaissance had not matched those numbers up with the dead. Dealing with potentially large numbers of zombies was something we'd successfully done many times but, as we knew, confidence was one thing and complacency was another entirely. This mission was crucial for our ongoing plans and failure was not an option, so even though confidence was high we all knew we had to be fully vigilant and on our game until we were back behind the safety of the castle walls.

Holding on to the side of the trailer I was surprised how quickly the journey passed. It was only one exit on the motorway along which took about fifteen minutes even at our slow and cautious speed to reach. Then it was only a few miles along A-roads before I saw the sign indicating we had arrived.

The closeness of where we were heading was why so many of us were on the mission. We'd only left a few knights and soldiers behind to help guard the others. Hannah, the young woman we'd rescued from the farm only a few days before, and the men and one woman from the pub we'd also rescued when returning from the Brough's farm had, to their credit, insisted on helping as well.

Their basic firearms training including a live fire exercise conducted on a quick trip around Warwick in the back of Shawn's tractor, after which we'd concluded they were ready to go. Hannah had shot many times on her boyfriend's farm and needed no instruction at all. After all, all our training had been 'on the job' so to speak, so throwing them into the deep end would not only advance their skills rapidly, but also increase our firepower if we needed it.

Also, if any problems arose at the castle, it had already been decided that the whole mission would be abandoned and we would race back to assist.

We knew the gates were closed, so the plan included breaking them open. We lined the trailer sides with our weapons ready as one of the Bushmasters peeled away from the convoy and drove up to the gates. Its rear door opened and a mix of soldiers and knights stepped out and one of them cut off the padlock with a pair of bolt croppers as the others formed a tight cordon around him. The Bushmaster drove onto the grass and they stood aside as the gates were swung open, which was the signal for the convoy to pull forwards and enter the base. They waited for the last lorry to pass before following, making sure the gates were secured behind them with a fresh padlock.

It was eerie driving through the base. We'd expected to see more zombies than the ones that had been shot by the gates a few days earlier, but not one was in sight.

Don't get me wrong, I was *not* complaining, but it just seemed strange that with the gates locked so no one could get in or out, I would have expected to see at least some shambling around.

"Where the bloody hell are they then?" some asked from the opposite side of the trailer.

I was about to open my mouth and tell him that was what I was wondering when we rounded a corner and the answer presented itself in its full, stinking glory.

Hundreds of zombies were bunched together in the middle of the wide road surrounding something, but from my position I couldn't see what it was. Most of them were in uniform, so my best guess was that they must be from the base's garrison but more than a few were in civilian clothes. I even made out a couple wearing pyjamas, which gave us an accurate time that the zompoc hit the base.

"There's a car in the middle of that lot. Looks like a Defender from what I can see," Shawn called over the radio before stating the obvious. *"My guess is we have possible survivors."*

Clarke spoke next, and I turned to look where I knew he was in the convoy, seeing that he'd pulled his Bushmaster out of the line for a better view. The zombies nearest to us had started to notice our arrival and some began to turn in our direction. The captain had been given command of this mission by the admiral following a meeting between just himself and the two other captains where the admiral wanted to make clear that he was choosing Clarke for overall command as he had first-hand knowledge of the base. He hadn't detected any inter-branch rivalry or any animosity between the two ever since Clarke had had his paradigm change of attitude not long after he had been rescued, but he'd wanted the mission to run smoothly and made his orders to the both of them clear.

Steve Hammond would remain in charge of the knights but would follow the SAS man's orders as to when to deploy them. We had forty knights on the mission, made up of most of the original group plus most of the new arrivals and a few of Steve's men who weren't needed for vehicle protection and overwatch duties. The majority of them were packed into the bus ready to deploy when called.

Clarke spoke over the open channel on the radio.

"*Mister Hammond, disembark your knights to deal with the threat ahead of us if you please. Nobody fire into the crowd in case anyone's still alive in that vehicle. Repeat, all units hold your fire. Bushmasters pull out to the flanks to provide cover. Shawn, pull forwards to secure our front.*"

This was one of the tactics we'd trained for, and as soon as Steve had confirmed the order the knights led by Ian filed from the bus and jogged past us to form a line before the slowly increasing number of the undead heading our way. Shawn, as soon as the knights were in position, pulled forwards at an angle so us in the trailer would be able to bring more of our weapons to bear.

Steve Hammond ordered the ones in his armoured car behind us to disembark also. They were there to mainly offer support for the knights, grabbing their pikes and spears when necessary and to provide close support with their rifles if needed.

"Ian," Steve shouted from his customary position high on the wheel arch of the armoured car. "I've got the best view, so listen out for orders."

With a cheerful, "Yes boss!" Ian organised the line of fighting men and women on either side of himself, shouting encouragement and war cries to raise their spirits and fighting ardour to fever pitch. The roars and return shouts told me they were as ready and confident as they could be.

Now more of our group had been trained and with a few of Steve's men now swelling the ranks, this was the largest platoon of knights we had fielded against our enemy. Ian had interspersed his friends – the most experienced medieval fighters we had – evenly along the line to act as sergeants or corporals would in a battle line to steady the troops around them with their experience and battle skills. With the nearest zombies now only twenty meters away he bellowed, "Pikes ready!" and everyone raised their pike or spear to form a wall of sharpened death that faced their closing adversaries.

"Now!"

He roared the command to strike, and the forty pikes and spears thrust forwards to strike the first blow of the battle. Those initial hits delivered by fresh arms were mainly accurate and well over half of the front rank were killed a second time. The knights held their ground and kept impaling the sharp heads of their pikes or spears into the skulls and bodies of the horde. With every thrust the body count grew until the mound of corpses once again created a natural barrier between the two groups. Ian looked around and judged the moment was right to change tactics.

"Pikes behind you and shields up! Great work everyone, now on my command, three paces forwards and start smashing heads...and make sure everyone you step over is dead first!"

"Move!'" came his one-word command, and they stepped towards the newly created moraine of bodies. Axes, maces, and swords began swinging and stabbing at every head they passed until they were in striking distance of the mound of dead. More shambling enemy were clumsily trying to climb over the pile, their simple brains not being able to work out the easiest route to their next meal was to walk around the blockage. The odd one at the extremity of the pack that did try that route though soon fell to a well-aimed shot from those protecting the flanks. At another command the line neatened up and they began to smash or impale any head that made it to the top of the stack until the mound was so high that none could surmount it.

"You've got most of them now," Steve called out. "Flanking manoeuvre when you're ready."

Ian stopped swinging his axe on hearing this and looked around to survey the situation. This was the first time the drill had been performed outside the practice field and was devised for situations such as this.

When the field of battle didn't need the tactics we'd performed before. To retreat and wait for the zombies to approach once more and then repeat the previous strategy. We had killed most of them, so the new idea we were going to try was to split into two groups and go around the sides of the wall of bodies and encircle the ones remaining to take the fight to them. When it had been thought up it seemed a good way to deal with another situation we may face, and it had been introduced into our drills.

Ian, in the middle of the line, raised his thumb to Steve to acknowledge his order and bellowed, "Okay, we know what to do...those to my right go that way, and the others go left. Stay sharp folks and listen out for me or Steve for any change of orders. Shields up and move on my command!"

As soon as the order was shouted the line of knights split and both halves worked their way around the small mountain of bodies, an occasional swing or thrust of a weapon marking the spot where one still lived as they moved past it. From my position in the trailer, I watched with interest as the two lines met again, facing each other with the remainder of the zombies between them. With raised shields they moved together, one commanded step at a time, swinging or thrusting their weapons at heads with every pace until the bodies became too thick on the ground to safely step over until another command from Ian stopped the lines moving forwards and let the remainder come to them.

I could see the ending was inevitable. Only a few remained alive and they'd soon join their former zombie friends on the ground; their rotting brains leaking out of the gaping cavities smashed or cut into their skulls.

With a mighty swing of his axe Ian removed the head from the last one standing. It took him a few seconds to realise they had got them all as he looked around for the next target; his eyes wild with the excitement and adrenaline coursing through his veins.

Steve shouted over to him once he had carefully surveyed the battlefield.

"You've got them all as far as I can see. Great work everyone," he said, then pointed to where the vehicle was.

It now sat lonely in the middle of the road and the ones who had trapped it lay piled together in front of us where death had found them a second time.

"Make your way over to the car and we'll join you," Steve called out.

Ian looked to where the Defender sat smeared by countless hungry fingers. Now it wasn't surrounded we could see that it was sitting at an angle caused by the bodies that had piled up underneath the wheels, telling another story of a desperate, failed escape attempt.

Clarke, who had had a front row seat of the battle, spoke over the radio in a voice firm but with a hint of incredulity to it.

"Captain Hammond…outstanding work. Outstanding. If you take your vehicle to back the knights up, I'll get the rest of the convoy moving."

With an affirmative reply Steve ordered those who had dismounted from his armoured car to accompany the knights. With a final check around, he climbed into it from the wheel arch and it moved forward to where the knights were gathering around the stranded Defender.

By the time the rest of the convoy had driven round the newly created heap of bodies and reached the stuck vehicle, I could see that the news was not good. Steve had dismounted his vehicle and was standing next to the open doors of the Land Rover. When we stopped, he walked over to us and handed some pieces of paper up to the admiral.

He had a depressed look on his face as he added an explanation to the notes he had passed.

"They're all dead. Shot themselves." He looked back at the Defender. "The notes they left explain it all. They were base guards who managed to reach the safety of the vehicle when it all started. They were trying to get to their families in the housing area when they got bogged down by the zombies as they were trying to push through them. Stuck, they could do nothing but watch as more and more surrounded them. For days they just sat there watching people they had known press their undead faces against the windows. They tried to hang on and wait for the mob to disperse, but with only the water in their canteens and no food, they were in a hopeless situation. It was only when the ones with families saw them amongst the ones trapping them that they knew all was lost. Eventually, facing certain painful death by dehydration they all took the only course they had left to them."

He gestured to the notes still held unread in the Admirals hand.

"They all wrote a note before they shot themselves."

Saddened by another story full of hopelessness and heartbreak we were all silent for a moment, most of us imagining the utter despair the four men must have endured before deciding to end their own lives. The admiral interrupted our silent, solemn contemplation as he carefully folded the sheets of paper and reverently put them in his pocket.

"Another sad tale we must remember when the time is right," he said solemnly.

He looked at Clarke who was leaning out of the window of his armoured car, listening to Steve's retelling of the events.

"Let's continue the mission," he said, replacing contemplation with action.

Even though he was the senior officer present he hadn't put himself in charge of the mission when he had specialist infantry officers available, stressing that he was there as an observer only. Not wanting to rely on second-hand reports from the mission of what the base contained, he had included himself amongst the personnel tasked with defending the knights on the ground from the back of Shawn's trailer and came without his usual entourage of aides. He was there to learn and to provide extra firepower if needed, and even though he had made the chain of command clear, Steve had still thought it appropriate to give him the farewell notes left by the unfortunate soldiers. With a silent nod Clarke picked up the radio.

"There's nothing more we can do here. Let's continue. Everyone back on board the vehicles."

Steve hung back and relieved the dead soldiers of their weapons as respectfully as possible.

CHAPTER TWENTY

The convoy reformed and moved off when the last knight was onboard the bus, and it soon became clear that most of the undead in the base had been drawn to the area around the beleaguered Defender as only a few individuals or small groups were seen elsewhere. The vehicles smashed through them without slowing, leaving barely a smear of blood, offal and tattered scraps of clothes on the tarmac after the last vehicle in the long convoy had driven over their remains.

Taking the road that cut through the forest we emerged back into the daylight to see row upon row of huge, turf-covered bunkers stretching into the distance. I'd been told the ammunition storage area was massive, but I don't think I appreciated how large it was, and I certainly had no reference to what the biggest in Europe meant.

Clarke had already told us during the briefing that stock records and manifests weren't available, so a methodical if lengthy approach was suggested. We'd start at the beginning, open the first bunker and search the crates or whatever there was inside, and keep going until we found what we wanted.

The first road I noticed was named Abu Sultan Road. I'd been told that all the roads, as were a lot on British military bases, named after battles or conflicts from the British armed forces' long history. The inquisitor in me wanted to reach for my phone and search for the significance of the name but as Google had disappeared into history, as did the battle or whatever it was referring to, I'd have to withhold my curiosity.

Cutting the padlock on the first door it took the soldiers, protected by the knights, some time to work out how to override the now defunct electric gear and to wind both doors slowly open with the manual controls. As soon as a large enough gap appeared the knights formed a shield wedge and the search team went inside. Tense minutes elapsed before Clarke ran back outside grinning like a Cheshire cat.

"It's a winner! It's full of pallets of five-five-six," he said referring to the ammunition for the rifles we all used now. "There's even a forklift in there."

As those of us in earshot cheered at the good news, he got on the radio and ordered a few of the lorries to drive forwards so we could begin loading them before positioning the armoured cars and the trailer where they needed to be.

This had already been planned so everyone involved knew where they needed to go. The knights disembarked the bus once more and formed a protective ring around us. Leaning on shields or pikes, they waited, keeping watch, ready to fall back behind the vehicles guns if whatever they faced became too dangerous for their tactics.

As soon as the lorries arrived, we pulled open their curtain sides and the forklift began loading the pallets of ammunition. The pace picked up when we detached the lorry mounted forklifts we had brought with us. They rushed around in an orchestrated ballet of heavy machinery, rapidly filling the lorries with their much-needed cargo.

Only the occasional zombies appeared alone or in very small groups which were easily dealt with by the knights, allowing the work to progress smoothly. Clarke, escorted by some knights and soldiers, began opening up more bunkers to check what they contained and it soon became obvious that the place was much more than a treasure trove.

Every bunker opened revealed more items to tick off our shopping list. We'd known that the base would contain far more ammunition than we could haul away, but items written on a list didn't compare to the visual impact of seeing so many munitions stored in one place.

One by one the empty lorries of our convoy filed down and we loaded everything we needed. As soon as one double-stacked lorry was full, straps were thrown over the load and ratcheted tight to secure it. Its curtain sides were slid back and shut and it moved out of the way to make space for the next in line to take position.

The mood was good and even though confidence was high, no one was complacent, and vigilance was kept to a maximum. In what seemed like no time at all, but actually was a few hours, we started to load the last lorry from a bunker that contained fifty-calibre ammunition.

The list had been completed; bullets of every calibre, mortar bombs, grenades, and even rocket launchers which the military contingent had decided they wanted to try against the zombies as a way of destroying large concentrations of them from a distance when mortars weren't an option. Everything we had wanted, and more, was loaded. Although the lorries were stacked way past their registered capacity, the return journey was on mainly low gradient roads and with the slow speed the convoy travelled, we were collectively happy that the weight the lorries carried wouldn't be an issue. Also, as there were no clipboard wielding policemen or government agency types to stop us, we were confident the return journey would be free of trouble. The road had been cleared of blockages, so it was just zombies that may slow us down, and they couldn't issue us with a ticket or a fine any easier than they could resist thirty-plus tonnes of lorry rumbling over them.

Our intention was to offload munitions from each lorry to stock the castle, so when they inevitably headed to the port to be transported to the Scilly isles, they'd be hauling a more comfortable amount of weight which would be safer for the longer journey.

Clarke's last act before climbing aboard his vehicle was to secure the final bunker door with one of the chains and padlocks brought with us just as the others had been similarly sealed. Even though with the right equipment the chains could easily be cut and removed, just as we had done with the original locks, it made no sense to just leave them open.

A lock only stops an honest thief, I thought, before adding, *and zombies.*

I knew we'd be returning to make use of the stockpile we had no hope of emptying quickly into less secure storage elsewhere, so when we left, we planned to secure the base and make it as hard as possible for anyone else to enter. Someone had suggested forming a garrison there, but the amount of personnel it would take to maintain an effective defence force would mean that M.O.D.

Kineton would effectively become a major base. Deciding that our nearby castle was the better option, the idea to simply mothball the base and not draw attention to it was deemed safer than actively defending it.

As very few zombies were approaching us now, it was a sensible deduction that most of the ones trapped within the secure fences of the base had now been killed. If another group discovered the base, we had already made the job easier for them by killing all the zombies, so not having the sweet shop doors unlocked and open as it were, may put them off accidently discovering what was there.

"Let's move," Clarke ordered as he climbed into the cab of his Bushmaster.

He led the way, going slow for the laden links of our road train to set off. The long convoy of overloaded lorries belched clouds of black diesel smoke and changed through the gears as their engines roared and strained to gain momentum.

Feeling satisfied with what we'd achieved, I leant against the side of the trailer and looked out. Reckoning we'd be back home in about thirty minutes; I was already looking forward to the celebration we'd hold tonight to mark yet another successfully completed mission. I was close to becoming lost in that thought when something in the treeline caught my eye and I snatched up the binoculars from their holder on the side of the trailer.

I couldn't see what it was at first, and then I spotted it. Someone was watching us from the edge of the trees. A person, man or a woman I had no idea from my unclear glimpse, dressed in camouflaged clothing was standing at the edge of the trees and watching us.

"Stop!" I shouted excitedly, pointing to where I was looking. "Someone's over there!"

All eyes turned to me then moved to search the place I pointed at. After regaining my balance as the vehicle jolted to a stop, I raised the binoculars again and focused on the person watching us. Steady now, I could see it was a man. His grey hair pointed to him being elderly and I could tell immediately he wasn't a zombie. His complexion looked normal, and his clothes weren't the usual tattered rags the zombies were mostly now adorned with after months of shambling around. He was standing still, not acknowledging us, but just staring in our direction.

His actions instantly made me suspicious. If he was a lone survivor, you'd think he'd be excited to see other living people. If it was me, I'd be *ecstatic* at meeting with another group but then again, we probably appeared to someone seeing us for the first time a threatening looking band. Our vehicles, all festooned with heavy weaponry, certainly looked intimidating, but if he'd wanted to remain hidden, he could've easily watched us from the gloom just inside the treeline and I wouldn't have ever noticed him.

I raised my hand to him, but still he didn't respond.

"*I see him now,*" Clarke announced over the radio. "*Everyone wait here and I'll drive over to him.*"

His Bushmaster detached itself from the convoy and headed across the grass to the tree line where he was still standing stock still. We watched as the captain stopped near to him and stepped out to talk.

Staring through the binoculars I could see they were in conversation, reading the body language and gestures as the words were lost to me at that distance. I wished I could lipread as I tried to follow their talk through their demeanour and gesticulations. Not being able to work anything out I was surprised when after a short period of time I saw them shake hands before the captain returned to his vehicle and the man turned and walked back into the woods.

As soon as he had closed his door the radio crackled into life beside me.

"Nobody move. Something's not right here. I'll come over to the trailer and we'll have a chat and decide what to do."

Completely mystified by his cryptic message my mind whirled like a windmill in a gale over all the possibilities that encompassed his phrase 'something's not right'. His vehicle pulled up next to the trailer and he stepped from it, shielding his eyes from the sun as he looked up at us.

"Admiral, as what I am about to suggest takes us off mission, I think command decisions should pass to you on this matter," Clarke said formally.

The admiral was clearly a better actor than me. All my puzzled brain could do was look at everyone on the trailer with a confused look on my face. He nodded soberly and replied formally.

"If that is your suggestion captain, then I agree. I am in command until we are back on mission. Now please enlighten us."

"Well, sir, my gut is telling me something is wrong."

Clarke indicated over to the tree line where he had talked to the lone man.

"He says his name is Brian Wilde, and claims to be the head groundsman on base."

Silence hung following the less than interesting revelation before Clarke went on to explain his feelings.

"It's just that I have been here many times and met most of the staff here when training for different scenarios. I have never met him; I have met the old head groundsman before and even if he has replaced him then usually, he would have been recruited from one of the others that worked here. That's the way it normally works on bases and as I've just said I've never met the man and I rarely forget a face…During our conversation I never let him know my regiment or that I had been here before, as from the start he just didn't seem…right."

"What are you saying captain?" the admiral asked, looking down from his position in Shawn's trailer.

"I know that almost all the groundsmen here are ex-military because they need to be for what's stored here. This is a high security base and it's better not to have any old contractor walking about who all they have to do is pass a basic security test. Here everyone needs to understand the official secrets act, so being retired ex-military works. They know not to talk and it's a nice way to give an old soldier a job to top his pension up."

"So did this chap not want to come back with us?"

Shaking his head in response, Clarke continued.

"No, he says he's secure in the gardener's compound and is happy. He's managed to gather enough supplies to feed himself for a long time but that's not what made me suspicious, sir. When I asked him if there was anyone with him, he was too quick to reply with a negative and couldn't hide the brief flash of panic on his face when I asked the question. Also, I'd bet my now non-existent pension that there's no way he's served."

"Takes one to know one, eh? The question is…do we want him left in the base when we know what it contains?"

The admiral raised his eyebrows to Clarke who had misunderstood the question for a rhetorical one.

"Is your gut to be listened to, captain? And do you know the location of this groundsman's compound?"

"Yes, it's along a track in the middle of the forest over there," he explained, pointing to the woods where we had seen the man. "It's fenced, and from memory there's a portacabin and a caravan or two in there. As it's in the middle of the forest it's not a bad place to hide out, as long as a huge horde don't find you that is."

He pointed in the direction all our vehicles were headed.

"The track that leads to it is probably about a quarter of a mile further on."

His mind made up the admiral said, "Okay, let's advance the convoy to this track. Captain Clarke, you divert from the route and find out what your gut is telling you. Take who you think is necessary, and I count myself among that number to save my own embarrassment, and the rest hold position until you return."

Clarke gave a nod and turned away, calling out to Steve that he was in command of the convoy until their return, then called out orders for the convoy to advance. Only his Bushmaster and Shawn's tractor and trailer would be breaking away when they found the track, and a small sense of tension descended over us.

The dense trees growing to the edge of the track dropped the light level as soon as we entered the forest. Everyone, including the admiral, looked outwards from the trailer; weapons held ready, on watch for any threats. After about a minute of driving I could see a clearing in the forest ahead.

184

The gardeners' compound was an assortment of open sheds that looked suitable for garaging vehicles, with a few structures that looked like workshops or office areas. A large static caravan was also sited neatly alongside one of the sheds. It was not hard to imagine it being the canteen and rest area for the ones who worked there. Surrounded by a sturdy looking chain link fence with a locked gate at the entrance, it was as had been described, a good area to take refuge in.

The man had clearly heard the noise of our engines as we approached. I watched as he emerged from the caravan, firmly shut and snapped a heavy padlock in place to secure it before walking quickly over to the gate.

"Oh yeah, my gut must have SAS training too. Getting a *serious* serial killer feel here," I said, instantly suspicious of the man who, now that we were closer, I could see looked as nervous as hell.

Clarke stepped from the Bushmaster as soon as it stopped and approached the gate.

"Bet you didn't think you'd see us again so quickly!" he said with a cheerful tone to his voice. "We had a chat about it, and decided to give you another chance to join us."

The man, Brian, responded immediately, his nasally voice instantly annoying to me.

"No, I told you I was fine here so please leave," he said sounding both defiantly arrogant and superior at the same time.

"That's not a very friendly way to refuse a genuine offer of help. Now why would you do that?" Clarke asked, still using the same annoyingly friendly tone I guessed was a deliberate tactic to wind the man up into revealing more.

His voice went up a few octaves as he stammered in indignation.

"I...I just don't need any help that's all," he whined, almost sneering the words before he completely lost it and screamed, "Now *please leave!*"

CHAPTER TWENTY-ONE

With the engines off on our vehicles the silence in the small clearing was palpable.

Clarke's face went from a mask of ignorant joviality to the hostile expression of a hunting predator in a transformation I'm not ashamed to say I found frightening. He lifted a hand to point at the gates and the big padlock securing them and raised his voice.

"Oh dear," Clarke said with mock drama. "Brian here appears to be locked inside this compound. Help him out, Pete."

The sergeant stepped forward without a word and produced a set of large bolt croppers from behind his back to begin sizing up the lock.

"Now, hang on a minute, I'm sure we can reach an amicable—"

He stopped talking as Pete grunted with the huge effort employed to unlock the gates. As the two parts of the now useless padlock thumped softly to the road a look of abject horror dawned on Brian's face.

I looked at the compound beyond the gate Brian stood behind. It appeared neat and well kept, and the caravan he had come from was clean and obviously cared for. The curtains were closed, and on the surface it all looked normal, but there was something wrong which, for the moment, I just couldn't put my finger on.

Maybe it was just his annoying manner which had roused first Clarke's suspicions and, now I'd met the guy, I understood what he'd meant.

Brian forced a fake smile onto his face and seemed to writhe inside his own skin.

"Sorry, I...I'm just a little..." he said, hands twisting together and eyes darting to the destroyed lock and back.

A barely discernible noise attracted my attention. Raising my head to try and pinpoint it, I heard it again. A muted banging noise was coming from somewhere. Furrowing my brows in concentration I turned my head from side to side to try and locate where it was coming from.

"Do you hear that?" I whispered to the admiral. "I can hear a faint banging noise."

"No," he replied. "But then again my hearing ain't the best these days."

The muffled noise which to me sounded more frantic than it had been when I first heard it continued. Still twisting my head from side to side to locate where it was coming from, my best guess was it was coming from the caravan.

"Captain Clarke, I can hear a banging noise and I think it's coming from the caravan," I called out, watching as Brian's eyes went wide with panic.

"It's my dog!" he shouted out rather too quickly. "Just my dog."

"You didn't tell me you had a *dog*," replied the captain wearing a disarming smile on his face. "We like dogs, don't we, Pete?"

"Yep," Pete answered flatly.

"We have a few ourselves back at our base. What breed is it?" Clarke asked.

He looked around and raised his hand to his forehead as if he was thinking hard as he stammered a few times before responding weakly.

"A…err, a Labrador?"

"Oh, it's a shame to keep it locked up in your caravan. I *love* Labs, don't I, Pete?"

"Yep."

"How about you let him out?" Clarke said as he took a very deliberate pace towards the gate. "Don't you think Brian here should let his dog out, Pete?"

"Yep."

"No, no. He's…uh…he's frightened of people. Please, just…leave us alone."

He stopped, his eyes wide with the fright of what he had let slip when he realised he had used the plural.

Immediately jumping on the conversation thread and not allowing him any recovery time the captain responded quickly.

"Us? There more than just you living here, Brian?"

His voice went even more nasally and higher pitched as he replied, desperately trying to correct himself.

"I meant me and the dog. There's no one here but us two. Us one. Me. And my dog."

"What's his name?" Pete asked menacingly, leaning ever so slightly forward.

"Um…Rich…ard?"

As soon as he said it and tried a pathetic, weak smile to convince us I heard the noise again, louder this time.

"Never met a lab who could bang on a wall," I grumbled before raising my voice much louder.

"Is there anyone else here? I can hear banging. If anyone else is in there we can hear you!"

Immediately the noise that only I had heard before turned into multiple bangs, and if I wasn't mistaken muffled shouts as well. Now they were louder I could tell they were definitely coming from the caravan.

Clarke had evidently heard it too. He kicked open the gate and advanced on Brian who didn't seem to know what to do. His legs tried to run but couldn't seem to coordinate with each other, and his upper body tried to fold in on itself to protect his vital organs on instinct, and the end result was that Clarke was met by a twitching ball of old man on the ground before he could lay a hand on him.

"Pete," Clarke said again, and between them they effortlessly straightened out his limbs as Pete Newman's expert hands began rifling the man's pockets.

"Go! Clear the compound," Clarke called back to his Bushmaster, watching as four of his troopers erupted from the vehicle to spill through the gates on fast moving boots with weapons raised.

Pete's right hand came back with a bunch of keys taken from Brian's pocket which he handed over to Clarke. Clarke tossed them up to me and the admiral, already down from the trailer via the side, and I reached out to snatch them from the air before running for the door of the caravan and trying to find the right one to unlock the padlock.

I could make out muted thumps and muffled shouts now, sending my heartrate soaring and making it difficult to breathe steadily because I never suffered that much adrenaline dumping into my bloodstream even when fighting a small army of the undead.

"Hold on! Just hold on, we're coming!" I yelled, knowing in my heart I wasn't talking to a Labrador called Richard but not yet able to fathom what I might find.

I still fumbled with the keys, finding it hard to work my fingers properly, when the admiral strode up to the door beside me.

"Stand aside," was all he said, barely giving me sufficient time to lean away before his right boot caved in not only the door but the flimsy wall beside it. Three more kicks set the door free and we both spilled inside only to freeze in horror.

I'd seen similar things on television. Heard about people like him and the things they did. I never imagined seeing it for myself.

Four girls, probably between four and eight years old, were tied up in the living area. Naked apart from their dirty, tattered underwear and with strips of torn sheets binding their wrists behind their backs. Yet more strips of cloth secured their ankles painfully tight together and gags that threatened to suffocate them stopped their screams from escaping fully.

"Oh my God, oh my God," I muttered as I dropped to my knees beside the nearest and reached out to remove the gag from her face.

She screamed and reared back, desperate to keep distance between my hands and her body. I held my palms open, trying to signal that I was there to help. She was probably about five or six, and was hyperventilating in fear and confusion while sobbing

191

with terror. She was struggling to breathe because the crying had filled her nose with mucus that bubbled from one nostril as her face turned red, but still she wouldn't let me near her face so instead I reached out for a strand of sheet securing her wrists and pulled, grabbing two parts with both hands to pry it open before she could squirm free and turn her red face on me again.

"We're here to help you," I pleaded, wishing her to believe me.

Still keeping my voice as low and gentle as I could I raised my hands again to try and show I was not going to hurt her, but she crawled into the furthest corner of the room and cowered in fear as she worked her hands free and pulled the gag away herself.

"It's okay, girls," the admiral crooned in a voice that made me think he had grandchildren. "It's all okay now."

He used a small folding knife to cut into the tight knots binding their limbs as I watched on in shock.

I tried to hide the rage building up inside me. There could be only one explanation to what was happening here, and it sickened me. Bootsteps behind me made me turn in time to see Clarke stopped dead in the shattered doorway.

"Oh dear god," he breathed, turning his eyes down to me. He seemed to be asking a question but I didn't know what it was, let alone the answer.

"Rest of the caravan?" he snapped, expecting precision and instead encountering only civilian incompetence.

I struggled to my feet fast and shoved open every other door, finding items of clothing and glossy pictures I couldn't look at for fear I might actually throw up.

"Empty," I said, walking back out to where Clarke watched the admiral talking to the girls, now freed from their bonds, and feeling captivated by the way they all clung to his soft words.

"How could…" I started, feeling my face contort in disgust and rage at the thought. "I mean, they're just kids…*babies*…how…"

"Don't try and understand it," Clarke said with a quiet rage burning behind his words. "You can never understand it because you're not an animal…Go get some air."

I nodded and went outside, only to find that Brian had been secured with plastic cuffs binding his wrists behind his back just as he had done to the little girls inside. I lost it, rushing the few paces to him to deliver a knee powerfully straight to his gut.

The air left him in a rush, prompting a second of silence before shouts of alarm erupted and Brian himself croaked a loud noise as his body fought for oxygen.

Hands grabbed me and things were shouted, but my rage had spilled over and it would not go back in the bottle easily. I broke free, aiming another kick at Brian's head and missing, succeeding only in scuffing my boot across his cheek.

"You fucking! Dirty! *Nonce!*" I screamed as I tried and failed to kick his head from his shoulders in one go.

The hands grabbed me again, only this time they came with calming sounds and pleas for me to regain my sanity. My actions and words clearly conveyed to everyone else what we'd discovered inside, and it seemed like others were about to take over from my attempts as one or two punches were delivered by the same hands that had just been trying to restrain me before Captain Clarke restored order with a sharp command.

"Secure him, and get him out of sight," he snapped. "Pete?"

The sergeant nodded, accepting the unwelcome task of keeping the man alive.

I stood over Brian as he was lifted up, eye bleeding from a lucky scrape of my boot but still very much alive. I wanted to beat the living shit out of the perverted, despicable worm of a man right there and then, and when he looked into my eyes in that one instant, he knew it. He saw his death in my eyes.

I groaned in disgust as a wet stain spread from his crotch and soaked his trousers, and in that moment my desire to murder him evaporated. He wasn't important, the children inside were our main concern now. We needed to look after them immediately. Once more I decided as we had when we'd found Hannah at the farm that a female face, rather than those of men dressed in uniform or armour, would most likely be better. I looked at the tractor where Louise was in her usual place beside Shawn. Faye and Aggie were also in the trailer, so I called for all three of them to join me.

Quickly explaining what was happening as we walked towards the caravan across the compound, they at first shot looks of pure hatred and venom towards Brian, who had been taken some twenty paces away and secured inside an open-front log shed. In case anyone worried that his jailer would be sympathetic to the man's pleas for help, Pete Newman had slung his rifle and now brandished a heavy splitting axe as an ambiguous promise of what he would do if faced with any escape attempts.

After I'd ushered the ladies through the door the admiral walked out, the relief evident on his face someone better qualified than he was had arrived. Looks were exchanged but no one said a word as we gathered together in stony faced, fury-filled silence until a radio call from the convoy asking for a progress report shattered the quiet.

Clarke took a moment to regain his composure before he updated them as to what we'd discovered. When he was told that no zombies had ventured into sight yet, he informed Steve that they would return as soon as it was possible, but to update them if their situation changed. In hindsight that was unnecessary because the surest sign they needed our help would be the volleys of gunfire that would precede it.

Eventually movement from the caravan got our attention as Louise, Faye, and Aggie slowly walked out of the door. Louise had her arms around two of the girls and the others cared for one each as they emerged blinking into the weak sunlight. The children still looked terrified, and their swollen, tear-filled eyes darted everywhere. All now had blankets draped over their bare shoulders which mostly covered the state of undress we had found them in.

Brian let out a high-pitched wail when he saw them which caused all four of them to jump in fright and cling to their escorts even tighter as they were led to the trailer and carefully helped up the ramp only for Louise to come back down the ramp moments later to stride purposefully up to us. The concerned and caring expression she wore when she led the children out had been replaced with one of cold fury.

Taking a moment to compose herself she told us what she had gleaned from the children so far, never taking her eyes off Brian's pathetic form cowering under the watchful gaze of the SAS sergeant.

They were the children of people based here and when the outbreak occurred, they'd been playing in the playground together near the housing area. Fleeing into the woods they knew from many adventures playing in them they hid, terrified after seeing people they knew being attacked. Days later, half-starved and severely dehydrated, they had come across Brian when they were searching for food in the groundsman's compound which had become their inevitable prison.

I asked the question we all needed to know the answer to.

"What did he do to them?"

Louise tried to answer but tears filled her eyes. Managing to give the only answer she was able to, she nodded until her fury boiled over. She turned and ran to where Brian was being held, screaming incoherent rage and hate. Pete made little effort to restrain her, using only idle hands around her waist as he lifted her up only for her legs to flail at the beast in her sights. She fought hard but made little real effort to attack Pete and force him to release her, instead she screamed abuse and lashed out to kick Brian over and over and to scratch deep gouges out of his face with her nails until he flattened himself into the jagged pile of split logs.

Panting with exertion and emotion but seemingly spent, Louise was released by Pete. She drew herself up, straightened her clothing, and as a final act spat in Brian's face before turning to walk back to the trailer pausing only to convey her feeling to us with a look. She didn't climb into the tractor with Shawn but went to continue helping to look after the children.

"Gentlemen," the admiral said solemnly. "That piece of filth over there has condemned himself by the acts we know he has committed, and he must answer for them. I believe we all agree on what the only course of action left to us is?"

The question seemed perfunctory as his eyes met each of us in turn in search of disagreement.

Part of me wanted to object, to say that we should do our due diligence and allow the man an opportunity to defend himself. The right to trial and all that. I wanted to object on the basis that nobody else did, if only to pay Devil's Advocate and attempt to be the voice of reason, but I couldn't utter a single syllable in defence of an animal who did things like that to children.

We all nodded as he looked each one of us in the eye, me included as last in line. He nodded grimly in reply as he drew his sidearm and checked it was ready. Lowering his voice, he continued dolefully.

"I will ask no other to do it. I will take full responsibility."

Brian couldn't hear our conversation, but from our mannerisms and seeing the admiral check his sidearm he guessed what was coming. He made a break for it, still with both hands bound behind him, begging and pleading for forgiveness.

"It's not me! I need help! Help me! I won't do it again, I promise. I can change, just give me a cha—*ugh*!"

His protestations and lies were cut off by the swift application of a balled fist, first to his face and then his solar plexus, delivered expertly by the sergeant who wasn't tested one bit by the escape attempt.

For me his words were a clear admission of guilt. We hadn't asked him for confirmation of what we suspected he had done, but there he was promising not to do it again as long as we let him go.

"I'll help, sir," Clarke said formally as he fell in step beside the admiral on his slow march towards the prisoner.

The admiral nodded a brief acceptance of the offer but I could tell even from his blank expression that he was grateful of any support.

Brian, now able to breathe again, squirmed and twisted in Pete's grip as the two officers approached.

"No, no, *please*," he croaked, still short of breath and struggling to form words after the brutal punches had shut him up previously. "Please, I swear, I…I'm not well. It's a disease, I can't help it, I—"

He stopped and folded himself up into a standing ball once again as Pete readied to deliver another shot that promised to rob him of the ability to speak ever again.

"Thank you, Sergeant Newman," Clarke said, still being formal as he approached and seized Brian's bound right arm.

Brian's face registered a glimmer of hope for less than a second, thinking that he had been rescued from rough treatment. That hope evaporated as soon as Clarke wound the strong grip of his right hand over the back of Brian's hand to stretch the tendons painfully enough that the old man let out a yelp of pain and tried to lift his knees up.

"Around the back of the building if you please, Captain," the admiral said, speaking just as formally as Clarke had as if both men treated the emotional task like an instruction to be carried out.

Clarke hauled on the limb held in a painful lock and marched Brian out of sight behind the outbuilding, all the while keeping him walking on his tiptoes through pain compliance as the man babbled and pleaded for an opportunity to do better if only they let him live. The admiral followed, head high and back straight, until only the faint sound of Brian's cries for mercy reached us.

The shot, even though I had been expecting it, made almost everyone jump.

***

I chose to accompany Shawn in the cab of the tractor for the return journey, both to make sure he was protected as Louise was in the trailer caring for the children, and to chat to him to discuss the day's events.

It was a tight fit as I squeezed my frame into the small passenger seat in the cab next to Shawns much larger and comfier drivers' seat, but comfort wasn't something I'd expected from life for a long time now.

"All in all, not a bad day, eh?" Shawn asked as if we were discussing a trip out rough shooting.

I nodded thoughtfully as I pondered the simple question. The mission had been an unqualified success, that was undeniable. Firstly, we had fielded the largest squad of knights against the greatest number of zombies we'd yet faced and slain them without any of us being even close to getting in trouble. We had confidence in the tactics we'd developed and were continually improving as our experience grew so that we could potentially face larger numbers of them and still emerge unscathed. Secondly, we'd secured a huge quantity of ammunition of all types for both us and the newly founded base on the Scilly Isles, but I did *not* feel like celebrating after what we'd discovered as we were leaving.

The roadblock where we lost Daniel, the attack at the Broughs' farm which had cost us two more lives, and the despicable acts Brian had perpetrated against four innocent children showed that evil existed.

I didn't mean the kind of evil posed by the undead millions roaming the land, but evil that lurked among the survivors. I was at a loss as to why people would choose to stay on the course of wrongdoing when we all needed, now more than ever, to band together to just survive.

I did *not* feel guilty for the end Brian had met. It was the only punishment suitable now there were no police or courts to fall back on to administer justice. I was just glad I'd seen him which led to the kids being rescued.

"Only thing for it, I reckon."

Shawn's words popped the bubble of thought I was lost in and brought me back to the uncomfortable reality inside the tractor.

"What's that?"

"I said only thing for it, I reckon."

I knew what he meant and I nodded in full agreement, yet I couldn't shake the feeling the whole situation had left me with. It was like a bad aftertaste in my soul.

"Yeah," I said. "I reckon so too."

Shawn said nothing else on the subject so neither did I. We simply sat in silence until we reached the point where I knew our radio would reach home and I could give them some advance warning of what to expect.

CHAPTER TWENTY-TWO

When the four children had been led from the trailer by Maud, Becky, and her willing helpers, Shawn and I drove my Volvo back to the carpark by the main gate to help manoeuvre all the heavily loaded lorries into position. Most of what they contained would be driven to the docks soon, along with the lorries loaded with food for their contents to be craned onto vessels bound for the Scillies, but a good portion would complement our own supplies.

This carried its own set of issues which we were trying to address and find the best solution for as, for obvious safety reasons, it wasn't a good idea to store a large quantity of explosives where you lived. The armoury we had created out of a storeroom at the castle already contained more than enough for our immediate needs, but where to store the rest was giving us a headache. It needed to be accessible if we needed it in a hurry, but far enough away that, if by some as yet unknown something happened, for example it caught fire, it wouldn't endanger us.

On the other hand, if we were attacked by an unstoppable horde of zombies that breached our outer fences, we'd need to be able to access it to resupply what was in our armoury. We could just park the lorries in the courtyard, but after the petrol bomb attack at the Brough's, even though it was probably unlikely, the idea of flaming death in bottles being launched at us over the walls to potentially cause a lorry full of hundreds of thousands of rounds of ammunition to catch fire was not a pleasant thought.

Who would have thought that having too much ammunition was as much a problem of not having enough? Still, it was a nice problem to have and as we returned to the castle, we knew that eventually the best solution would be reached.

At dinner that evening Maud, Becky, and the others that were caring for our new arrivals did not join us. They had made the decision to keep them away from the noisy bustle of the communal areas until their needs and what help they required to cope with the trauma of their imprisonment and treatment could be properly worked out. Maud told Willie he was being temporarily turfed out of their luxuriously appointed suite of rooms as she knew that they would be the best place for the children to be for now. Their rooms were self-contained, with a separate dining area, sleeping area, and bathroom that would provide them with the peace and quiet they needed to begin their recovery.

Willie, with a duvet and pillowcase tucked under one arm and a prized bottle of whisky he had been given in a way of compensation held in his free hand, cheerfully claimed the comfiest sofa in the Great Hall as his for the duration of his exile. Becky would also be staying with them which put my plans on hold to have some late-night whisky fuelled fireside 'planning meetings' with Willie when she popped down to get something and overheard us discussing our plans like naughty excited schoolchildren. Of course, I agreed it was a stupid notion we were planning and immediately told her there was no way I would have done it anyway. I just hoped she didn't come down later that night and catch us in the lie.

She did, and I got into trouble. Again.

***

In the morning we put the finishing touches to the mission to Bristol docks. The food lorries and the ammunition lorries were all now armoured, checked over, and ready to go. Royal Navy ships, boats and personnel were also preparing at the Scilly isles to depart to assist us. The sea distance between the two locations was only about one hundred and fifty miles, in other words an easy day's sailing in most sea conditions. When the chosen day arrived, they'd hopefully be positioned just off the docks waiting for us to arrive and secure the initial beachhead.

The plan was to use shipping containers to create a protective wall around the loading area. From the aerial shots taken by the helicopter we knew there were thousands of containers stacked in long lines at the port along with the huge forklifts used to move them around. Initially the plan was to create a small area and then expand it when our theories had hopefully been proved to work. Helicopters, transported on the ships, would provide overhead cover and reconnaissance duties. Once the initial perimeter was formed, they'd disembark more of their own people to help and, as long as all went to plan, to staff and protect the base. Once we deemed the facility was as secure as it needed to be, we'd return to the castle with a complement of the arriving marines and sailors. With us escorting them, they'd drive the first supply convoy back to the port. The boats and ships the navy had selected for this mission all had cranes which would be able to lift the supplies unloaded from the lorries onboard. The process we imagined wouldn't be very fast as each pallet needed to be craned one at a time onto the waiting vessel, but it was the best option that us and the planners had been able to come up with using the resources we had available or knew were at the docks. Once this routine had been proven, they would provide extra manpower to begin raiding more warehouses and supermarkets in an expanding radius around Bristol which should keep a constant flow of foodstuffs and others supplies heading towards the Scillies.

This was good news for us at the castle, because whilst we had no problem helping in the initial phases of the operation, they had more than enough service men, women, and civilians to fulfil the many roles required to not need much of our assistance going forwards. We'd already agreed that Warwick Castle would always provide refuge for their convoys to rest up if needed, and of course if anything unexpected happened we would, without question, come to their aid.

We had plans and ideas we wanted to start or continue doing, but since making contact with the navy most of these had been put on hold. These included identifying and gathering or at least securing for later, more foodstuffs. We definitely had enough weapons, but we all agreed that it would be for the best if stocks of known weapons from places such as gun shops were under our control and not able to fall into the wrong hands. After all, a gun gathering dust in an armoury was better than one being pointed at us.

When the weather allowed, we also wanted to go flying again. The last time we went flying we had discovered the Brough's and what an asset they had become. Chris and I had poured over maps and already decided on the grid pattern we would fly to carefully cover different sections of the country within the range of the plane on different trips. The SAS soldiers had their own missions to undertake as well. They needed to go and investigate the known locations of the other trapped military forces around the country. Depending on what they found they would either deal with the problem themselves or involve us in their plans. Something we'd already told them we would be happy to do.

All those plans though needed to wait until we had secured the resupply route, but the lack of forward momentum of all our collective plans filled us with a sense of frustrated urgency. We knew we would always have a never-ending and always growing list to work through, but with the successes we had had so far, we just wanted to continue while things seemed to be going our way.

All morning we discussed and finalised routes, personnel, equipment and the many other facets we needed to consider before we reckoned the plan was good to go. The admiral was in continual contact with those in the Scilly isles. Even though he'd been with us for almost two weeks, he had long daily radio calls with the ones he'd left in charge to continue making the Scilly isles a viable location.

From the news and updates he gave to us at our regular meetings or just when we were collectively enjoying a drink at the end of another long day, we knew they were making real progress. Over four thousand Royal Navy, Merchant Navy, and civilian personnel now called the islands home and the logistical task of organising, housing and feeding all of them was an immense undertaking. Luckily one of the things the Armed Forces were good at was logistics. Service personnel by nature of their job, were used to hierarchy and taking or giving orders. It was the civilian refugees that they needed to concentrate on.

Teams of them were coordinating and organising them based on what skills and experience they possessed. Most were just ordinary people still coming to terms with, that by luck or fate they were on or were able to get to a boat in the initial hours and days of the outbreak and then were fortunate enough to firstly receive the broadcast from the fleet and secondly be able to make it to the Solent. The one fact we would never know was how many had perished trying to reach the sanctuary the radio broadcast offered.

By nature, a lot of the island's new inhabitants were sea-faring folk, so the first resource they were exploiting for food was the sea. The Scilly Isles did not have a large offshore fishing industry but relied on smaller day fishing boats to supply the hotels, restaurants, pubs, and shops on the islands. Those with the most experience of fishing or at least some knowledge of the local waters were formed into teams and allocated boats. Without the detailed local knowledge of the waters that the fisherman who had lived on the islands would have learned after years or in some cases generations, those chosen were learning on the job. Harvesting the bounty of the sea, they were busy discovering their new roles and also the waters around them to identify the best places to find their catch. Their success rate was improving and already they were supplying a regular yield of fish, crab, and lobster to supplement their food supplies. Expeditions to the nearest mainland fishing ports had been dispatched to locate and acquire more suitable fishing boats to expand the fleet, giving it the potential to be a large, all-year-round food source supplier.

Any with experience of agriculture, which for most just meant having a vegetable patch at home for a qualification, were allocated to the farming projects. The Scillies did have numerous farms and small holdings which again supplied the locals along with all the hotels and restaurants which catered to the thousands of tourists that flocked to the archipelago. These teams were working together to keep a steady stream of vegetables, milk, eggs, and meat flowing into the food chain. The timing of the apocalypse was weirdly fortunate as all the fields and vegetable plots were planted, and most crops were available for harvest. The skills they were learning were how to stretch those resources out for as long as possible.

One of the islands largest exports had been flowers, which proliferated in the warmer climate the location offered. Now a useless resource in the new world, the large commercial greenhouses that grew them were being repurposed for growing food.

With the nutrition that the land and the sea surrounding the islands could provide, it was all looking positive for the long-term viability of the islands as a permanent base. The winter would be a different challenge, but with the food they already had in store and what we had ready to send to them and could keep sending, the future looked bright.

Another positive note was that, even though the islands were connected to the national grid for their electricity requirements and so the supplies were cut when the power stations on the mainland stopped working, there were numerous large diesel generators on each island that would kick in to maintain the electric supply as a viable backup plan. These generators were well maintained and ready to fire up at a moment's notice even though, until more fuel supplies could be scavenged, they were only used for a few hours each day, the inhabitants had the luxury of a working electricity supply which made their lives a little more comfortable.

It was encouraging to know the progress they had made collectively. Another group of heartbroken survivors, who this time with the help of what remained of the Royal Navy, were forming a viable community on British soil.

All we now had to do was find more likeminded people until we could create and mobilise a large enough force of trained warriors to take the fight to the zombies.

CHAPTER TWENTY-THREE

Hard-earned experience had raised confidence in our abilities, so driving around the countryside now didn't invoke as much fear as it had in the early days. We had the skills and knowledge, and most importantly the right vehicles to deal with most situations we might encounter. If we stumbled upon something we couldn't collectively handle, then we could always just turn around and find a different route.

I was feeling relaxed as I drove my Volvo with Dave Eddy in the passenger seat and Noah standing up in the back, as much to enjoy the cooling effect of the breeze as to be our overwatch. He also claimed it was to avoid the boring 'dad' conversations the two of us in the front normally engaged in to pass the time.

The mission to Kineton seemed much longer away than the three days it had been.

Noah still shot the occasional zombie we came across, doing his best to get everyone he saw to save any others following the trouble of raising their weapon. The high spirits of the whole group showed in the banter that continually rebounded in the meaningless conversations that we reverted to in times like these. The tone and level of ridiculousness of these conversations varied greatly depending on who was, or more accurately, was *not* in ear shot at the time.

The long convoy stretched out behind us as we followed our planned route to Bristol, which was basically the reverse of our initial route to the castle. The convoy carried all the original knights. Bristol was their home after all, and not only did they want to return to see what had become of the city, their local knowledge might prove invaluable if problems arose and we needed to alter our plans or routes. Coming along as well were most of our newer knights, minus ten who were selected to stay behind and guard the castle, all of the SAS troopers in two bush-masters, and most of Captain Hammond's men in the bus with the knights. Every vehicle we bought was either equipped for fighting, a personnel transport, or a reconnaissance vehicle. Shawn with Louise by his side was driving his tractor pulling the trailer holding the admiral, Captain Digby, some aides and sol-diers as guards. Two military lorries were also transporting equip-ment and supplies carefully selected for our first run.

This was the first time my Volvo had been used for some time as Simon's Defender had been deemed, much to my continued denials, to be a more suitable reconnaissance vehicle than mine. But now my Bren gun had been fitted to a bracket above the driver's seat and another machine gun had been mounted for backseat passengers to use, I insisted we bring it as an extra recon-naissance vehicle. Only having fired the Bren once after we had ventured out on a short trip as soon as the gun was fitted, I was overjoyed with it. Not only because it just looked very cool, but when I'd fired a few magazines at some approaching zombies, the slower rate of fire and the heavier bullet it shot compared to the light machine guns we had mounted on almost every vehicle, proved it to be an effective and surprisingly accurate weapon. The door bins on both the driver and passenger doors to my vehicle were also just the right size to securely hold a decent quantity of the curved, banana shaped magazines which gave the weapon its distinctive and classic look. Becky quite rightly mocked me after she had kept finding me 'practising' with my new toy after it was fitted. Luckily, she hadn't caught me, as others had done, unwittingly making childlike machine gun noises as I performed the magazine changing drill, standing on the driver's seat with the butt tight into my shoulder swapping the magazines and charging the weapon in one slick move as I familiarised myself with it.

We had decided that the two reconnaissance vehicles we had would be useful when we got to the docks as they would be quicker to reconnoitre the entire area that should be surrounded by a secure fence, firstly when we got there and then to patrol the docks on the lookout for any zombies and breaches in the fences which might need repairing.

The route was easy to identify in places by the cleared blockages which now made our journey easier, and the corpses of the former zombies we had dispatched on our initial path through the area leading us onwards like a trail of breadcrumbs. The corpses littering the route were mainly in the process of being picked clean by the multitudinous birds or scavenging animals that flew away or scattered into the undergrowth when our approach disturbed their feast. Some lay untouched and were just rotting, swelling and bursting open in a nauseous display of corruption and decay.

Looking out of the side window a glimpse of one corpse seared an image of dried, blackened flesh in stark contrast to the bright white of exposed bone into my mind. That vivid image was replaced almost instantly by another, but this bloated, rotting carcass had been enigmatically ignored by the opportunistic birds and animals.

"Why are some being eaten and others not?" I asked, wondering out loud more than expecting a coherent answer.

Beside me, Dave's eyebrows met in the middle to answer my question with a silent one of his own, so I added.

"Some get picked clean, right down to the bone, but others they just…ignore."

The smells, even though we'd grown accustomed to them before we'd used a bulldozer to push the thousands of rotting corpses near the castle into a funeral pyre, weren't ones you could easily forget. I could tell the approaching smell was particularly disgusting when Noah sat down in his seat to try and shelter himself from the revolting odours wafting over the vehicle.

"Not a clue, mate." Dave said after a long, thoughtful pause. "Come to think of it, there were always some that were untouched in the piles we've seen before. I just put it down to them being killed more recently and the animals preferred a proper ripe one to eat…But these were either killed by us or by Steve and his lot a few days later."

It was my turn to ponder in silence as the road hummed under our tyres.

"Luckily there's no scientists with us, or they'd probably want to stop and experiment on them or something," I said.

Dave didn't answer because he was leaning forward to squint at the road ahead as if that would somehow enhance his view, then began to pull himself upwards.

"Anyway, on your feet, Noah me lad, there's a group of live ones ahead of us that need to be eaten by the rats. I'll give you a hand."

Noah scrambled back to his feet and pushed a cartridge into the chamber of his shotgun. To avoid slowing to use the spears, as thinning out the zombie population even though a good idea wasn't the main agenda today, everyone had been told to use their firearms to kill any we encountered on the route. With the speed we were going, if the first to attempt to get them missed there would always be someone else behind to finish the job.

Shane had been busy, after having a lightbulb moment a few days before, converting the semi-automatic and pump action shotguns recovered from the gun shops from their usual two-plus-one in the chamber set up, to take up to eight-plus-one. Under normal UK law this would be illegal unless the person held the right certificates, but as that no longer mattered and as increasing the magazine capacity of our shotguns could only be considered a good idea. Shane had the skills to do this and after berating himself for not thinking of it earlier, had busied himself convert-ing the ones capable of being tampered with.

Having a semi-automatic shotgun with a cartridge chambered was never a good idea unless you were just about to fire it and it was pointing in a safe direction, so everyone who carried them had had it drilled into them to only push the final cartridge into the chamber when it could be done safely. In other words, point-ing towards the things you wanted to kill and not those you called your friends.

Trial, error, and logic had proved to us that it was easier to hit a target using a shotgun from a fast-moving vehicle rather than using the more precise, powerful rifles we carried. For that matter, hitting anything with a shotgun was much easier and required far less skill and training.

Dave and Noah readied their converted shotguns to lean out and take aim as I slowed as much as I dared while approaching the flank of a small crowd of undead. I knew their healthy competition wasn't just among one another, but for bragging rights over their friends on the convoy.

"Ready?" Dave yelled, earning an enthusiastic double thump on the roof of the Volvo.

Shotgun blasts boomed out, and I matched the sounds to the odd imagery of heads disintegrating and chunks being blown from bodies as they were thrown down under the weight of heavy lead balls.

When the final one had had the top of its head removed from a blast from Dave's shotgun, he made his weapon safe by ejecting the cartridge that was in the chamber, catching it deftly before using it to reload the tube magazine. As he pushed more cartridges into the gun grabbed from an open box in the centre console, he continued the conversation that had been rudely interrupted by the zombies a few minutes before.

"Sorry, you were saying?"

***

We couldn't come up with a single viable reason why some zombies remained untouched.

"What about crocodiles?" Noah asked, making both of us frown in confusion.

214

"They kill whatever then stuff it under a log in the river so it goes off a bit. Something about it being easier to digest?" he said.

I had to admit he had a point, but I couldn't think of anything else that didn't prefer their meat fresh and recently killed. The rest of the conversation offered even less in the way of logical explanation, but it still played on my mind as I saw the occasional roadside corpse left to fester and rot in disgusting loneliness, unwanted even by the scavengers who were getting fat on the fresher flesh of their companions.

CHAPTER TWENTY-FOUR

Knowing the roads well, I didn't need to look at a map or ask for directions from my passengers as the miles passed. We only had one planned stop on the journey, and on reaching what was left of the roadblock where Daniel had been killed, my mood darkened. Anger rose in me at the needless waste of a young life as we drove through the burnt-out vehicles, bones, and corpses that littered the area marking such a sad day in our lives. The memory of stroking his ruined head, telling him he was going to be okay as I sped away from the barricade with his brains leaking into my lap, was one that was never far from my mind in my very occasional quiet moments of reflection.

We stopped at the place where we'd hurriedly buried his corpse and while others stood guard, those of us who were there on the day he was killed gathered silently around his grave. Noah, who had been friends with him for years, had lovingly crafted a beautiful wooden cross with his name elaborately carved in it. As I watched him carefully dig the small hole to seat the cross into the ground, I marvelled at how long he must have spent making it, and whether the hours dedicated to it had been his own form of therapy to cope with the loss.

We spend a short time tidying the grave before Noah, with tears of a friendship gone too soon running down his face, hammered in the cross with a finality that felt to me like he was getting to say goodbye on his own terms.

Aggie, who hadn't been as close to Daniel as Noah but had known him from their time at The Royal Fowey Yacht Club where they'd both worked, read a short eulogy that she and Noah had written together.

Daniel's final resting place was on a picturesque stretch of the motorway in an elevated position overlooking the stunning countryside that stretched away into the distance. It had always been one of my favourite views when travelling down the M5 motorway and I looked forward to taking in the vista every time I had passed it, so it felt right that Daniel stood permanent sentry over such a place.

In planning the mission we'd decided that it would be a good idea to regroup and refresh ourselves before we reached Bristol, and Daniel's grave site had sprung to our minds as a good place. Being only about thirty minutes' drive from our destination, it would give everyone the opportunity to stretch, get some food and drink inside them as well as offering the opportunity to answer a call of nature.

The wide-open areas all around us offered a sense of security. As long as someone kept an eye on our perimeter, then nothing could sneak up on us undetected. Flasks of tea and coffee were opened and mugs handed around, as others passed around the sandwiches and chocolate we'd bought with us until almost the entire convoy enjoyed a picnic beside what was once a very busy road.

When I'd finished my snack I looked around for Noah, realising I hadn't seen him since the brief ceremony. Finding him atop my Volvo with keen eyes glued to the horizon, I guessed he had chosen sentry duty as a way to be alone.

"Did you eat?" I asked gently so as not to startle him if he'd been mentally miles away.

"Yeah."

His voice was low and cracked when he uttered the single syllable.

"Did you get a drink?" I asked, seeing him turn angry, red eyes on me.

He was about to shout at me, to tell me he wasn't a kid and to leave him be, but he saw my outstretched hand bearing a thermos cup of steaming coffee and the reassuring smile I wore behind it, so he deflated instead.

"Thanks," he said, taking the coffee as I grunted and heaved my way up onto the roof beside him.

"Beautiful spot, isn't it?" I asked, looking out at the miles of rolling countryside and leaning my head back to let the sun fall on my face.

"Yeah. Good place for him to be, you know? Good…" he swallowed, trying to clear his throat so the words didn't fall into a sob. "Good that he's here and not…"

I knew what he meant and knew it didn't need saying, so I just leaned over and gave him a gentle shove with my shoulder.

"Yeah. It's good that he's here."

Little were we to know as we sat there together in the sun, that in the coming months and years, Daniel's place, as it became known, would become a regular rest area for the crews touring the country on whatever their chosen mission or task was. It became a tradition, even, to those who only got to know Daniel through stories passed down, to tend to the grave before resting on the eclectic mix of tables and chairs that were left over time by the side of the road and afforded the best view over the beautiful landscape.

More people joined him there in time, making him the pioneer of lives lost on the road, but at that time it was just a stop on the road for us.

***

Trepidation built as I led the convoy over the Avonmouth bridge, its high, elevated position giving us all a good view of our destination down to our right. Radio calls had already informed us that the Royal Navy vessels and other commandeered boats were in position just offshore, and we could see them in the distance. I didn't know one warship from another, but even from a distance the grey ships looked solid and dependable, stirring something very British in me at a true sign of the power of the Royal Navy. We had been told that two frigates and numerous smaller patrol craft were escorting other boats that would also be suitable to carry the cargo they wanted to load were in the flotilla we could see, but I wouldn't be able to tell a cargo ship from a carrier without binoculars.

Dave and Noah both had binoculars raised to their eyes. Wedged against the sides of the vehicle, steadying themselves against the gentle rocking motion of the moving car they were both staring at the ships and then the dock trying to spot anything that didn't look right. They both reported, and other radio calls from many pairs of eyes from the other vehicles, confirmed that the whole area looked deserted. Looks could be deceiving but as first reports went, they were about as encouraging as possible.

Turning off the motorway at the next junction the main convoy stopped and our two recon vehicles scouted the roads ahead. I listened as Dave, who had a map provided by the Navy of the layout of the docks held in his hands, directed me into the maze of roads that took us deeper into the industrial area surrounding the docks.

We knew there was no housing in the immediate vicinity, which would hopefully limit the zombie population, but the docks had operated twenty-four hours a day and boasted a sizeable workforce.

Just how many remained was something none of us knew. Saying that, we had bought enough firepower with us to destroy a far larger horde than we'd ever faced before. It was purely a matter of how many bullets we fired and how much noise we made before the job was done in a lot of people's opinions but still, as we headed into the unknown, I felt my nerves tightening.

"The gate coming up on the right should be the main entrance if I'm reading this damn thing right," Dave called down to me from above as he was standing on his seat with his upper body outside.

That's not good, I thought to myself as I looked at the wide-open entrance ahead of us.

The gates had been left open, most likely as those whose job it was to operate them had other things on their minds on their final day working there. The large open area beyond it looked clear of anything that looked dangerous, so I stopped, stood on my seat, and called over to Simon in his Defender.

"Let's enter and do a quick loop of the docks and if it's clear, I'll go and guide them in while you wait here to close the gate when they're all through."

"Yes," he replied, any trace of the humour from our previous radio conversations gone as he entered full business mode.

Ten minutes later, satisfied the immediate area was safe, I drove off to guide the convoy in.

As I drove through the gate the convoy following all confirmed our instructions. Pulling myself to my feet as soon as I had looped back round to be near the gate and stopped, the other vehicles filed past. Standing on my seat I removed the bolt that stopped my Bren gun swinging around everywhere when the car was moving and rested my shoulder into the buttstock. I slowly swung the weapon around, checking my arc of fire and finding no undead in sight, but I now knew the limit of my weapon's reach.

When the last vehicle was through the gate and had formed themselves into a rough defensive square, two from Simon's Defender climbed down and ran to it, finding the override lever that disengaged the motor that would normally open and close the gate remotely. With a bit of strenuous pushing they soon had the gate closed.

Once they were back onboard we began the next stage of the operation: full reconnaissance of the site. I looked over to the admiral who, knowing what the next phase of the operation was, was already looking in our direction awaiting our signal. I gave him the thumbs up, and he indicated he understood before turning to one of his aides next to him and issuing an order I couldn't hear.

We waited for the distant sound of a helicopter taking off before we moved. Knowing it would be overhead in a few moments, our plan was to follow the perimeter fence looking for any other open gates or areas we would need to secure. The helicopter, with its bird's eye view, would be able to tell us of any zombies ahead, giving us advance warning to get ready.

As it swooped overhead, looking like it was too cumbersome to be up there as the downdraft buffeted us, I glanced up to see both side doors and rear ramp were open and every gun it had was manned. It looked mean, intimidating to the extreme with two machine guns at every door, and very, very warlike. Having proved itself as an effective gun platform when it had provided us with overhead cover during the mission to rescue the SAS soldiers and others from the base, it gave me an extra sense of reassurance knowing it was overhead again today. If they saw anything they would communicate to the people in the trailer who would then relay the message to us via radio. Simple, like every plan needed to be.

"*Zombies ahead, just beyond the next building,*" the radio broadcast making me look hard ahead as I sensed Dave and Noah point their weapons forwards. Simon, who had been following me as I tracked the fence line, pulled up alongside as we approached the big steel building ahead. Rounding the corner together we both stopped. A horde a few hundred strong surrounded the base of one of the high dockside cranes that were used for lifting shipping containers on and off docked vessels.

"They haven't moved since the helicopter took pictures when it flew over the place." I said remembering the photo of a crowd of the undead surrounding one of the cranes that had been on the table when planning the mission.

Agitated by our arrival and the noise of the helicopter, the crowd slowly turned and moved towards us as one. Dave had his binoculars out and was looking up at the crane.

"Looks like some poor guy's trapped up there," he reported.

"Alive?" I asked, shock robbing me of my common sense.

The look Dave gave me told me I was being stupid, but I couldn't shake the idea there was a survivor.

"What? He might've climbed up there just before the helicopter took the picture for all you know!"

"Fine, but a hundred to one he's dead…" he pointed up at the glass-encased cabin of the crane and spoke to Noah. "Aim a shot near the cabin and I'll watch for a reaction. If he's been up there since it began, then there is no way he's survived."

"But it wouldn't hurt to check," I insisted.

Noah lifted his rifle and steadied himself for a few seconds before firing a single shot sending sparks flying from the metal.

"Nothing." Dave said. "He's probably dead, but you can climb all the way up to check later when we've got the whole place secure."

I said nothing to that, not relishing the thought of the endless ladder heading into the sky, instead I pointed to the slowly approaching mass of undead making its way towards us. Most were dressed in high-viz vests and workwear which told us they were probably the resident workforce, turned traitor on one of their own like the world's strangest piñata.

"Let's deal with those first," I said.

Just as our tactics dictated, Simon and I positioned our vehicles so we could bring the greatest weight of fire to bear. The metallic sounds of charging handles sliding rounds into chambers rang out as we prepared to fire.

There was no subtlety to the plan we'd devised to clear any zombies found trapped inside the docks. Firepower and lots of it was the idea. We waited a few moments while Dave radioed to warn the others waiting by the gate we were about to open fire, and not to be alarmed. Nodding silently at the acknowledgement he put the radio down and rolled his shoulders ready to give the order.

"Fire."

Multiple machine guns opened up at the mass of undead flesh shambling towards us. The front row was flung back by the weight of lead hitting them as blood misted in the air where once a body had stood as the corpses were punched into the ones behind them, making the whole mass distort as they fell. Heavy calibre rounds punched through one, two, three bodies before the projectiles were either robbed of their kinetic force or else sent off on tangents from an errant ricochet off bone. Those behind blindly trying to reach us stumbled over the corpses of the leading ranks until they too were destroyed by the volleys of bullets striking home.

Firing my Bren gun in controlled bursts, just like I had been shown how, to avoid overheating the weapon and causing a stoppage, it bucked against my shoulder as I kept adjusting my aim in my search for the next target. Spent ammunition spewed from ejection ports and bounced off the cars to cover the ground around us with hundreds of the shiny, smoking cases. The sounds of firing echoed off the buildings near us as we kept up the deadly barrage with the deeper, slower bass booms of my weapon contrasting with the lighter, more rapid snaps of the more modern weapons. Brand-spanking new and direct from the manufacturer or nearly seventy years old made little difference to the outcome; bodies piled up until none were left standing.

We didn't need to be told to cease fire. When the last one fell either twitching on the ground or still, contorted at the angles with their bodies meshed together, all shooting stopped. The barrels of our guns smoked and emitted metallic *plinks* as they cooled. We stood for a moment to survey the carnage, finding not a single zombie left standing. Some still writhed with shattered limbs, unable to articulate their broken bodies to reach the fresh meat. Their heads still turned, mouths snarling, as their teeth snapped with futility at the uncrossable distance between us.

The next stage of the operation, getting the beachhead set up, couldn't begin until we'd checked and cleared the entire dock area, so with the pressure of time being against us I dropped back down to my seat and drove. Dave and Noah picked up their shotguns and aimed at the more ambulatory undead as we passed, picking off the crawlers and the draggers with headshots. We were satisfied they were all incapacitated by our fire and couldn't harm us, but every survivor of our attack would need to be rekilled at some point, so if a few more could be ended as we passed the mound of death, it would save work later.

Following the fence line and escorted by the helicopter that was flying a slow, circular pattern overhead as it tracked our movements, we continued. Zombies either on their own or in small groups were dealt with as we drove through them. Stopping

225

and quickly checking any other gates we passed were secure, we completed the circuit, leaving a trail of corpses behind us.

Knowing how zombies are attracted to noise, we completed another circuit just in case any of the undead had made their way out of buildings after we had passed by before we called the docks clear. This also gave us a second chance to spot anything we had missed first time around and added a few more to the tally for the day. No huge horde could have remained hidden from the noise our firing had made unless they were trapped inside a building which, if that was the case, was where they could stay as far as I was concerned. Their basic brain function didn't possess any tactical ideas such as opening doors or turning locks, or to lie in wait and catch us off guard. Such methods simply didn't feature in whatever thinking they could do. If they detected us and could reach us, they would.

The many offices and buildings at the docks would have to be checked and cleared one by one at some point, but if they hadn't made themselves known to us by now then we could safely assume that any large concentrations of them were trapped and couldn't do us any harm currently which was good enough for us. Going door to door wasn't part of the initial plan, so we headed back to the main gate, radioing on the way that the next phase could begin.

CHAPTER TWENTY-FIVE

As soon as the radio called was received the convoy joined us and together we drove through the docks to the waterfront. From the overhead photographs we knew it was a vast, clear area which allowed the huge forklifts to manoeuvre the shipping containers either away from the ships when they'd been unloaded or positioned for the dockside cranes to lift them onboard the waiting vessels. I knew this, but still the sheer size of the operation astounded me.

When the docks would have been busy, the orchestrated ballet of heavy machinery moving purposely around the area would undoubtedly have been a sight to see but now it was just acres of empty concrete. Only the occasional container broke that monotony of open space, sitting beside a few of the heavyweight forklift trucks abandoned months prior when their operators had been forced to run for their lives.

If only at the time they had been thinking more clearly because the size and power of the trucks would have taken their drivers most likely wherever they had wanted to go.

The Royal Navy frigates, now I was closer to them, were even more impressive to see. As they manoeuvred into position they towered over the docks. Personnel manned the extra machine guns mounted on the rails of the ship which were clearly a later addition to the ship's defences as normally they would rely on their missiles and automated weapon systems to defend themselves from any threat. The only hazard they now had to contend with wasn't a barrage of missiles fired from miles away or even over the horizon, but one within line of sight that could be dealt with by the much more low-tech option of hot lead sent from the barrel of a gun.

While the ships were creeping towards the docks we set up an all-round defence. Simon directed all our vehicles so they formed an arc-like perimeter around the dock where knights and soldiers disgorged from the bus and other vehicles to form a loose cordon around our position and fill in the gaps between the vehicles, while others remained manning the many machine guns pointing outwards.

Looking around I felt very satisfied, thinking that it would take a huge number of zombies to get through our defences, and as we knew there shouldn't be many more hidden around the docks my level of concern was low. The helicopter maintained its overwatch, circling slowly around our perimeter ready to warn us of any approaching undead. When it needed to refuel another one was waiting to take over and continue patrolling overhead.

My level of concern was low but it was never at zero, although I had to admit with the level of protection we currently had surrounding us, it was as good as it could get. I felt like we were an army in that moment. An unstoppable force.

Lines were thrown from the ships and secured around the large bollards that lined the quayside as they completed their docking procedures. It felt surreal to be standing, watching a warship tie up just yards from where I was positioned. Naval Dockyards were, for obvious reasons, secure areas, so being this close to not just one but two of the grey behemoths was a new and exciting experience for me. A quick glance around told me I wasn't alone as it was clearly as special for the other civilians in our group who seemed to be spending more time looking behind us rather than outwards for danger.

The moment the ships were secured, gangplanks were lowered from both and with shouts of commands echoing around the area, orderly ranks of uniformed men and women filed down them and formed up on the quayside. The military, despite the tumultuous events, were still maintaining the strict procedures and discipline which enabled them to function as a multi-level cohesive force. As soon as they had been formed up by the sergeants, or whatever they were called in the Navy – petty officers maybe? – the admiral walked along the ranks, chatted to a few servicemen and women before he addressed the whole group from a hastily erected dais of ammunition boxes.

"It is good to be reunited with you once more! The work completed so far on the Scilly Isles has been heroic, and I thank you all for your continued efforts. Now, I won't keep you long as we all have a lot of work to do, but this marks the occasion when both our offshore and onshore assets meet in large numbers for the first time."

He indicated to the groups of us still guarding the perimeter.

"There is now no distinction between those of us who uphold the proud tradition of Her Majesty's armed forces and fulfil their role admirably to defend this beautiful country from all enemies and threats and those who recently have combined together to not only help whoever they have found to survive the desperate events that have overtaken us, but have aided their country greatly in the process. We all have a vital role to play and much work to do, but now we will be doing it together as one."

He paused as his head turned to take in the whole scene around him.

"You know your tasks, so please strive to fulfil your orders to the best of your abilities and continue to make me proud of our accomplishments."

He saluted the massed ranks and waited as the salute was returned crisply as one, before turning away for the officers to start their tasks.

***

Our role was to protect the navy personnel as they worked. They had enough expertise not to need our assistance in the next phase of the operation, so the moment the parade was dismissed, individual groups split off and gathered to start whatever task they had been allocated. I knew the warships were going to stay quayside until the initial barrier of shipping containers had been formed so if anything went wrong and we were faced with an unstoppable wave of zombies, the ships would afford refuge for any that needed it. With their gangplanks raised, their high sides would provide ample protection and their close-in weapons systems would devastate a horde in a heartbeat.

When the first abandoned forklift trucks had been coaxed back into life with large, portable starter packs that had been wheeled off the ships, they began to move the nearest containers to begin forming a perimeter. Containers at a dock are rarely empty because they've either just been unloaded from a ship and are waiting to be moved by road or rail to their next destination or are filled with cargo and waiting to be loaded on to a ship. The dockyard had many thousands of these containers stacked on top of each other or standing alone waiting to begin their next journey, so running out wasn't a concern.

The design of the protected beachhead had taken this into consideration. Therefore, the plan was to build an initial barrier quickly by stacking the nearest containers end to end to form a three-sided square that enclosed where the two frigates were docked, giving the living the run of the massive expanse of concrete to form our base.

Before being placed each container would be opened, searched, and its contents noted just in case whatever it held was deemed useful. When this initial ring had been completed, they would begin construction of a much larger fort. Trial and error were a factor in how this would eventually look, but the plan was to have a double stacked ring of containers with some placed with their doors facing inwards to create, once their contents had been disposed of, spaces that could be used for accommodation or storage.

An hour or so of frantic but coordinated work achieved the first objective, and the initial barrier was finished with a neat half square of containers stacked end to end now enclosing the quayside surrounding the frigates. The container at each end of the line hung over the edge of the quay ensuring that no one except those with ninja like climbing skills could squeeze past and gain entry to the inner cordon. For a gate, a gap was left in the centre where one massive forklift sat silent carrying a double stack of containers ready to move into place and seal the gap. The engineers, not resting on their laurels, had already began marking out with cans of spray paint where the next layer of protection needed to be placed, and forklifts were already racing around gathering more of the huge steel boxes.

Whilst this was happening Simon and I drove around the dockyard together, our passengers armed with maps to check every roadway and the external of every building inside the vast area to check for any danger. Overhead coverage was still provided from the helicopter and, working together, we reconnoitred the whole place and eliminated the further few zombies we discovered. There were very few of them and we could only surmise that as we knew they preferred to gather together, the man trapped in the crane had inadvertently done us a favour as had happened at M.O.D Kineton with the unfortunate base guards, by ensuring the majority of the dead population of the docks remained stubbornly immobile in the one place where we could kill them easier.

Noah volunteered to make the climb to check on the person we suspected was dead up in the crane's cabin. The flies had already begun to swarm around the mound of corpses we'd recently created and as we stood on our seats to watch him climb the ladder, we were forced to keep swatting them away with a free hand. Thankfully Noah was nimble and the climb up and down the ladder didn't take him too long. We didn't have to ask him because even from the height the control room was at, we could see his reaction when he opened the door. He had recoiled, most likely from the stench of the rotting corpse that had been trapped for so long and slowly roasted in a hot, glass box. His actions as we watched him retch a few times over the guard rail before steeling himself to enter the room had those of us who witnessed it chuckling in mutual sympathy and understanding. He returned, much sweatier than when he had left us, and after he had wordlessly climbed into the back of my Volvo and used his canteen to swill and spit the taste out his mouth before taking a long drink from it, he then handed Dave a piece of paper.

"I haven't read it, but it was taped to the door. Must be from the poor bugger up there…He was dead by the way, thanks for asking."

I smirked at him.

"Yeah, we guessed that when you threw up" I said with a smirk. "You okay mate? Never nice to see, but at least we know now and no one needs to go up there again."

Dave, who had opened the piece of paper and scanned it as we were talking spoke up.

"Poor bastard spent days up there before he realised all hope was lost…It's a goodbye message to his wife and kids."

He handed it over to me, looking thoughtful before continuing, this time with a real edge of emotion to his voice.

"There must be lots of these everywhere. Desperate last messages of love and affection from people who realised that no help was coming. Just a few words scrawled onto whatever scrap of paper they had to hand to mark their end."

"How about we keep every message we find and start a record of sorts of them? Along with where they were found and whatever else we know about them" Noah asked. "The admiral said something about it when we found the ones in the Land Rover at Kineton, and I think it's a good idea. When this is all over, and it has to end at some point, then these notes might actually end up in the hands of someone they were written for."

He went silent again before he concluded, his voice barely above a whisper this time as memories of his own family and their almost certain demise saddened him.

"Even if they don't then it's a record of someone we know who died, and there aren't many we'll be able to say that about."

We were all silent for a while as Dave took the note back and carefully folded it before sliding it into a pocket. My own emotions and looking around at both Noah and Simon and those in his Land Rover who had listened to Noah's short speech, had come to the fore. With sad sighs and melancholy mutterings we all agreed it was a great idea and one that we must adopt in future.

We continued our patrol until a short while later a call on the radio ordered our return to the quayside. Pulling up we could see the admiral surrounded by uniformed men and women. He waved, indicating for us to join them, so Dave, myself, and Simon walked over leaving the others to have a break now we were safely back behind our own lines.

"Good job so far," the admiral began. He wasn't one to beat around the bush and usually got straight to the point, so we all waited for him to do so. "The operation here is ahead of schedule, mainly due to the excellent job you did on arrival in clearing the base of all threats. I know the plan was to wait until the morning to transport the drivers to Warwick Castle but" – He indicated the work going on around us. Forklifts, carrying containers bustled everywhere and each one placed completed the encirclement a little more – "I've been informed that the main wall will be complete in just a few more hours before they start double stacking. My suggestion, therefore, is that as no problems or delays have been encountered so far, we advance the plans and send a selected few vehicles back with the extra drivers we have standing by ready to go to the castle. They can then set out at first light and get back here when the transport ships will be safely docked. I'm assured the loading will prove to be a time-consuming process, so if we can get a head start on that it seems sensible. Does anyone here see any issues with my proposal?"

I thought for a few moments but couldn't see any concerns with what he was suggesting. He was right: we weren't needed here now that the area was zombie-free and hundreds of service men and women guarded the efforts of the engineers. If we could get the new drivers back to the castle there was no reason why they, with us guiding and guarding them, wouldn't be able to start heading back first thing in the morning.

"Sounds good to me," I said with a shrug that didn't seem to do the decision justice.

Once again I was filled with a great sense of accomplishment and achievement. After weeks of planning, which we all had input into, the mission was proceeding to plan and ahead of schedule. Our tactics had ensured that not once had anyone come close to danger so I felt I had a right to be proud of achieving another landmark, but as I stood in the sun preparing to head home, I had to rein it in as the job was a long way from being completed.

Yes, the hardest part of establishing a deep-water port bridgehead on the British Mainland was done, but the continual noise from the traffic that would now begin to echo around the empty wastelands as lorries continually made their way to and from the port would potentially attract zombies from miles around.

Another problem for another day though, so we got on with it.

The admiral turned to captain's Clarke and Hammond.

"I trust one can leave it to you two gents to arrange this?"

"Yes Sir," Steve answered for both of them and with a salute he indicated for Clarke to join him for a chat. Ten minutes later they called me and the others included in their new plan over to them.

Steve clapped his hands for attention and, with a nod of assent from Clarke, laid it out for us. "Right. We send the tractor and the Volvo back along with the bus to carry the extra drivers and half of the knights who can then remain at the castle. Do you think that will be enough?" he asked with a quizzical look sent at Clarke who pulled a mildly pained expression.

"Yeah. On second thought, if sar'nt Newman brings along a Bushmaster as well, that should be enough to get through anything you encounter. If the bus then stays at the castle, I reckon the three vehicles will be ample coverage for the lorries on the way back."

I looked at Shawn and nodded and he smiled in agreement. Including the Bushmaster was a good idea. The remaining Bushmaster, along with Simon's Defender and the couple of army lorries, all which were up armoured and bristled with extra machine guns, should give those at the docks enough mobility and protection until we returned. The docks were already swarming with hundreds of personnel from the ships and gun posts were being constructed atop some of the containers. Their protection looked in good shape and would quickly improve as more containers and firing positions were added.

"Yes," I replied for both of us as I addressed the two captains. "If you get the drivers we're taking back organised, I'll have a word with Ian so he can decide which of the knights he wants to send home."

My stomach rumbled as I spoke and I realised I hadn't eaten anything with only the occasional sip from my canteen since we'd stopped many hours earlier at Daniel's gravesite. I pointed to a canteen area that had been set up under a tent near to the bottom of one of the ship's gangplanks.

"I don't know about you lot, but I'm going to get some scram inside me before we set out. It's a good couple of hours to get back to the castle and I'll be chewing my arm off with hunger by then if I don't eat now," I said before heading towards the food only to find Ian had beaten me to it.

I was hardly surprised that he'd sniffed out the food before anyone else. He called it maintaining his fighting weight, but his friends called it staying fat.

CHAPTER TWENTY-SIX

Leading the convoy, I paused to check Simon had secured the compound gates before we began our journey home. No stops were envisaged and, if all went to plan, the journey should take us around three hours. Not unsurprisingly most of the drivers returning with us had wanted to ride in the trailer as it would, after all, afford them the best view of the land they had been so desperate to see ever since the apocalypse began. The knights and soldiers having seen it all many times before, agreed to ride in the bus leaving just a few of the more seasoned of them to instruct the new passengers in the art of zombie sticking, just in case that skill was needed. We didn't expect it to be, but we hadn't made it this far without being prepared.

Slowing occasionally as I led the convoy in my Volvo to let the eager new arrivals in the trailer behind me practice their new skill on the odd zombie we encountered, the journey back to the castle went smoothly. They'd been radioed to expect our arrival and we updated them enroute as to our progress and our expected arrival time.

Used to the reaction every time someone new arrived at the castle, we let Maud greet them first and show them to their allocated rooms before we gave them the well-rehearsed tour before gathering for the evening meal. The new arrivals mingled well with our group and even though they were only staying for one night, we did our best to make them feel welcome. With what would be going on in the future, we knew that we'd most likely have an endless stream of visitors as they rotated duties with those stationed at the castle or just used us as a rest station on their way to or from somewhere else. These people would clearly tell those who hadn't visited us yet what the experience was like, and pride demanded those reports to be as positive as possible.

Eager to be off in the morning I gave Becky a quick hug, after I woke her attempting to quietly get dressed in the dark of our bedroom. We gathered in the dining room just as the first light of dawn was peeking over the high walls of the castle, drinking coffee and eating the breakfast Maud had kindly risen early to make.

The talk centred around the job in hand, which was to drive the fully laden food and ammunition lorries back to the docks. Even though we were retracing our route of the previous day, we still ensured that the new drivers each had maps and had studied the route in case any diversions needed to be made, or worse, they got separated from the convoy. Satisfied we were as ready as we could be, we washed up our mugs and dishes, grabbed the flasks of hot drinks and packs of sandwiches which were piled on the table and walked out to the vehicles.

The returned knights would stay to help defend the castle which gave me comfort, as yesterday we'd left the defences spread thinly. A calculated risk that had proved worthwhile, but naturally as my family were at the castle, I selfishly wanted them protected as best we could. No other jobs or tasks outside the castle walls were planned until the resupply operation was running smoothly, and our involvement reduced as the Scilly Isles garrison took over the main responsibility for it.

Waving a thankyou at the knights who'd accompanied us to the main gate as we passed, we set out once more, driving slowly at first as the drivers got used to their new charges. The crunches of gears and hisses of air with the accompanying squeals of complaining tyres as brake pedals were pressed too heavily, reminded me of my first few attempts to drive the huge, heavy lorries.

Time behind the wheel was the best cure and, as the miles passed, I slowly picked up the pace as I could tell their competence was increasing. The twelve lorries all with extra protection added and a passenger manning the machine gun mounted on them followed my lead. Shawn was positioned in the middle of the convoy and the Bushmaster brought up the rear.

Driving along the M5 motorway near Tewksbury, Dave who was standing up on the seat by my side scanning the way ahead with some binoculars, called out a warning.

"Zombies ahead…A lot by the look of it."

Staring ahead, I could just make out the darker shadow of something in the distance. Slowing down I reached for the radio and instructed everyone we were stopping before standing on my seat and raising my own binoculars to focus them ahead.

"What now?" I asked as the magnified image showed a horde of at least a few hundred heading towards us.

"They most likely were attracted by the noise we made passing this way twice yesterday," Dave replied.

I looked around and with a start realised we were on the very bridge where we'd stopped and met Graham and Arthur. Only a few weeks ago we had discovered they had made it to the Scillies after their story had filtered through the chain of command there, and the significance of their requests to pass on the message we'd given them had been recognised.

I'd spoken to them since via radio and had to keep deflecting the thanks they piled on us. The supplies we'd given them had made their journey possible, and they'd reached the Solent without the need to refuel. They'd arrived exhausted but in good shape, and it turned out that the shotguns we gave them had come in useful. When passing under one bridge they'd found that in desperation to get to them, some of the zombies had thrown themselves over the low parapets onto their boats. They had some dangerous and scary moments ridding themselves of their un-wanted guests using the shotguns and boathooks, but after a few desperate minutes, all those that had landed on their decks had been killed and pushed overboard. Learning from this and not wanting a repeat, at every subsequent bridge they passed under they had their weapons aimed and ready to shoot any that tried to reach them. Bonded together by the trials of the journey, the two families now shared a house on St Mary's and were adjusting to their new life as farm workers. The news had warmed the hearts of our community and reinforced that our willingness to help others had always been the right action to take.

Dave was still concentrating fully on the problem ahead of us, and I could almost hear the gears of thought turning in his head so left him to his musings for a few more seconds until he spoke.

"If Shawn cleaves us right through them we can do that with no problems, but the issue won't end there...This route is going to become well-travelled soon, so leaving a horde to get in the way in the future is not a good idea. I say we get Pete in the

Bushmaster up here along with Shawn and just blast 'em to noth-ingness. It'll also be a good opportunity to see how the grenade machine guns deal with massed groups of them."

"Oh *hell* yes," I said, rather too excitedly as I knew I was going to get the chance to use my pride and joy, my Bren gun, in anger again.

Dave smiled and shook his head in mock despair at my words, raised the radio to his mouth and asked Shawn and Pete to bring their vehicles forwards to join us.

With a bit of shunting the three vehicles positioned themselves in front of the long line of lorries so the greatest number of weap-ons could be brought to bear. The approaching shuffling, sham-bling mass of dead flesh was still some distance away as Dave shouted out.

"Okay, ladies, get your personal weapons out and see if you can hit them from here. Life isn't all about blasting them from close range, so a bit of sharpshooting practice while we are here won't go amiss. God knows some of you could do with the prac-tice…you know who you are! When they get closer we'll use the bigger stuff".

With mock groans of outrage from us at his disparaging words about our sharp shooting abilities, he waited until we'd picked up weapons and performed the quick safety drill, which for all of us non-military types was becoming second nature. Any sloppy weapons drill noticed, especially by the sergeants, got the unfor-tunate recipient a public and sarcastic dressing down. The con-tinuous training and guidance we received from them though was never taken half-heartedly or with bad grace. It helped us tip the life-or-death balance into our favour.

Single shots rang out as we all tried to aim at the distant bodies. Dave didn't raise his own weapon but held his binoculars to his eyes and helped to call shot corrections to Noah and myself when he was able to discern which missed shot was ours and not from one of the many others trying to outdo each other in accuracy. Reverting to his sergeant's voice he kept up a continual tirade of advice or abuse depending on the shot he had witnessed.

"Are we at Rorke's drift now Dave?" I sniggered after he'd said for the third time. "Take your time, mark your target."

"No Tom," he replied immediately. "These are not highly trained warriors you are facing who want to disembowel you with their assegai, but a bunch of putrefying corpses, so don't treat them with any respect. They are not running at you but walking slowly."

His voice hardened.

"And you are still bloody missing them. *So, take your time and mark your target like a good boy will you?*"

Noah, proud of his Welsh heritage and therefore had an unassailable belief that his rugby team were the best in the world began singing Men of Harlech loudly. Knowing the song from the film and many rugby matches I'd attended over the years I joined in. Somehow, I began to get more shots on target much to the pleasure of Dave who seemed to be enjoying himself so much he even joined in the chorus.

The hi-tech sights on our weapons made the job easier, but it was still difficult to get a hit at a long distance even though the rifles had the range. An inch of movement in the rifle's barrel translated to missing by the proverbial mile downrange, but zombies still dropped and the numbers thinned until Dave called out for us to cease fire and prepare the machine guns.

I eagerly made my gun safe and stowed it before pulling my Bren gun's stock into my shoulder before I yanked back on the heavy bolt to charge the weapon and prepared to fire.

Shooting a machine gun was just plain…fun. There's literally no other word I could use to describe it. The destruction that spewed from the barrels soon began thinning out the crowd far quicker than our rifles had, but the grenade machine guns, lobbing their deadly 40mm high-explosive munitions, caused the greatest damage. Each explosion within the approaching mass blew body parts skywards and swept an area clear within its blast radius, causing many more injuries as its flying shrapnel cut through soft rotting flesh. The weapon couldn't have been more aptly named. It could fire dozens of deadly grenades per minute accurately over a long distance, but discipline and a mind conscious of ammunition conservation filled the air with rapid *chung-chung-chung* sounds as the little bombs were fired in reserved bursts.

Only having the ones we had taken from the SAS base they were a weapon we could do with more of in my opinion. Many more. In the convoy behind us, I knew one lorry was stacked with pallets of extra ammunition for them gathered from M.O.D Kineton, and we had another full lorry still at Warwick. The base still contained hundreds more similar pallets, and now their effectiveness had been proved beyond doubt locating more of them would definitely be included to the list of 'must haves' we were always adding items to.

The gunfire petered out as the numbers facing us were decimated by our intense firing. Emptying a magazine from my Bren at a small crowd left untouched at the edge of the field of destruction, I was satisfied with my accuracy as they all were thrown back to lie twisted together in a bloody, gore-splashed heap. With no more left in sight, I changed the empty magazine for a full one but didn't charge the weapon, and let the barrel swing skywards on its bracket as I surveyed the destruction.

None were left standing and, as I raised my binoculars to get a clearer look, all I could see was a sea of still or twitching bodies piled together.

"That'll do for now," Dave said simply as he also inspected the carnage before picking up the radio and saying.

"Shawn, when you are ready lead the way and plough through that pile of shit ahead of us. Then slot in where you were before, please."

He acknowledged and after a minute's pause, he pulled forwards and the convoy followed.

I grinned at the radio calls from the lorries as Shawn lowered his plough and cut a clear path through the tangled corpses. Some of them as I had discovered when talking to them last night had been involved with the mission to clear the Scillies, and so had experience of meeting them face to face, but the closest the rest had got was observing from the side of a ship. As Shawn's plough easily cleaved through them, their chatter was a mixture of both excitement and disgust, but we had proved to yet more people, that with the right tactics, the zombies that plagued the land could be dealt with and weren't the unstoppable wave of flesh-eating death that imaginations would conjure up.

Once Shawn had cleared the way he pulled to one side ready to re-join the middle of the convoy, and I led the way to the Docks.

CHAPTER TWENTY-SEVEN

Five days later, with our part in the mission to resupply the Scilly isles now officially over as enough military personnel were stationed at the docks to defend it and drive the lorries, we decided to be helpful in other ways. We had the experience and know-how to find, adapt, and deliver them the vehicles they needed to protect the convoys that soon they would send out to scour the area themselves. We added the finishing touches to a pair of Defenders we'd acquired from a local Land Rover dealers' forecourt, along with two more tractors and trailers scavenged from nearby farms.

All the lorries gathered so far containing both the food and ammunition had been delivered to the docks. The loading process was, we were assured, running smoothly and the last of what we'd helped to deliver was on its way to the Scillies and Fort Bristol, as it had been named, was now fully operational. On my last visit when we delivered the vehicles to grateful soldiers and sailors, we'd been invited to inspect the facility and advise on any improvements we could suggest from our experience.

With the quantity of containers they had to hand, a large area surrounding the docked ships had been created. Double-stacked perimeter walls with another single layer behind it for good measure, it looked impressive. At regular intervals containers had been placed facing inwards to create usable rooms for accommodating the garrison, and looking inside I saw that air beds and camp beds filled the ones designated as sleeping quarters and others were in the process of being fitted out as canteens, breakrooms, and bathroom-type areas. The gateway had been constructed by stacking containers facing inwards three high on either side with one placed to bridge the top of it. It was high enough and wide enough for the lorries to drive through where they would be unloaded. The engineers had designed and built a strong gate from steel sheeting, which when closed and with a massive locking bar made from a steel beam dropped into place, the base was sealed completely. Gun posts connected by walkways had been placed at regular intervals around the walls, and huge floodlights snaked wires back to generators at ground level. We were introduced to an officer named Linell, who was the engineer in charge of constructing the base. He eagerly wanted to give us a tour as if needing our seal of approval on what he had completed so far.

I looked up at the containers and asked, "How do you get up there?"

I could see no steps or ladders but the gun post atop the containers were manned and others walked sentry duty between them.

"Initially we used ladders," he explained "but now we are working on stairways going up internally through the containers. Ladders were okay to start but made it difficult and slow to fully man the walls when we held our first emergency drill. Plus hauling heavy ammunition boxes to resupply the gun posts was downright dangerous from a ladder."

He pointed through the open gateway at the many buildings surrounding them.

"Fortunately, most of the buildings are steel framed and so most have prefabricated steel staircases in them. It's not hard with the amount of labour we have to remove them, cut 'em up a bit to make them fit and repurpose them here. Come on I'll show you."

Leading us through a doorway cut in the side of the nearest container. I was surprised to see a well-lit corridor extending into the distance.

"Does this extend right through them?" I asked impressed at the labour needed to achieve it.

"Not yet but it will eventually. We are making doors so if an area gets breached, we can isolate it and contain the threat."

He pointed behind us.

"The nearest stairs are just through there if you'd like to follow me. We're building more but this was the first."

Feeling already impressed I followed as he led us up a set of stairs to another level similar to the one below. Our footsteps clanged and echoed along the empty steel lined corridor as we were led up another flight of stairs to emerge into daylight.

"To achieve this in the time you've had is impressive," I said smiling in genuine pleasure at the man. Everyone else joined in with praise. He flustered a bit with the approbations we were giving him, but I could see his chest swell with pride and he showed more confidence as he continued the tour.

The structure, if the steel walls were replaced with stone, would have been called a castle in any other age, impregnable and well protected against attack. The gun posts were simple sandbagged emplaced positions currently sheltered from the elements by only a tarpaulin stretched over poles. Linnel saw me looking at them and said quickly as if he knew what I was going to say next.

"I am trying to work out a better way to provide protection from the elements, but it's low priority as there are many other projects to complete first," he explained almost apologising that I had noticed a flaw in his design.

"Hey, don't worry, we've only just built shelters for our sentries, and we've been at the castle at lot longer than you've been here." I then used the expression overused as an excuse but one that I hoped would allay his worry.

"Rome wasn't built in a day you know, and with what you've completed so far all I can say is it exceeds my expectations."

I thought for a while as an idea was ruminating in my mind.

"Why don't you use containers as gun posts? Plonk one up here, cut a hole in either end for access and a big hole in the front for a gun port, it'll be more weatherproof than most things I imagine."

He stood staring into space for a while as he worked through my suggestion until his face brightened.

"Brilliant idea, now why in the hell didn't I think of that?"

Walking back through the containers he showed us more accommodation areas that had already been started. Currently everyone was sleeping back on board the ships but when the dormitories, bathroom facilities, and rest areas were completed it was planned that the garrison would be independent from the ships, only needing to retreat back to them under dire circumstances.

None of us could pick any fault in what had been built, and we heaped praise on their achievements. The walls were high and strong enough, and the weapons facing outwards would be able to destroy all hordes of the size we'd encountered so far. Inside the walls, the accommodation areas would provide them with a reasonably comfortable living environment, and if the unexpected happened then they could always board one of the docked vessels. All in all, Fort Bristol proved to be an excellent blueprint for further bases, with the added benefit of the sea providing secure evacuation and resupply options.

The empty lorries were parked at the fort waiting for us to deliver the vehicles we'd adapted for them to use as escorts. They would, after starting small and clearing every inch of the docks, begin to search for their own supplies. As their experience and confidence built, they could expand the missions and widen their search areas. Searching new areas would also fulfil the objectives to continually be on the lookout for more survivors, and to fulfil the promise made to see if any family members of the many personnel, both military and civilian who lived close enough to Bristol to make the mission viable, had made it.

My highlight of the trip was the tour we were given of the frigate moored at the docks and the meal served to us in the officers' mess, waited on by crisply uniformed stewards just before we were due to leave. Touring the ship was hardly mission critical, but it did show us the firepower they had available if it was needed. The Phalanx weapon system, basically an automatic twenty-millimetre gatling gun which could destroy anything it wanted to in less than half a second. Eddy was standing beside me as the weapons officer was explaining its capabilities absentmind-edly tapping his shirt pocket.

"You still carrying it around?" I asked, knowing what he was doing.

He looked at me and blinked in surprise as he realised what he was doing.

"Sorry. It's becoming a bit of a habit checking it's still there…it's kind of a good luck charm to me now, and I never go anywhere without it."

He was referring to the single shotgun cartridge he had re-trieved from the floor of a farmhouse we were searching before we reached the castle so long ago. As he put it in his pocket he had said that if he ever found himself reaching for it, he could pretty much guarantee that we were fucked. Hearing him talk of saving his last round for himself sobered me then and still did to that day.

"As nothing bad had happened to you since then I'd keep it there nice and safe," I said before we returned to listening about the fearsome looking weapon.

It was normally used as an independently operated autono-mous system which activated when incoming threats such as mis-siles or aircraft were detected by the ships defence systems. Now, he explained, they were on manual mode where the operator just needed to flick a switch to turn it on and use its inbuilt camera systems to aim and fire it using a joystick and a tv screen. Imag-ining the destructive power of thousands of rounds pouring out-wards in a solid stream of metal at the massed soft flesh of an approaching horde it wasn't hard to believe they had a weapon that could be described as the goriest games console ever invented.

Before we left the ship, conscious that Stanley, Eddie, and most likely all the other children at the castle would have loved the chance to have the tour we'd had, I blagged a few souvenirs such as caps and badges from the ships company as gifts for them.

CHAPTER TWENTY-EIGHT

At the castle life slowly returned to us looking after ourselves. Captain Digby and a detachment of marines were still stationed with us, primarily to help bolster our defences, but also to assist with the scavenging missions we turned our efforts back to. The captain admitted himself that he had pulled on the admiral's heartstrings to allow him to be based here so he could continue to spend time with Eddie. When he was at the castle and not on duty, Eddie was never far from his side.

While we began concentrating on gathering foodstuffs and other essentials of life, the military faction of our community split into two different roles. Captain Clarke and his men left on days-long missions to rescue the personnel trapped at the few other known locations around the land. We eagerly awaited his return and his description of what the state of the rest of the country was in, although unsurprisingly his reports mirrored what we'd experienced for ourselves. Zombies were still everywhere and a few times he had to rely on firepower and the strength of his vehicles to break through them, leaving a trail of corpses in his wake.

Once all the survivors from the bases they knew of were rescued and safely transported back to the castle or Fort Bristol, he and his men continued to empty the vast quantity of ammunition stored at M.O.D Kineton, albeit on a much smaller scale than our first mission there. It would be the work of months, but every lorry that delivered another full load to us or to the garrison at Fort Bristol was another large quantity of ammunition under our control and able to be employed against the enemy. The survivors, trapped for so long, recovered at the castle before being sent to where their skills were best suited. Some stayed either with us or went to Bristol if they were more from the fighting end of the military hierarchy, while others with skills in logistics were better suited being part of the command structure based on the Scillies.

Captain Digby and Captain Hammond worked together to start gathering all other known military stores. When they informed us of all the known locations of military weapons, it surprised us how many places held such arsenals. Every mainline barracks and reserve regiments barracks would obviously hold a quantity of them, but none of us had considered the weapons held at many schools which had Combined Cadet Force, or CCF, units. Local police forces also held weapons for their armed police units, and all these were earmarked to be added to our stores or sent to the Scillies. The potential quantities they could get made our efforts to empty the gun shops in an ever-increasing radius around us seem insignificant by comparison, but when one was near where we were heading to on a scavenging mission it never hurt to bring back a car full of shotguns, rifles, cartridges and bullets to add to our ever-growing haul.

The military bases not only provided us with a wide range of weapons but with more armoured vehicles than we knew what to do with. Some were sent to Fort Bristol, once we had added the usual extra protection to them, but with such a surplus we ended up filling one of the castle's visitor car parks with fresh mounts ready for use.

One base even provided a challenger tank that was just asking to be taken as it was already sitting on its low loader heavy transport lorry. We had no idea what we would use it for, but it worked and a tank after all, was a tank, and who the hell wouldn't want a tank?

M.O.D Kineton provided reloads for the main gun and we placed it in pride of place at the castle. For a while it became the latest tourist attraction for those of us, young and old, who wanted to play with it. That was until Maud stopped our fun complaining that we were pointlessly churning up the grounds of the castle and should be spending our time on more productive pursuits. The admiral, knowing that possessing all these vehicles would be pointless unless they were in working order, dispatched a team of mechanics to keep them all in operational condition. Every day they started up, inspected, and moved each vehicle in turn, keeping them in prime operational condition and ready to move at a moment's notice if required.

One delivery from the Scillies created a lot of work for us. Captain Clarke returned from Bristol with a few pallets of fruit and vegetables along with a cockerel and some hens from the farms on the Scillies. We'd been eating well mainly using our stores of canned meat and vegetables to feed ourselves, but fresh produce was something we didn't know we were craving until it arrived. After we'd devoured the strawberries, raspberries, and fresh vegetables – which tasted far better than anything out of a can – we were immediately dispatched to locate as many green-houses as we could find so we could begin to grow our own produce straight away. Areas for cultivation around the grounds were also marked out and work parties began preparing them for crops once the coming winter was over.

The children insisted on taking on the job of caring for the chickens, once we had constructed a coop for them against the castle walls, which seemed to mostly entail chasing them. After being told that they weren't pets and were there to provide us with eggs which would hopefully hatch to expand the population until we had enough to provide both eggs and meat, they still insisted on giving them names and spent much of their off time getting them used to being handled.

The south-facing wall of the castle soon got filled with greenhouses and cold frames which were tended to by enthusiastic, green-fingered volunteers who were eagerly and regularly tending to our future crops. They were excitedly awaiting to report when the first green shoots started to show.

If our life could be described as routine, then we settled in to one. Our food, ammunition, and weapons stores were being added to continuously and whenever we were out on scavenging missions we chose to use as many different routes as possible to continue our endless search for survivors. Every time we went out, even though fewer and fewer zombies crossed our paths, the kill tally mounted.

It rose slowly but we still lived by the mantra set by Shawn on the first day I had met him: one less is still one less. We didn't know where they were, or if their numbers were reducing as the availability of food sources, i.e. living bodies, left the food chain. It was a turn of events we weren't complaining about but neither did we allow ourselves to become complacent. Every time we left the sanctuary of the castle walls we still maintained the highest level of vigilance, ready for anything that may cross our path.

Chris and I, with advice from the fleet regarding weather conditions, took the plane out when the skies permitted. We flew the slow, predetermined search pattens, one of us always searching the ground below us for any tell-tale signs of life or a horde of the undead crowding around a house or a building. A few hopeful places were spotted, and ground teams were dispatched to investigate them further, but these always ended in disappointment. We either found places empty or, after we had dealt with the undead encircling the place, we discovered the heartbreak of those that had survived and found shelter but had starved to death or chose to end their own lives to avoid any more suffering as they waited in vain for a rescue that never came.

The weeks and months began to roll by as summer changed to autumn and the weather grew colder and more unsettled. The admiral or one of his aides was always in constant contact, updating us on the progress of both Fort Bristol and the Scilly Isles. He visited occasionally when he joined one of the regular convoys that toured between Bristol, us, and the Brough's farm, which acted as both supply runs and allowed for changing of personnel. Most of the garrison at the Scillies had passed through the castle by now, as the missions expanded and the garrisons of all places swapped in and out as the rotas changed.

The Scillies were becoming well established as a permanent base. The farming and fishing programmes were producing a regular yield to supplement the supplies being gathered on the mainland and continually shipped to them. In return we also received regular deliveries of fish, meat, and vegetables on returning convoys, which were always gratefully received. The island's power supply had become more regular and was on for longer periods every day as fuel supplies had been located and shipped there, but it was still being rationed as sensibly they realised the electric supply and the fuel needed for it would be best used to provide lighting and heating when it would be needed most during the winter months. The bunkering facilities at Bristol were extensive as they needed the capacity to refuel the container ships which travelled the globe continuously, only ever stopping to load, unload, and replenish their fuel and food supplies in port before continuing to their next destination. The fuel contained in the huge tanks, we were told, should be sufficient for the fleet's needs for many months before an alternative supply needed to be secured.

The garrison at the Brough's had also not been idle, and were continually searching and scavenging a wider radius around their farm. Again, no more survivors had been found and we began to depressingly believe that no one else was left alive in the country. If any were out there then they must be in a secure location and either have sufficient food or at least the ability to gather more like us, in which case hopefully they'd be able to survive in the long term and we might come across them in the future.

With the coming of winter proper, our world shrank to be mainly just inside the castle walls and grounds. We didn't need to venture out to gather more supplies as we had enough to last us all for many months if not years, so keeping warm and maintaining the structure of the castle became our main concern. Storms and heavy rainfall caused leaks and damage to the ancient building which needed constant attention and work.

Patrols ventured out weekly to keep the routes between our three mainland bases clear. Fallen trees, floods caused by blocked drains, and many other tasks which usually would be the job of the local authority to keep its highways open had to be worked on by our teams. It was essential to keep the routes between us open in case we needed to rush to help each other, and stopping to attack a fallen tree with chainsaws could cause a delay that meant the difference between life and death.

Reducing our travel to the main routes meant that we'd actively stopped looking for survivors. Every building and obvious place where we might have found people had already been searched many times when we'd passed them over the previous months, so it was deemed a waste of time and effort to keep repeating it just in case. The garrison at the Brough's, in their much smaller outpost, felt the isolation of winter much more than we did at the castle. They were the most at-risk base, even though their defences had been continually added to and improved, it would never be as safe as behind the high walls of our castle or the walls of containers at Fort Bristol. We knew that, as did the defenders posted there, and the constant worry of it wore them down.

Regular shift changes on every visit helped to keep their spirits up. The Brough's, on the few occasions they requested it, came to the castle for a break from the monotony of staring at the same walls for weeks on end. On these infrequent visits, we made sure they were treated as honoured guests and had very little to do apart from rest and join in the banter and conversations that continually flowed round the much larger group of companions the castle provided.

A lot of meetings, both formal and informal, took place about what we would collectively do when the weather improved in the coming year. Nobody wanted to be just satisfied with all the great things we'd already achieved, and our long-term aim was not to be stuck sheltering behind walls, but to be out there freeing the land from zombies, so maybe one day we could live, not behind walls lined with guns but somewhere where we could live as normal and free a life as possible.

CHAPTER TWENTY-NINE

The colder weather bought a change to the remaining zombies. Always pulled by a primitive urge to gather together by some base level of understanding still in their brain giving them the knowledge they could hunt better as a pack, the basic rule of strength in numbers rang true.

The first frost heralding the true start of winter caused a change in their behaviour. The sun and rain of the summer and autumn hadn't affected them. Rotting bodies so sunburned they blistered until their skin and flesh fell off in sheets, seemed unaffected. The rain did not affect them. Their bodies needed the drops of rain that fell into open throats when they raised them to the heavens in an unconscious act of self-preservation. These few drops helped to sustain the basic needs which kept them still functioning as an organic being.

The cold was another matter.

A frozen body could not function. Blood, even though in the zombies it was a thick, blackened, virus-laden soup, would stop flowing to the extremities as the cold forced the body to shut down and protect its vital organs, in exactly the same way a healthy human body would. These body parts cut off from the blood supply would turn gangrenous and die. Legs and arms would fester, making the host unable to move and rendering its sole objective, to spread the virus, impossible.

The winter had the potential to kill the virus's host and, by definition, the virus.

Viruses have existed for tens of millions of years, however, pre-dating everything that exists on the planet today. They have un-consciously ensured their survival by adapting and changing when their existence is threatened. This virus, tweaked by humans and the hand of fate into its current form, was no different. It must survive to spread, and that required mutation.

The lowering temperatures manifested this change. Zombies, most of whom with no external influence to urge them to hunt human flesh had fallen into a state of hibernation. Their bodies shut down, barely using any energy to enable the virus to still live on in their catatonic carcasses. This helped them survive until their primitive senses detected another source to hunt, devour, and pass on the virus to.

They now felt a greater urge to seek out others. To gather to-gether where their combined body heat would keep the host virus alive as it coursed through their veins. Drawn to shelter by the basic animalistic instinct for survival, the gathering masses grew as the low, rhythmic breathing of those in power-saving mode attracted others by some unknown means.

Across the country a great migration occurred as millions gath-ered in houses, barns, warehouses or anywhere the first one found which offered dry, protected shelter and sent out the near-silent signal. Forming tight knots of flesh and bone they merged into one organic mass and once more fell into their catatonic state to preserve their corpses until the urge to feed awakened them.

The surviving humans saw none of this. It happened out of sight and hence out of mind. Concentrating on gathering supplies and searching for survivors, these dark places they gathered were not entered as it was known nothing useful would be there and no survivors would be found.

Even though sheltered, these nests of zombies were still affected by the cold. The last to arrive, the ones forced to remain on the outer edges, froze and died. Their dead bodies though, still insulated the inner rings and kept them from freezing. So surrounded by the thousands encircling them, the heat generated by the packed masses of undead kept the inner rings, the first to arrive and send out that signal, heated above normal body temperature. Their bodies baked in a virus-filled mass of flesh, blood, and sinew provided the perfect conditions for the virus to adapt and change once more.

The virus, in its current state, had run its course. Even though the carriers still numbered in their countless millions, the slow, shambling state had become obsolete having consumed or infected all easily located sources of fresh meat.

Not just that, but those sources of fresh meat had adapted also, and changed as they learned to live in the world the virus had created. When the winter was over, the virus would not be able to spread and survive in its current state. It needed to spread to survive, and it knew, if such concepts could be applied to a virus, that doing so would be impossible if future hosts stayed safely beyond their reach.

It changed once more in a last throw of the dice to fulfil its objective: To infect every human on the planet. It no longer needed the massed armies of the undead it had created. They had served their purpose, but now were obsolete as a method of transmission.

Mutated once more, the new virus spread outwards from its warm inner cordon. It knew the temperature it needed to be at now to live and spread. The temperature dropped nearer to the edge of each group and the virus did not transmit to anymore when it reached it. Those inner groups, though, needed energy to feed the changes the virus wanted to make on their bodies. They did not need much, but for what the virus had planned they needed fuel for their bodies to regenerate, they needed flesh.

Zombies from the outer ring on some unheard and undetected command pushed themselves inwards and were consumed one bite at a time as if willingly sacrificing themselves for the greater good. Great hunks of rotting flesh were ripped from their bodies by the teeth of their former comrades as they pushed through the masses, offering themselves as willing unhuman sacrifices until only bones remained.

The virus was clever enough not to decimate its outer ring of protection too much, as it still needed the insulated protection it gave to stop the inner core freezing. When the insulating layers of those sacrificed to save the few was not needed when winter ended, then they would be eaten in a frenzy as the inner rings needed to go through their final change and take the fight back to the only enemy the virus had to stop it spreading over the whole planet.

EPILOGUE

March the following year.

"Still bloody freezing," Kip Ferris complained as he hunkered down trying to shelter against the rain that sheeted down.

"Oh for the love of…will you stop moaning for one day? Just one day? It's not that fucking cold anymore, the snow's all gone, we're just bloody soaked," Stu Marks groaned, sick of the constant stream of pessimism from the man he had been partnered with to watch the walls of the Brough's farm.

"Well, what are we even doing out in this anyway?" Ferris went on, undeterred by the anger in Marks' tone. "When was the last time you even bleedin' saw a zombie, eh? Tell me that."

"How about I break your ankle and toss you over the wall? See if that attracts one?" Marks growled with a smirk on his face in an attempt to diffuse the situation.

Ferris watched him warily, unsure if the threat was genuine or not. He knew he was getting on the older man's nerves, but it wasn't in his nature to let grievances go unaired, so he doubled down in a vain attempt to make his point despite the olive branch thrown in his direction.

"Months, mate. It's been months. Not even the road crews reported seeing any, so I reckon the cold's done for 'em."

Marks said nothing, holding his tongue lest he lose control with the whining man beside him, but his silence was taken as a piqued interest.

"They've all froze, right? Must have. All we had to do was make it to winter and *poof!* No more zombies. It's meant to be spring now despite this bloody weather, I bet we won't see a single one of the ba—"

"Will you, for the love of *everything holy*, shut the f—" Marks snapped with real venom in his voice for the first time.

"*Movement!*"

The shout from far to their left ended the argument before it could take hold, snapping both men's attention to the empty ground ahead of them.

"*Lights!*" came the next order, and Marks fumbled with cold hands to work the large spotlight attached to the wall of their post and activate it.

In an instant the dull grey of predawn was banished by the harsh beam of bright white light cutting swathes over the flat ground surrounding the farm's walls. He scanned it left and right, tried to maintain a methodical pace but fought the urge to whip it around in a desperate search for what had caused the alarm. They didn't possess night vision optics, they were told it was because the batteries for them were a finite resource so only the watch commanders were given them, but Marks knew it was more likely that idiots like Ferris would mess around with them probably dropping and breaking them in the process, so like all the good toys, they'd been taken away and kept under lock and key.

"Where?" Marks called out as his nerve broke.

"*Your eleven o'clock, two hundred metres,*" came the shouted reply.

Marks turned the light to the right direction and lifted it slowly, estimating where the beam would land on the right distance to hold it steady.

Nothing. Nothing moved and nothing stood there, waiting for a sniff of them to animate it into moaning and shambling in a futile bid to eat them.

Marks relaxed, sagging with relief.

"Probably a fox," Ferris grumbled.

"*Stand down. Probably a fox,*" came the orders in a voice that sounded almost disappointed.

"Told you," Ferris said smugly. "And it's still bloody freezing."

But Stu Marks didn't hear Ferris renewed complaint. As he killed the powerful beam of light, he had seen a glimpse of something that his brain failed to register. His eyes sent the images, but they hadn't been interpreted correctly, at least that was what his first conscious thought had been, because there was no way what he thought he'd seen could be real.

He switched the light back on and jerked the beam over the area he'd recently lit up, only to invite an angry question yelled at him.

"*Bloody hell what are you playin' at? I said stand down!*"

Marks froze at a scratching noise and a low, rhythmic panting like that of an animal. His eyes locked onto Ferris' in the weak light cast by a sun not yet peeking the horizon. Before either man could think sufficiently to make words the noises from below them, from outside the walls, turned both of their heads down in time to see a pale-faced body leaping high like no human had the ability to do so.

Both men screamed.

Both screams were cut off by wet, sinewy rips, and the pre-dawn became a nightmare for the living.

Chris Harris is a UK-based author, well-known for his post-apoc-alyptic and zombie book series.
Find his website at www.chrisharrisauthor.co.uk
Facebook @chrisharrisauthor

UK Dark Book 1: The Blackout

By Chris Harris

"What would happen if......?"

Many people ask themselves the question, but how many actually do something about it?

Tom lives in Birmingham, England with his family. After asking himself the question and researching what could happen, he decided it wouldn't do any harm to be a little bit prepared. Just in case.

He discovers the world is going to be hit by a massive Coronal Mass Ejection from the sun, which will turn the whole planet dark.

He only has a few days to get ready.

Will they survive?

People want what they have, but is he prepared to kill to protect it?

The UK Dark series, out now!